PRAISE FOR SHOLES & MOORE'S
AWARD WINNING BESTSELLING THRILLERS

THE SHIELD

"Sholes & Moore have done it again. Their latest thriller, *The Shield*, combines exciting historical speculations with tantalizing extrapolations about science--both real and theoretical. But best of all, the book rocks on all cylinders, delivering a topical political punch and a riveting adventure story. Can't wait to travel with Agent Decker on her next assignment!" ~ James Rollins, *New York Times* bestselling author of THE EYE OF GOD

"Sholes & Moore have written a gripping, adrenaline rush that combines science, conspiracy, and the realities of nuclear war. *The Shield* will grab you and have you screaming at the characters as you become engulfed in this terrifying ride. Sholes & Moore will leave you rethinking what you know about Roswell and Area 51 and leave you longing for the next Decker and Gates adventure." ~ *Suspense Magazine*

THE BLADE

"Sholes & Moore are at the top of their game in this dark, chilling cat-and-mouse race to stop an unimaginable act of terrorism. THE BLADE is full-throttle thriller writing." -- David Morrell, *New York Times* bestselling author of MURDER AS A FINE ART.

"Completely kept me guessing. THE BLADE delivers a razor edge of suspense. As fast as you think you know what's going on, you're wrong. An absolute thrill ride." -- Lisa Gardner, #1 *New York Times* bestselling author of CATCH ME

"Fast. Fresh. Fascinating. THE BLADE is another razor-sharp thriller from one of my favorite writing teams!" -- Brad Thor, #1 *New York Times* bestselling author of BLACK LIST

"You will need THE BLADE to cut the tension as you turn the pages to the shocking climax. Sholes & Moore have painted a stunning portrait of suspense that leaves you wanting their next collaboration." -- *Suspense Magazine*

THE PHOENIX APOSTLES

"Fast-paced, exciting story that grips the audience." -- *The Mystery Gazette*

"Once again, Lynn Sholes & Joe Moore have produced a novel that is as revelatory as it is packed with action and suspense. THE PHOENIX APOSTLES takes their talent to new heights in a story that will leave readers breathless and wanting more. Bold, taut, and masterfully told, here is a book that demands to be read in one sitting." -- James Rollins, *New York Times* bestselling author of THE DOOMSDAY KEY

"A fascinating, compelling page-turner. Lynn Sholes & Joe Moore hit all the right notes with THE PHOENIX APOSTLES!" -- Carla Neggers, *New York Times* bestselling author of COLD DAWN

"Lynn Sholes & Joe Moore have created a knockout apocalyptic thriller with THE PHOENIX APOSTLES. An epic tale of gold, archaeology, mass murder, ancient prophecy and terrorism, it propels the reader at light speed from its opening chapters to its stunning climax. An outstanding read!" -- Douglas Preston, #1 *New York Times* bestselling author of IMPACT and THE MONSTER OF FLORENCE

"An ingenious thriller with an audacious plot. Awesome; a reminder why fiction is fun." -- *Library Journal*

"What do you get when you cross Indiana Jones with THE DA VINCI CODE? THE PHOENIX APOSTLES, a rollicking thrill ride with so many twists and turns that you won't have time to catch your breath!" -- Tess Gerritsen, *New York Times* bestselling author of ICE COLD

"Sholes and Moore have been writing stellar thrillers that use religious themes for some time, and their fifth effort, the first to feature archaeologist Seneca Hunt, is their best yet. Hunt and her fiancé are on a dig near Mexico City when explosions rock the site. Hunt is the only survivor. Still grieving, she teams up with a journalist who has evidence that the explosion was meant to cover up a robbery. All over the world, tombs are being invaded and bodies stolen, while valuable jewels and gold are left behind. Who are the thieves, and do all the missing bodies belong to infamous mass murderers throughout history? The breakneck pace and sharp characterizations immerse the reader into a surprising and frightening story that posits what the future might look like if science is allowed to run amok. Fans of historical thrillers and mysteries with a religious tint will devour this one while eagerly awaiting the next Seneca Hunt adventure." – *Booklist*

THE GRAIL CONSPIRACY
#1 Bestselling Kindle Book on Amazon

ForeWord Magazine Book-Of-The-Year

Independent Publisher IPPY Award Nominee

"Cotten Stone is a heroine for the ages." ~ Douglas Preston, #1 *New York Times* bestselling co-author of RELIC

"Action-packed, twenty-first century Indiana Jones." ~ Harriet Klausner, ReviewCentre

"If you love books by Steve Berry and Dan Brown, you will love this one, too. The search for the Holy Grail is an exciting adventure and definitely worth reading." ~ Bookreporter.com

"In this time of Dan Brown, here are fresh voices. THE GRAIL CONSPIRACY is everything a mystery should be." ~ Stuart Hecht, The Book Vault

"Gripping!" ~ *Mystery Scene Magazine*

"Spellbinding!" ~ *BookSense*

THE LAST SECRET
"Sholes & Moore have the magical ability to keep you on the edge of your seat. From the first page to the last, you won't be able to put it down." ~ ReaderViews

"Skillfully crafted page-turner." ~ Debra Hamel, Book-Blog.com

"A blend of international thriller and religious fiction, it's an attention-grabber that kept me up at night feverishly turning pages because I just had to know what would happen next. (THE LAST SECRET is) one for those who want a really good "DA VINCI CODE"-esque read." ~ Lelia Taylor, Creatures 'n Crooks Bookshoppe

"Superb thriller. Sholes & Moore write some of the best apocalyptical thrillers on the market today." ~ Harriet Klausner, ReviewCentre

"Demonic possession, strange suicides, and Biblical prophecy collide in THE LAST SECRET, an intelligent religious thriller with bite. Once again, Cotten Stone proves herself to be a heroine for the new millennium. A female Indiana Jones with a press pass! Insightful, engrossing…but more importantly, a suspenseful thriller from first page to last!" ~ James Rollins, *New York Times* bestselling author of BLACK ORDER

"Fascinating and breathless, THE LAST SECRET will leave you glued to your chair. The story sweeps across centuries in a quest for the secret key to surviving Armageddon. Sholes & Moore are true story-tellers with unerring eyes and the souls of artists. You'll love this one!" ~ Gayle Lynds, *New York Times* bestselling author of THE LAST SPYMASTER

"THE LAST SECRET grabs you and won't let go. This is a page-turner with an awesomely creative premise and a surprise around every corner." ~ Lewis Perdue, *New York Times* bestselling author of DAUGHTER OF GOD

"Engaging. Sholes & Moore are experienced authors whose expertise is evident. THE LAST SECRET is entertaining and recommended." ~ BookPleasures

THE HADES PROJECT
"THE HADES PROJECT is an exceptional novel, a dark labyrinth of suspense, international intrigue and apocalyptic horror. The characters, the pacing and the amazing premise of this series are all first-rate. Sholes & Moore are very talented writers indeed." ~ Douglas Preston, #1 *New York Times* bestselling co-author of RELIC

"Short chapters and a pulsating storyline make this a quick read, and those looking for well-drawn characters will be pleased as well. Fans of religious-themed thrillers like THE DA VINCI CODE will enjoy. Recommended for all public libraries." ~ *Library Journal*

"A compelling thriller!" ~ Harriet Klausner *The Mystery Gazette*

"Smoothly-written, nicely paced page-turner." ~ Book-Blog

". . . the tension builds as Stone and her mortal and otherworldly allies race to avert catastrophe." ~ *Publishers Weekly*

"THE HADES PROJECT is a briskly-paced read combining Christian fantasy with mystery. Fans of THE DA VINCI CODE should find THE HADES PROJECT a satisfying read. ~ *Mystery Scene Magazine*

THE 731 LEGACY

"Sholes & Moore are the new Preston & Child. From the very first chapter, THE 731 LEGACY wraps a rope around your neck, pulls it tight, and never lets go! This is what masterful storytelling is all about!" ~ Brad Thor, #1 *New York Times* bestselling author of THE LAST PATRIOT

"What an outrageous and terrifying read. I can't get enough of Cotten Stone!" ~ Lincoln Child, #1 *New York Times* bestselling author of DEEP STORM

"A superb blend of science, myth, history, and imagination. Strap yourself to the chair and get ready for a heart-thumping ride. Sholes & Moore are clearly ahead of the pack, able to satisfy even the most finicky of reader. THE 731 LEGACY is a labyrinth of mystery, crisply plotted and paced, with throat-grabbing twists." ~ Steve Berry, *New York Times* bestselling author of THE TEMPLAR LEGACY

THE 731 LEGACY "has a bit of everything found in popular thrillers: destruction of civilization, ancient religious lore, modern science, and non-stop action. It could be entitled Angels and Demons, and is far superior to the book that bears that title." ~ *Mystery Scene Magazine*

THE TOMB

LYNN SHOLES & JOE MOORE

THE TOMB

Published by Stone Creek Books
Oakland Park, Florida
www.stonecreekbooks.com
Interior design by Joe Moore
Cover design by Joe Moore
Cover image © 2015

Excerpt from THE BLADE
© 2013 by Lynn Sholes & Joe Moore
Published by Stone Creek Books

Excerpt from THE SHIELD
© 2014 by Lynn Sholes & Joe Moore
Published by Stone Creek Books

ISBN: 0692486283
ISBN-13: 978-0692486283

DEDICATION

For Margaret Dinn, who instilled in me
the wonder of the written word.
~ Lynn Sholes

For Sydney Archer Moore
~ Joe Moore

Special thanks to The Unknown Brewing Company in
Charlotte, NC, and especially to Lisa Shell.

"The rhythmical vibrations pass through the earth with almost no loss of energy. It becomes possible to convey mechanical effects to the greatest terrestrial distances and produce all kinds of unique effects. The invention could be used with destructive effect in war."
~ Nicola Tesla

"They died to make the desert bloom."
~ Inscription on plaque at Hoover Dam

AUTHORS NOTE
Because of the 112 lives lost during its construction, the
Hoover Dam is sometimes referred to as
The Tomb.

Lynn Sholes & Joe Moore

CHAPTER 1 – MOST WANTED
Acapulco, Mexico

I sat in the backseat of the unmarked SUV and watched the armor-plated Mercedes limo pull up in front of La Pampa, an Argentinean steakhouse a block away. "Is that his car?"

"Yes, Agent Decker," said Colonel Marquez from the front seat as he studied the limousine through binoculars.

Marquez headed a special unit of the Mexican Federal Police whose mission was to capture Pablo Garcia, the man at the top of the most wanted list and ranked by *Forbes Magazine* as one of the richest men in the world. Besides being responsible for the lion's share of all drug trafficking in North America, Garcia collected priceless art objects, most of which were stolen and moved through the black market. That's why I was involved—a former OSI agent and now a consultant for the FBI, I was often requested by foreign governments to help in the recovery of missing antiquities—my specialty.

Marquez turned to the driver. "Tell all units to stand by." The officer relayed the message into a hand-held radio to the police commandos positioned throughout the surrounding business district.

"Agent Decker," Colonel Marquez said, "just a reminder that once I give the order to move in, you are to stay here and wait until the all-clear. Do you understand?"

"Yes, Colonel."

"You are here to identify the stolen art objects at Garcia's home—not to get involved in this capture operation." He looked at me using the mirror on the back of the sun visor.

I nodded. He'd already reminded me of my role several times earlier, and his constant recaps irked me.

"There," the driver said and pointed.

Marquez raised the binoculars. "That's Ernesto Cesar, Director of Banco de Nacional. Most of the cartel's money is laundered through Cesar."

"Can I see?" I asked. Marquez turned toward me, paused and frowned, but he handed me spare binoculars. We both watched the two men, obviously bodyguards, who had already exited the limo and stood curbside. The one Marquez identified as Cesar was a slim, well-dressed man who strolled into the restaurant. A moment later, a second man, short, pudgy, dressed in jeans and open collar shirt, stepped from the limo. He held a cell phone to his ear that partially blocked his profile, and wore a pulled down baseball cap. Unlike the banker, he moved briskly into the restaurant.

"That's our mark," Marquez said.

"Are you sure the second guy is Pablo Garcia?" I put the binoculars down. "Seems his face was too obstructed. What if he's a decoy?"

Marquez didn't answer but kept his focus on the entrance to La Pampa. Finally, he said to his driver, "Tell all units I'm going in for a positive identification." Again his eyes met mine in the visor mirror. "Stay here, Agent Decker."

Dressed in civilian clothes, the colonel and the driver got out and casually crossed the busy city street, heading for the restaurant. I knew I had placed enough doubt in the colonel's mind that he had to confirm it was Garcia before giving the order to begin the takedown.

I grabbed the binoculars again. Marquez and the driver moved as if they were tourists, pausing to glance in the storefronts. There was serious doubt back at the FBI Task Force in Dallas that the Mexicans were on the up-and-up when it came to corruption, payoffs, and taking down a man as powerful as Garcia. So far, they appeared to be as tight and focused as any law enforcement organization I'd dealt with. But they hadn't captured the drug kingpin yet.

I rested the binoculars on the seat and glanced in several directions to see if I could spot any sign of the commandos. Nothing. Only tourists and others moving along the sidewalks. That's when I spotted the Cadillac Escalade pulling to the curb thirty meters behind our SUV. A dark-skinned man got out, opened the side door, and retrieved a slender object about a meter long, wrapped in what looked like brown butcher paper. *Too big for a gun.* He moved across the sidewalk, opened the door of a building and disappeared inside.

A second man stepped from the Escalade and surveyed the sidewalk in both directions. As he turned in my direction, I saw the thick curly head of hair, the round, boyish face with a bushy mustache, and small black eyes set too close—those distinctive features I had memorized from a photo of him during the flight down to Mexico. I watched as Pablo Garcia followed his friend through the door and into the building.

I put the binoculars to my eyes and searched in the other direction for Marquez and his driver. They were standing a block away in front of La Pampa Restaurant with their backs to me, the colonel talking on his phone. If I called him, he'd see my caller ID and no doubt ignore me. For all I knew he was giving the command to start the assault. I thought of blowing the car horn to attract his attention, but that would also draw the attention of the two targets in the restaurant—the same problem if I got out and started yelling for the colonel's attention. With no other choice, I pulled up the right leg of my jeans and removed the Walther PPK strapped to my calf. Slipping out of the SUV, I moved at a swift pace to the door on the side of the building Garcia had entered. I reached for the knob, determined to follow the most wanted man on the planet.

CHAPTER 2 – DEAD OR ALIVE

The building was much older than the surrounding structures. I found a well-worn set of dry-rotting stairs leading up to the second-floor landing. With each step the wood creaked. My heart stuttered fearing someone would hear me. If caught, I'd be a dead woman within seconds. I wasn't dealing with some penny-ante punk who'd shoplifted. Garcia's barbaric reputation was well established.

Sweat dribbled down my back as I entered a short hallway ending with two doors that I guessed to be offices. Falling plaster powdered the floor, leaving evidence of footsteps made by the men I followed. Whatever the occupants paid to rent these offices, it was too much.

I stopped to listen but heard nothing.

I tracked the prints to the next flight of stairs that continued up to the third-floor landing. There I found a repeat of the second floor—a couple of doors with faded names of bygone businesses. Again I stood and listened to the distant sounds of traffic beyond the old walls.

One of the doors opened, and a gray-haired woman came out. She had a mop in one hand and a bucket in the other. At least one office in the building had to be somewhat clean. She didn't seem surprised to see me holding a gun aimed at her. I pointed at my FBI ID hanging around my neck.

In my best Spanish, I said, "*¿Has visto a dos hombres?*"

She studied me, cocked her head, and turned her gaze to the last set of stairs. I nodded a *thank you* and motioned with my gun for her to go back into the office. Then I took the stairs that ended at a metal door. The powdery footprints faded. I assumed I'd found access to the roof.

The floor creaked again with my last step. I froze, waiting

for the door to burst open and a hail of bullets to come my way. I stood as still as possible, gripped my Walther and aimed at the door. Thirty seconds passed, but it seemed like hours. When nothing happened, I opened the door a narrow crack. Sunlight streamed in. I peered through. No one was in sight. Had the woman with the mop lied? Garcia was a folk hero to many in Mexico—a Spanish Robin Hood. I needed to be vigilant.

I pushed the door open a bit more and saw a tar rooftop with shingle patches too numerous to count. From what I could see, there was a handful of metal vents, rusted with age, and an equal number of corroded air conditioner coverings.

Near the front of the building, the side that faced the street below and the La Pampa restaurant, two men stood peering over the edge. One I recognized as the driver of the Escalade. He had unwrapped the long object—the butcher paper curled in a light breeze at his feet. The object, a rocket-propelled grenade launcher rested on his shoulder. His eye pressed against the scope, and his hand gripped the trigger handle. The angle of the RPG told me he must be targeting the restaurant.

Two meters to his side stood Pablo Garcia.

I gently pushed the door open enough for me to pass through, estimating I was twelve or so meters away from the men. Aiming my Walther on Garcia's back, I took a step forward. A loud whoosh filled the air, followed by an earth-shaking blast. A second later, black smoke billowed up from below.

The two turned away from the scene and headed across the roof toward the door—and me.

At the sight of my gun leveled at them, both stopped.

"Drop the weapon! Hands up!" I shouted over the screams, car alarms, and chaos from the street.

The driver looked at Garcia. Receiving a nod, he slowly lowered the RPG launcher to the rooftop. The drug lord took a step away as the driver pulled a gun from his waistband. Before he could raise it, I fired, hitting him in the abdomen. He dropped onto the roof, yelping like an injured dog and gripping his stomach. His gun skittered away.

Garcia turned and ran for the cover of a nearby storage shed.

"*Alto!*" I yelled. I had the Walther trained on him, ready to fire, never figuring he would halt, but he did. "Put both hands on top of your head. *Ahora!*"

He didn't respond, so I took a few more steps toward him, both hands steadying my PPK. "Now, asshole, or you're toast. *Muerto.*"

Garcia complied.

"If you move, the wind will be whistling between your eyes and out the back of your skull. I hope the hell you understand English."

I stood in front of him. "How's your day going, Pablo?"

"Who are you?" His eyes seemed to be gauging me.

"Sorry about your friend." I took a quick glance at the driver. He had stopped moaning and looked unconscious or dead. Back at Garcia, I said, "I'm Maxine Decker, a consultant for the FBI here to identify all the stolen property you've stashed away back at your *hacienda.*

"A consultant? You're not even a federal agent?"

"Retired OSI Special Agent. Now I travel around capturing super villains on rooftops."

"You have a smart mouth."

"My mom used to say that. Now drop to your knees. Nice and slow."

As he eased down, he said, "I can make you one of the richest women in the world."

"That's very generous. Lean back on your heels."

"You can have anything you want. Nothing will be too much. You can live like a queen."

"Thanks, but I'm not into the royalty thing so much. Reach back and grab your ankles."

"Simply turn the other way until I'm gone, and you'll have all you ever wanted."

"You're pushing my buttons, Pablo, and you don't want to do that. Grab your damn ankles."

Garcia reached behind and grunted as he leaned back—his overweight body didn't help.

"Why did you blow up the restaurant?"

"Ernesto Cesar was a traitor. He stole from me."

I leaned forward until we were eye to eye. "Open your mouth."

"*¡Vete al diablo!*"

I didn't understand much Spanish, but I got what he said. "No, I'm not the one going to hell. That would be you, my friend. Open your mouth or I'll simply blow your face off right now."

As he reluctantly did so, I shoved the PPK in so hard I knew I must have chipped some teeth. "I'm very nervous right now. Don't make this gun go off by accident."

Spittle built up in the corners of his mouth, and I could smell the stench of his sweat. His breathing burst in and out as his eyes filled with fear and rage. That was good. He got the message.

With my left hand, I removed my cell phone and dialed Colonel Marquez. I prayed he would answer. There was a good chance he could have been caught in the explosion.

"Agent Decker, are you all right?"

"Yes," I said.

His tone turned from concern to being pissed off. "I ordered you to stay in the SUV. It's total destruction down here. Where the hell are you?"

"On the roof across from the restaurant."

There was a moment of silence. I could hear frightened voices through his phone. "Get back down here," Marquez said. "I don't have time for your disobedience."

"I shot and may have killed the man who fired the RPG. And I have Pablo Garcia here gagging on my gun."

Another momentary pause. "We're on our way."

I was pretty sure it would annoy Marquez to have to come to me to collect his prisoner. I'd stolen his thunder. But if he'd listened to me in the first place when I suggested the man he pegged as Garcia might be a decoy, he'd be up here rather than me.

I smiled at the drug lord. "Some of my friends want to meet you."

He tried to say something, probably his final offer to make me rich. But the gun turned his words into gibberish.

It couldn't have been more than one minute before Marquez burst through the door followed by so many Federales that I feared the roof might not support the weight.

Once we were surrounded by an abundance of assault rifles aimed at Garcia, Colonel Marquez placed his hand on my shoulder and gently but firmly pulled me away. "I'll take it from here, Agent Decker."

Yeah, I guess so. I backed up until I was standing with the circle of commandos. Marquez hovered over Garcia. Then he leaned forward and whispered into the drug lord's ear. He spoke for about thirty seconds, and I watched Garcia's expression shift to pure terror. His face ashened.

The colonel took a step back and spoke in Spanish. *¡Chinga tu madre!* He raised his gun and fired. The bullet made a neat, round hole in the Mexican's forehead. There was nothing neat about what it did to the back of his skull. He collapsed, his life gone in an instant.

Everyone stood silently until the colonel holstered his gun. Then, as a group, they moved to the roof exit. The finality and brutality of the action struck me. As Marquez walked past, I said, "You killed him. I thought you wanted him alive?"

"We did Agent Decker. Long enough for me to pass sentence and perform the execution. Why waste money on a trial for this pig? All of Mexico thanks you for that. You are the hero who brought down the great Pablo Garcia. Be proud."

"What did you say to him?"

"I simply recited the names of all my family members that he murdered or had killed."

"And the last thing you said?"

"It is not fit for a lady's ears."

EXCERPT FROM MAGDA SCARLET'S
JOURNAL – CONFESSION
Otter Brook, South Carolina—**1988**

I feel sick. I'm devastated. Maybe if I write some of this out, it won't be so bad.

This evening I sat on the couch beside my husband while I studied some of Nikola Tesla's patents. Craig wasn't acting normal. I put the Tesla book down and stared at my husband. Earlier, I tried to start a conversation when he came home from work, but he just sat watching TV. I thought he was unusually quiet. His excuse was that he'd had a long day.

I knew something was bothering him. There was something wrong.

Were we going off track again?

This wasn't the first time I felt his distance recently. Of course, being pregnant didn't make me the most alluring woman. And keeping up with all the new research in my career stole time away from him. We'd been through some rough spots, but that was behind us now, I thought. This baby was the symbol of our new beginning.

When I asked him what was on his mind, he didn't answer.

Then Craig clicked the remote control, and the television went dark.

I reached for the lamp on the end table, but he told me to leave it off. My first fear was that Craig had been diagnosed with some horrible disease.

He stared at the ceiling and said he didn't know where to start.

That's when I figured out that he was going to tell me something I didn't want to hear.

*Craig said he wished he **was** sick. Wished he **was** dying because of what he had to tell me. Then he stood and paced, his hands laced over the crown of his head. He did something bad, he said. It sounded as if the words came out on their own, like he didn't want to say them.*

He sat beside me again and held both my hands and started talking about the difficult time we'd had a few years back when I was studying so hard for my Ph.D. He rehashed it all—how I'd stay late with my study group, and he'd stay home drinking, mindlessly watching television.

I stopped him because that wasn't what he'd said back then. He'd told me he often met up with friends and have dinner once in a while. Or met for drinks.

He said he'd lied to me. He hadn't had friends. He'd had one friend. It was a woman.

I slapped him and then slapped him again. I started crying, and he did, too.

He said me he felt so guilty. It had been over for a long time, and he'd never told me about it because he didn't want to hurt me. But now he had no choice.

CHAPTER 3 – INTERVIEW
Acapulco, Mexico

Soledad Conseco smiled at me with deep brown eyes and red lips. "So, Agent Decker, you took down the infamous Pablo Garcia on your own—by yourself—on a rooftop. I'm impressed."

It sounded like she wanted to chalk up Garcia's death to me. "No, I apprehended him and held him until Colonel Marquez arrived, which was only a matter of minutes."

I had agreed to the interview on TV Acapulco's En Las Noticias News talk show, but now in the middle of it, I wondered if I should have declined. I was certain that the cartel intended to come after me. I hadn't fired the shot that killed Garcia, but I was complicit. Less visibility meant fewer guns aimed at me. Secondly, I thought Conseco would ask more questions about the stolen works of art and artifacts recovered from Garcia's mansion. I kept attempting to steer the conversation in that direction and away from my involvement with the apprehension—busting drug lords was not my expertise, and I didn't want that kind of notoriety.

"Aside from removing the kingpin of the Selinas Cartel off the streets, I believe there's another remarkable outcome of this event," I said. "Are you familiar with Tucker's Cross?"

Conseco's expression clearly told me she was taken off guard, and not particularly pleased about it. "No, I must admit, I am not."

"It's one of the artifacts recovered from Garcia's estate. It has an interesting history."

I hoped I had turned the interview. "In 1955, Teddy Tucker

returned to a shipwreck he had found five years earlier. This time, instead of just wreckage and canons, he found treasure. One of the objects he salvaged was a heavy gold cross, studded with seven huge emeralds the size of musket balls. He tried to keep his find a secret, but Bermuda is small, and rumors began to fly. The Smithsonian appraised the treasure and artifacts at $250,000."

"That was a long time ago," Conseco said. "I can't imagine the value now."

"Way up in the millions. Still, $250,000 was a lot of money in the 1950s."

Across from where I sat, I could see the weather set and a technician prepping it for the next report. Maybe my interview was coming to an end. I hoped Conseco would ask a few more questions about the reclamation of treasures. I gave it one more shot. "Every time poor old Tucker went out in his boat, he was followed. And when the government threatened to confiscate the goods, he stuffed the cross in a potato sack and hid it in an underwater cave. Eventually, he displayed the cross and other treasures in a museum he and his wife ran. Then they sold the museum to the government. Just before Queen Elizabeth II was to visit the museum—I think it was in 1974— they discovered that the cross had been stolen, and a replica left in its place. It's been missing ever since. But not any longer. Those are the types of mysteries I love to solve."

"You must take great pride in finding so many stolen riches."

"I do. I've spent the last three days identifying and inventorying Garcia's stolen and black market collection, and making arrangements for returning them to the rightful owners or other appropriate destinations. That's my job, and I love it."

"So where did you get the nerve to take on an international criminal?"

I had to commend the TV show host for her persistence.

"I didn't have a choice. I was in the right place at the wrong time." I could see she was annoyed. Like most other news shows, to get good ratings, they thrived on grisly details. And she wasn't getting that from me.

Finally Conseco thanked me and then turned to face the camera and described what would be coming up next. A huge relief swept through me. The interview was over.

I thanked her for having me on her show and headed to the lobby feeling the tightness in my chest release so I could breathe normally again.

My ex-husband, OSI Special Agent Kenny Gates, sat on the couch beside my Mexican police protection escort. "How'd it go?"

The Mexican didn't say anything. He never did. I wondered if he even spoke English.

"Crappy. I'm not fond of recounting that I witnessed the killing of someone, good or bad." I moved close to him as he stood. "Damn, I'm glad you're here." I pecked him on the cheek. He'd flown in the previous day, and this morning he came along with me to the interview. We hadn't had much time to talk, other than his congratulating me and asking if I was okay.

Kenny and I had a complicated relationship that most people had difficulty understanding. We were divorced on paper, but not from one another. He was always there for me, and me for him. He was still my best friend, and I trusted him more than any other human on Earth. Now and again, we both needed each other for company—to share what was going on in our lives. And even though I often rebuffed his advances, sometimes I gave in, and once in a while lapsed into what we do best—sex.

"I'm not good at the press circus," I said. "And I feel like I have a big X on my back. I keep looking over my shoulder. I don't want to be stupid and ignore the dangers of staying in cartel country. I can't wait to get back to the U.S."

Kenny took my hand and walked me out the glass doors, the policeman in tow. "Never stupid, Max—well, except for when you left me."

I jabbed my elbow in his side. I thought the poke would make it seem as if I thought his remark was funny in some way. But in actuality, his statement hurt. "Don't you remember? It was a mutual decision."

"I let you think so."

We walked to my rental car in silence.

My Mexican shadow got in a car parked behind us. I assumed he would hang with me until I boarded the plane.

"You sit back and relax," Kenny said. "I'll drive us to the airport."

And I let him.

When we landed in San Diego, I was cranky. My least favorite parts of flying were landing and taking off. Our long flight made two stops, ramping up my anxiety enough to rip me out of my Johnny Walker-aided naps. It didn't seem to bother Kenny at all. Every time I had glanced at him, his head appeared comfortably resting against the back of the seat, and his eyes were closed. His mouth didn't even gape, nor did his chin fall to his chest. How could anybody relax and drift off like that?

We'd no sooner gotten through customs and made our way off the concourse when a cluster of lights flashed. Reporters. *Damn.*

They started hurling questions about how I captured Pablo Garcia. Was I afraid? Exactly how did I subdue him? What about the man I shot? Did I know I had mortally wounded him? Why didn't I shoot Garcia? Did I think of myself as a hero?

We walked faster.

Kenny suddenly stopped and turned around. "Back off. Leave her alone."

One reporter got up in Kenny's face, and I tensed. I knew my ex, and crowding his space was one thing he didn't tolerate with much patience.

"I'm telling you as nice as I can, pal," Kenny said. "I'll be happy to bust that camera and even buy you a new one once you're out of the ER. Got it?"

Kenny took my arm, and we continued. He read the stress

on my face. "I'm keeping my cool, Max. You hang in there. We'll be out of here in a minute. We're not taking the shuttle."

Kenny led me to a car rental kiosk. It didn't take long for the paperwork, and in a short time we picked up the car and headed to the Hilton on Harbor Island. We only had a day layover before our return flights—mine to my mountain cabin in Colorado and his back to OSI headquarters in Maryland.

"Thanks for making all the arrangements," I said.

Kenny let me unwind, tuning the radio to some soft jazz. He didn't talk to me or ask questions. The mood was blissful.

After a little while, he reached for my thigh. "What do you say we get away from it all? I can take a few more days, and hell, you set your schedule, so that's not a problem. We can get a decent night's sleep and leave in the morning."

I leaned my head back on the seat and left his hand on my leg. His touch was comforting, and in some way made me feel safe.

"That would be wonderful. I'd love it."

"Ready for a short road trip? I've got just the place. No one will know where you are. Not the press and not the cartel."

I rolled my head to the side to look out the window. My eyes caught a reflection in the side mirror, one I'd already noticed before. I sat up.

"You see it, too?" Kenny said.

"Yeah. That car's been with us since we left the airport."

CHAPTER 4 – RICARDO
The Hilton, Harbor Island, San Diego, California

When the phone rang next to my bed, I jumped. I'd been dead asleep. I had no trouble remembering that the dream I was awakened from was bizarre, but couldn't recall the details.

I fumbled for the receiver in the dark. "Hello."

Kenny's voice came through, sounding much too cheerful for whatever time it was. "You gonna sleep all day or what?"

I slid off the bed, padded to the window and drew open the blackout curtains. A brilliant shard of sunlight nearly blinded me.

"What time is it?"

"Time to get up and at 'em. Ten AM."

"Holy crap." I swept my hair away from my face and rubbed my eyes that felt gritty. "I must have been tired. I crashed."

"Let's get this bus on the road."

"Where are you?"

"Down in the lobby. I've already read the paper, watched the news, and checked my e-mail."

"You're not going to tell me where you're taking me, are you?"

"Nope. Not yet. Working on a couple of last minute details to make sure everything is going to be perfect. By the way, to put your mind at rest, I went out early to Starbucks for a coffee, and nobody followed me. If it was the paparazzi or some splinter of the cartel behind us yesterday, they changed their mind."

I sighed. "Glad to hear that. I'll meet you downstairs in a few minutes."

After a quick shower, dressing, and applying a swish of lip gloss, I headed down to the lobby, wet hair and all.

"Hello, beautiful," Kenny said as I emerged from the elevator. "Hungry?"

"I'm starved. I think I could chow down on the south end of a northbound anything."

He led me to the restaurant where I ordered a Belgian waffle and bacon, and he had steel-cut oatmeal.

"What's the mystery destination?" I asked, after my first sip of coffee.

"And spoil the surprise?"

"Yep."

"Never could keep a secret from you for long. San Felipe. It's a little village in the Mexican Baha on the Gulf of California. Plenty of sun and beach, and a selection of cold drinks with little umbrellas."

"Sounds like Paradise."

San Felipe *was* paradise! Kenny had rented a villa on a gorgeous stretch of sparkling white sand beach that eventually vanished beneath the turquoise water. Above, the blue sky was cloudless. Palms moved with the breeze like performing a tropical dance. Postcard perfect. I stood at the window staring out at the breathtaking view, trying to ignore the fact that I was back in Mexico. "I can't believe this," I called to Kenny who was putting our luggage in the bedroom.

He came up behind me and wrapped his arms around my waist. "Think you can relax here?"

"Silly question. How can I not?"

"Wi-Fi and satellite if you want to connect with the outside world. And a kitchen for midnight snacks. Look out there, see the little tiki huts, the *palapas*, on the beach? We can dig our toes in the sand, take a swim, and then chill in a hammock in the shade of a hut."

"You amaze me. You always know just what I need."

"Oh, and I had them stock the fridge with my grocery list. Cost a little extra, but what the heck. And the minibar of course. How about I fix you one of my famous piña coladas."

"I'd love one."

While he went into the kitchen, I removed my ankle-holstered Walther PPK and placed it in the nightstand drawer next to Kenny's Glock G41. As an active OSI special agent, he was always armed, and for my protection, so was I. I heard whirring and then ice grinding. A moment later, he handed me the fresh piña colada. In his other hand was a bottle of Tecate. "Cheers."

I raised my glass to his bottle, but just before they clinked, there was a knock at the door.

I tensed.

Kenny went to the front window and peeked between the blinds. "Some guy. Probably wants to wash the car or something for an easy American dollar. Not the cartel type."

"How can you be sure?" I retrieved a kitchen towel then my Walther and Kenny's G41.

"Trust me, Max. But just in case." He took his .45 auto from me and draped the towel over it.

"Wait." I positioned myself flush against the wall where I wouldn't be seen through the doorway.

Kenny opened the door. "Can I help you?"

"I need to see *Señora* Decker."

I raised the Walther.

"Who are you?" Kenny moved forward to make the kid step back. My ex closed the door behind him, but I could still hear bits of conversation.

A moment later, Kenny opened the door again. "Max, he wants to talk to you about something his brother found."

I nodded and stuffed the Walther in the back of my waistband.

Kenny openly carried his weapon back to the counter and offered the young man a drink of water, but he refused. And he didn't sit until he was invited.

"My name is Ricardo Delgado. I am from San Luis Rio

Colorado, Mexico. I see you on the television. I pray for to see you in person. I ask God for help. My brother, he find something."

His accent was thick, but I didn't have much trouble understanding him.

"Vincente, my brother, was in the water." Ricardo stopped as if searching for the right words. "A month ago, he wade in the river. New water put in the Colorado from the dam. That is where my brother go in the water."

Kenny stopped him. "I think he means the pulse water recently released from the Morelos Dam upstream in the Colorado River."

Ricardo looked excited. "*Sí!*"

Kenny turned to me. "That's part of a program to restore the Colorado River delta."

"*Sí,*" Ricardo said. "Yes. Restore. We live not too far away. Vincente wade in the water." Ricardo pulled a bandana from his pocket and unfolded it. *Mira.* Look. My brother, he find this. He take picture." He handed me a photograph.

I stared at the image, and so did Kenny.

My eyes shifted to my ex's. "What in the hell is it?"

CHAPTER 5 – THE PHOTO

Holding Ricardo's photo to catch the light, I examined it. He told us his brother had taken the picture with his cell phone. "Excuse me a minute." I went to retrieve my suitcase. I took out a small leather pouch, and then dumped the contents on the bed. Among the articles was a plastic case containing my illuminated jeweler's loupe, a necessity in my line of work.

I went back to Kenny and the young man. Peering through the magnifying lens I made out more of the photograph's detail. What I saw was an object that had a slight resemblance to a large toolbox—about one meter long with a handle on top. I got an idea of the scale because someone stood behind the object with one hand touching it. But this was no toolbox. Unlike a toolbox, there were no latches to secure a lid. And out of one end extended a metal tube, about the diameter of a paper towel cardboard roller. I estimated its length to be 30 centimeters. The photo had been taken at an angle, so I was able to observe two multi-prong connectors, much like modern power plugs, on the other end-panel that faced the camera. There appeared to be an abundance of oxidation and corrosion all over the object. "Certainly looks metallic, maybe copper or brass. I'd have to see it to be sure."

My eye stopped on what appeared to be an engraving or stamping. Maybe even a metal tag. "Kenny, look at this." I handed him the picture and the loupe. "Bottom right corner of whatever this is."

Kenny stared through the lens. "Yeah, I see it. The name Friedrich Krupp AG."

"Right," I said. "A German company."

Kenny glanced up. "And there's a damn swastika on it. That

dates it from World War II."

I turned to Kenny. "Not in such bad shape if it was from that era. What do you think it could be?"

"Could have been a vet's war souvenir, and he lost it. But I have no idea what it is."

"Kind of big for a souvenir," I said.

"No," Ricardo said loudly, taking me by surprise.

Kenny returned the photo. "What do you mean?"

"No, souvenir. No memento. My brother die because of this. Vincente murdered."

I felt my eyes widen at his statement. "You told us your brother was wading in the water when he found it. Why do you say he was murdered?"

Ricardo rewrapped the photograph in his bandana. "New water rush down from Morelos Dam. Everyone in San Luis Rio very excited. Everyone play in the water. Little *niños* and *adultos*. Vincente—my older brother—he find this washed down with water. So he think it interesting and start looking up information on computer. He tell me it is important find. Some secret from war."

"I can't imagine what that could be," I said. "Looks like nothing more than an equipment part or perhaps a power converter. Not worth enough money for someone to kill him for it."

"Vincente think it was big deal. Very important. I tell him, 'You crazy, man.' That was all he do all day, search for stuff on computer about this." Ricardo held up the wrapped bandana. "He take this picture and put it on the Internet. It made no sense to me. *Loco,* I say." He tapped his finger to his temple.

Kenny scratched his head. "What did your brother tell you about what he found in his research? Did he say why he thought it was so important?"

"Vincente find someone on the Internet. He didn't tell me who, only that this man knew something. My brother, he very excited. He convinced he find something special. He hide it in the shed behind our mother's house. Every night he go there and look at it. Sometimes I would go with him. I keep telling him, Vincente, you are crazy. One night he get a phone call. My brother's face full of fear."

I glanced at Kenny and then at Ricardo. "Who called him?"

Ricardo shook his head. "I wish I know. Vincente did not know who it was, either. But my brother say the woman on the phone threaten him. My brother was afraid. He say I should not tell anyone about what he found or about the phone call. Then he tell me the woman on the phone say she would kill my brother if he keep looking for answers about the object. I say what are you afraid of? It's just a woman."

He teared up, and Kenny offered him water again. This time he accepted.

"You okay?" I asked.

"*Si, si.* I apologize. My brother was like a father to me." Ricardo raised his eyes to the ceiling as if peering through the roof. "Our father, he is with God." Then his gaze met mine.

I let Ricardo take a moment to sip the water and recollect himself. His story was getting to me, too. I swallowed back my memories at the tragic death of my twin sister, Francine—at my own hands. I believed I knew how he was feeling. Calling his brother crazy was probably tearing him up. I understood what guilt boiling inside felt like. Even now, the nausea of blame rolled inside my belly. I gave us time for the daggers in our guts to retreat. Though I didn't want to, I finally asked him a question I knew would agitate his emotions again. "How did your brother die?"

Ricardo cleared his throat. "I give him a party for his birthday. Vincente was twenty-five. We all stay up late celebrating. Everyone leave about two in the morning. My brother and I have one more drink. '*Salud*,' Then go to bed. *Policía* come to our house early in the morning. Seven o'clock, maybe. They tell me Vincente is dead. They tell me he fall from bridge, and they find his body in the water. Too much to drink, they say. I can't believe it. So, I go check, and his bed is empty. I say it can't be. Vincente went to bed when I did. He would not go out and walk to the bridge. But the *policía* say they have no reason to inv … invegis … what is the word?"

"Investigate?" I said.

"*Si*. They say it was accident." Ricardo's chin quivered. "If only I had believed him. I call him crazy. Tell him he is *loco*. Maybe this would not have happened if I listen to him. If I take him serious. I should have believed." Ricardo wiped his nose with the back of his hand.

My heart went out to him. My throat tightened as I remembered the death of my sister—like he was remembering Vincente. I shoved my feelings into a dark room in my mind and slammed the door.

I could think of nothing to say to Ricardo that would diminish his anguish. No one had ever been able to speak any words to me that relieved my guilt about Fran. What was so sad was that the Mexican police were probably right—a night of partying, and one thing led to another. Ricardo went to sleep, but his brother wasn't done celebrating. The truth wouldn't matter. Ricardo still had a long difficult road to travel to forgive himself for calling his brother crazy.

He stared hard at me. "I see in your eyes, you do not believe me. You believe the *Federales*. I did, too. At first. But then everything changed."

CHAPTER 6 – *POR FAVOR*

Ricardo's voice quavered, and again I connected with his pain.

"How did everything change?" I asked. "What do you mean?"

"I grieve for my brother and hate myself because I was angry at him. Why my brother go out on the bridge drunk? I feel guilty for being mad, and I pray to God for help." Ricardo put his hand on his heart. "I hurt so bad. The heart aches. I realize others want the object, too. Maybe his killer want it because after Vincente die, I discover our house broken into. Back window is smashed. It is old bedroom used for storage. I never go in there. Thief come in window while I am at church for Vincente's funeral. Vincente was warned. He had threat call from woman."

"Is the object still hidden in your mother's shed?" Kenny said.

He took a long time before he answered—staring at our faces as if considering our trustworthiness. "No. The secret to object's hiding place went to the grave with Vincente. He was killed for what he find that day in the water. This is why I come to you."

I hated to tell Ricardo, but I didn't work murder cases. He must have been reading my mind because he started explaining why he had sought me out.

"I see you all over TV news, and I think to myself, you are the one I must talk to."

"But how did you know I was here? How did you find me?"

Ricardo smiled for the first time since he had arrived. "Small report in my town *periódico— periódico*, how you say?"

"Newspaper," Kenny said.

"*Si si.* Reporter follow you from airport. He write you were in San Diego hotel restaurant and talk about go to San Felipe. I check around." Ricardo shot his eyes to Kenny. "Aha, I find you by Kenneth Gates name, right here at these villas. I drive down in my truck. Long trip for you. Short trip for me."

Terrific. If he can find us, anyone can. I glanced at Kenny. "Well, so much for being under the radar."

"Sorry, Max. I did that test ride to Starbucks and nobody followed. I guess that's why I'm not a field agent."

"Maybe because I wasn't in the car," I said.

"Probably. And I didn't think anything more about it because nobody followed us here. I kept checking in the rearview."

The drug cartel swept into my head like a roaring wind. *Did they know I was here, too?*

I returned my attention to the young man. "Ricardo, I'm sorry. I don't think you've come to the right person."

Ricardo bolted up out of his seat. "*Si*, I have. I have. You find Tucker's Cross and take care of cartel drug lord. You can help me find who kill my brother and why." He sank into the chair again. With an apologetic expression, he said, "Please, *Señora* Decker. I no rest until I find who did this. Every day I do not know, a piece of me dies."

I heard a little crack in his voice again and was afraid if I responded, he and Kenny would hear the crack in mine. Waves of heartbreak washed through me. *Francine.* I'd been tricked into shooting and killing my sister. My twin. Why hadn't I been smarter? I understood how Ricardo's insides felt, ripping apart with guilt. As much as I wanted to help, I knew that taking this on would tear me to pieces. Besides, I had my commitment with the FBI task force. They gave me a great deal of flexibility but had exclusive use of my time. I had to tell him no. And I was going to witness his expression and feel sick in the pit of my belly.

"I do not have much to pay you," he said. "But I will give you all I have. Everything. My money. My truck."

I put my elbows on my knees and rested my face in my

hands.

"You find lost and stolen things," Ricardo said. "And you take care of bad people. *Por favor.* I beg."

Kenny spoke up. "Ricardo, we're sorry to hear about what happened to your brother. This must be a difficult time for you. I'm sure Ms. Decker would love to help you. But she has another job. And right now, she needs to have some personal time. You can see this is distressing to her."

I looked up and watched Kenny go to the door and open it followed by Ricardo, the young man's steps slow and heavy.

"Hang on," I said. "Let me see the picture again."

EXCERPT FROM MAGDA SCARLET'S
JOURNAL – OVER THE EDGE
Otter Brook, South Carolina—1988

*T*his *morning when I was fixing coffee, Craig came in the kitchen. The only word I could get out of my mouth was* **who**.

He told me I didn't know her, that he'd met her at a bar one night.

I wanted to know her name. He kept saying it wasn't important, that it was over and done. But I couldn't help it. I wanted her name. I wanted to hear him say it. I screamed at him, and he finally said that her name is Ellen Osterling. He blamed it all on the drinking and the loneliness like it was my fault. He admitted there weren't any excuses.

I asked him how long.

He confessed to a couple of months before calling it off. He told her he loved me, and it was over. He said Ellen didn't want to end it—that she'd been like a crazy woman when he told her.

I had one question ripping through my brain. It hung up like an old scratched record that kept repeating and repeating and repeating. I asked him if he loved her.

He denied it with a loud, NO!

The power a man can display with his voice is scary. Craig frightened me. Then I asked him about what he'd said last night, that he had no choice but to tell me.

He didn't answer right away. Then he finally said he was afraid for me—that Ellen Osterling had gone over the edge. She'd sent letters to him at his school address. Recently he'd gotten one almost every day. A few were kind and understanding, but most of them were foul rants. Even her handwriting was bizarre. Then he told me that sometimes he sees Ellen sitting in the school parking lot, but she's never approached him, and he pretends not to notice her. But then the other day, she'd stopped him before he got in the car. She made threats and said she was going to come to the house and tell me everything. She made up a bunch of lies. Even "sick, sexual stuff."

When I heard that, my mouth dried, and my words sounded sticky when I asked if any of it was true. Craig said she is insane, and that she wants to hurt me emotionally or maybe even physically. She wants to punish him and to hurt me.

I hate him. I love him. Shit, I don't know how I feel. I'm numb. I don't know if I'll ever be able to forgive him. There were a million things I wanted to say but kept biting my tongue. My dad always told me it was okay to argue, but always check your weapons to make sure they're not deadly. Probably good advice.

We were drinking our coffee and the doorbell rang. I knew in my gut it was her. I said I'd answer the door. I wanted to see this woman and look into the eyes of the person who was bent on destroying my family.

Craig insisted I go to the bedroom. If it was Ellen, there was no telling what she might do. I'm not sure if it was courage or anger that made me step past him and open the door. She wasn't what I expected. The woman on the porch was trim, tall, with large dark brown eyes and sandy hair that was pulled back, leaving behind a few tendrils that softened her face. She was no floozy with big cosmetic boob implants. No bleach blond hair. No stilettos. She had a classic look about her, and I felt frumpish, especially with my big belly. It was so easy for me to hate her.

Craig was nasty, cursing and telling her to get the hell away and leave us alone.

I butted in and informed her that my husband had already told me about their affair, so there was nothing she could say.

She asked me if I believed he'd told me everything.

I couldn't resist lying. I put on a big smile and said yes, every little detail. I said she'd be surprised at how much I knew about her. And then I told her I was used to Craig's skirt-chasing. She wasn't the first and probably wouldn't be the last. Then I made myself laugh. The astonished look on her face made my day. Then, I slowly closed the door.

What she didn't see, thank God, was me holding my belly and sliding down to the floor and crying like a baby.

CHAPTER 7 – STING

I relaxed on the patio outside our room and studied the picture of the German-made object that Ricardo allowed me to take with my iPad. He wouldn't leave the original with us. Kenny was beside me on a matching chaise lounge sipping a beer. The setting sun lit up the thunderheads over the Sea of Cortez. Despite the threat of the distant storm, the ocean remained calm as it lapped gently against the sand ten meters away.

The young Mexican had shared lunch with us and then left somewhat upbeat after I agreed to investigate. No promises—only that I would research and investigate. This annoyed Kenny since he felt I already had enough on my plate with the FBI task force and didn't need to take on a side project. And he worried about my emotions. But I felt sorry for Ricardo and told him that I'd look into it. I didn't expect to find anything earth shattering, but he needed closure, and I understood how that was.

My mind drifted back to the horrifying time when I'd taken my sister's life. I'd been tracking a brutal smuggling and trafficking professional, and he'd drawn me to Cuba by threating to kill my sister. He was holding her against her will. He set me up, challenging me to a kind of duel. I fired first, but...

The memory slammed my heart. In my mind, I heard the thunderous blast from the pistol. I knew I'd hit him and expected to see him drop. Instead, a mirror shattered into thousands of pieces. I hadn't realized that I'd been looking into that mirror—one mounted at a 45-degree angle. The man I wanted hadn't been in front of me at all. I'd fired at his reflection. When the mirror collapsed in splinters and shards, I saw what I'd hit—my sister who was gagged and tied to a post in the same spot where the man's image appeared in the mirror. I'd been duped by a cheap carnival trick. I didn't know if I'd ever forgive myself.

I glanced at Kenny. He understood how traumatized I'd been. My ex didn't want those horrible memories to stir in me again. He feared that if I got involved with Ricardo, my guilt over Francine would rise like a monster, and I'd slump into depression again.

I took a deep breath and tried to shake off the gloom. I didn't want Kenny to see me so down. I put on a peppy voice. "Now, I'm going to take a shower so you can wine and dine me at—"

"La Hacienda de la Langosta Roja," Kenny said with a Spanish accent straight out of a Cheech and Chong movie.

God, love him, he was doing all he could to cheer me up. "Sounds perfect." I drained my margarita and stood. "Make sure your credit card limit is sky high because I'm having lobster with a shitload of tequila, and you're buying."

"Price is no object for the badass lady who brought down Pablo Garcia." Kenny hoisted his bottle of Tecate. "You need any help in the shower?"

"The night is young," I said and wiggled my ass.

In the bathroom, I looked down at my string bikini-clad body. I wasn't 20 anymore. I noticed the tiny muffin top, and my breasts weren't where I'd prefer them. Gravity had taken its toll, even though I tried to stay in shape. There was no way you could stave off age.

Kenny came up behind me. "Not bad for forty-something."

"I don't know if that's a compliment or not. You could have left out the age reference."

"It *was* a compliment. You had told me before we got married that age didn't matter. You didn't care that I was older."

"That's different. A woman's body just…"

"Will you stop and look at yourself? You don't even have to suck in your tummy." He turned me sideways and asked me to take a look in the vanity mirror.

"Well, I see a few things that could use a tuck, snip, or lift."

"Hush." Kenny pulled the strings on the bikini top, and it fell to the tile floor.

"You're not going to let me take a shower are you?"

"Sure I am. I'm even going to lather you up until you beg me to stop."

I knew if I spoke, I'd let on how good his promise sounded to me. So I kept quiet. As I slipped off the bottom of the bikini, Kenny undressed.

In another minute, we were beneath the steaming shower, and Kenny was kissing me. He knew everything to do that set me on fire. He'd always been an expert. Pressing me against the shower wall, I felt the length of his body against mine and let out a little pleasure groan. From that point on, I was lost in a feverish realm that blotted out all distractions, thoughts, and dark memories.

It was quick and bone shattering for both of us. Afterward, we clung to one another, breathing hard, letting the water stream down our bodies. His face was nuzzled in my neck, and I ran my fingers up and down his spine.

"A little age never hurt either of us," I said.

"It's you, Max. You."

Kenny got out of the shower. "I'm gonna get dressed and finish that beer."

I shampooed my hair, still basking in the slow burn that eventually faded. Sex was one of the things we *always* got right.

Our marriage had been an enigma. We met right after I joined the OSI, fresh out of college with a degree in archaeology and just getting started. On the other hand, Kenny was an experienced agent, ten years my senior. Few stepped up to help this rookie female agent, but Kenny made time to guide me through the ins and outs of my new job. He acted as a mentor, even though our fields of expertise were different. He was an OSI Computer Crimes Investigator specializing in computer forensics and encryption while I covered the black market in stolen antiquities. If Air Force military personnel committed a crime, OSI agents were usually called.

After a decade of marriage came our divorce. I'd become obsessed with my drive to succeed, wanting to spend more time working on my career and less time working on our marriage and starting a family. Kenny wanted a family, something that always seemed to take a backseat as I rose through the ranks at OSI. It hurt him. But too much time had passed to start digging up those bones.

Then the incident in Iraq—five years after our divorce. I was on a joint OSI-Iraqi sting operation when I was forced to shoot a fellow agent and became critically wounded in the process. First there was the long physical rehab then the Department of Justice investigation. It came just short of accusing me of being an accomplice in the smuggling operation, and nearly destroyed me. I bought a cabin in the Colorado Mountains and said goodbye to OSI and the world. That was until Kenny showed up and enticed me to come back and consult for the agency. He pulled me back into the job I wanted so desperately in which to succeed. And here I was on yet another assignment, wondering if I should have stayed in the rocking chair on the front porch of my cabin.

I stepped out of the shower. I was so ready for a delicious lobster dinner, lots of alcohol, and maybe even another but slower and tenderer round of sex with my ex-husband—for old times' sake. When I came out of the bathroom, I noticed that the living room was dark as was the patio beyond. I thought I'd left some lights on. Maybe Kenny turned them off. He was such a romantic. I wrapped myself in the plush robe provided by the villa and took a few steps down the hall into the living room. Looking out on the patio, I expected to see Kenny dozed off.

The moon had risen, and its light reflected off broken glass beside Kenny's lounge—his beer bottle shattered on the patio tile.

I spun around. My Walther PPK was in the nightstand drawer.

I felt a sharp sting on my neck.

CHAPTER 8 – THE EXAMPLE
Near San Felipe, Mexico

I can't breathe, I can't breathe right!" were my first thoughts as I came out of the fog of unconsciousness. I tried to open my mouth to take in air, but I couldn't. Air hungry, panic set it. I wanted to rip off whatever was over my head and the binding that sealed my mouth. I jerked my hands to separate them, but couldn't, and whatever tethered them bit into my wrists. *Plastic tie wraps?*

I lay face down on a hard surface, unable to move. The head cover, mouth binding, and tethering of my wrists sent blistering waves of claustrophobia through the circuitry of my nerves. I wriggled, and the grit under me abraded my body. *Was I naked?* Movement was limited with both wrists and ankles bound. My eyes were of no use, but my sense of smell and touch were intact. The dank, sour odor of moist concrete filled my nostrils.

Calm yourself, Max. Slow your breathing or you're going to pass out. My chest rose and fell, rose and fell, rose and fell, in a runaway rhythm. My heart beat with the same flying tempo. Concentrate. Slow. Breathe in—deep. Now, let it out in a slow, even exhale. Take control. I repeated this in my mind over and over until the panic subsided enough that I could think and recall what had happened. Assess the situation. Think back. What do I remember?

The last thing I could recall was seeing Kenny's broken beer bottle and then feeling a sting in my neck. The needle prick must have been an injection to knock me out. My head thumped like a kettledrum from the aftereffects of whatever drug was used. I'd been wearing a terrycloth robe. If I still wore it, the robe had fallen open because I detected the harsh texture of the floor.

I ached from being in this prone position, although I had no idea how long I had lain here or where I was. But I was working on remembering every detail I could perceive. Keeping my wits about me was important.

I accessed my senses once again. Aside from the smell of what I assumed was concrete, I also detected a mixture of motor oil and mildew. I listened. No voices. The only sound was the buzz of a fluorescent light.

Beneath the darkness of the hood, time became muddled. An hour, maybe two, or even only thirty minutes passed when I heard the sound of a door unlocking and the squeak of rusty hinges, followed by crunchy footsteps that grew louder as someone approached. My throat and mouth felt like they'd been doused with alum. I tried to ask for water, but the tape made my words garbled. Trying harder only produced a louder garble.

"*¡Silencio!*" It was a male voice.

Even through the thick material of the bag, I smelled him—sweat, chili powder, and alcohol. He checked my bindings, and I flinched at his touch.

The man rolled me onto my back. I'd been right about my robe being open. He took his time fondling my breasts. I thrashed, but my effort produced little motion. *Get away from me!* I screamed through the gag, throwing my head from side to side. I feared that I might vomit and then choke due to my mouth being gagged and taped closed. I struggled, holding back my urge to throw up. "Stop it! Stop!" I screamed, but my words were unintelligible. His sweaty hands wandered my bare flesh, and his hot breath seeped through the cloth of my hood. My grunting only seemed to provoke him to touch more of me. His hand trailed down my belly.

"Ahh," I heard him say as he explored between my legs. Then a voice rang out. His hands were suddenly off me, and the near heat of his body disappeared. I heard him walk away and the door close and lock.

I had drifted off into a ragged sleep when the sound of the door opening brought me back to reality. This time there was the sound of many footfalls, and then the clicking of what I figured were light switches being turned on or off.

"Time to get up, Agent Decker." The man spoke with a heavy Spanish accent.

I tried to clear my mind as I came out of sleep and the last vestiges of the drug's effect. The feel of a beefy hand grabbed me by the arm and pulled me to my feet. A second later, the bag over my head was yanked off. Blinded by the lights at first, it took a moment for my eyes to adjust. I turned to the man who had pulled me to my feet. He was a good 30 centimeters taller than me, and built like a Sequoia. A dark stocking mask hid his face. But I saw his eyes. Black as tar without even the slightest glimmer of empathy—like looking into the eyes of a shark.

The left side of the room was in shadows. To the right, powerful floodlights lit up a section of the wall as if it were a stage waiting for a performance. An expansive banner stretched across the wall with a logo consisting of a circle filled with a stylized skull—Xs for eyes, and bullets for teeth. The whole image brought on a hitch in my breath—a bandana wrapped around the skull's neck, crossed AK-47s, a marijuana plant between the gun stocks, and two hands gripping knives. Above the illustration were the words *Cártel de Selinas*.

Pablo Garcia's drug cartel. A shudder rattled my backbone.

Focusing better as I became more alert, I noticed a chair positioned in front of the banner with a camera on a tripod aimed at it. Around the chair, dark stains blotched the concrete. Blood? Within a second it registered with me what had happened here. The images of terrorist beheadings exploded in my mind. I shivered, not from the fact that my robe hung open, but from the paralyzing horror that I was likely the next person to sit in that chair.

I stared at the wire cutters the big man held. Was he going to take one of my fingers? Like slow motion, I watched him move the cutters around to my back. I squinted, anticipating the pain, but then I heard a click and my hands fell free. I closed my robe around me. He cut my ankle ties and then ripped the tape from my mouth. My face stung, left raw from the stripping of the tape. I rubbed the tender skin around my mouth and jawline.

They wouldn't have kidnapped me just to release me. There had to be some other plan. I glanced again at the chair in front of the wall. And the camera.

Another man approached from the dark side of the room. He also wore a mask and was dressed in faded military fatigues, an automatic pistol holstered on his hip. When he spoke, I recognized his voice. He was the one who had ordered me to wake up.

"You are a very beautiful woman," he said. "It is a shame I cannot spend time giving you the best fuck of your life."

Accommodating this pervert's desires seemed less dreadful than what I feared was going to happen. "What do you intend to do?"

"We need to send a strong message to all of Mexico and your American *cabróns*—make an example of you, so others do not try to do what you did."

"I didn't kill Pablo Garcia."

"I am aware of that fact. It was Colonel Marquez who pulled the trigger." He looked at the stains on the floor and smiled. "But he has already his price. Now it is your turn." He motioned toward the chair. "Please take a seat."

I stood firm for a second before the big guy shoved me. "Make sure your robe stays closed," he said.

Another shudder ricocheted through me. It wouldn't play as well in the world to show a half-disrobed woman being beheaded. That would be a distraction from their message.

Other men, also shrouded in dark clothing and black hooded masks, stood around the perimeter of the room. One stepped forward and manned the camera. The one I assumed to be the leader handed me a piece of paper. A single, handwritten paragraph.

"Sit, look into the camera and read it out loud," he said.

I clenched my jaw and glared at him before I spoke. "My death is not going to accomplish anything."

The big man slapped me across the face so hard that I flew to the floor. He quickly jerked me up and threw me into the chair.

The leader said, "You get one more chance."

My cheek burned, and I tasted blood. I was dizzy and fought to see the writing on the paper. I ran options through my mind, and realized I had none. I looked at the camera. Like the Devil's eye, the red light stared back. My parched throat felt scorched, and my mouth filled with desert sand. The first attempt to read came out like a scratchy croak.

"Do it," the leader demanded.

I tried once again. "I am Maxine Decker, special consultant to the FBI. I am responsible for the death of Pablo Garcia. I regret my actions and understand that my execution is justified. I now prepare to suffer for all eternity for what I have done."

The large guy pulled a long serrated knife from under his jacket and moved behind me. He brought the cold edge of the blade to rest against my throat.

The paper in my hands shook. The knife pressed my skin, and then the pressure of it suddenly disappeared. My body trembled. Then I realized it was not me that shook, it was the chair and the floor and the building. The men stumbled around as if trying to maintain their balance. Dust and dirt drifted down from the roof.

A corner of the banner flew free from as a low rumble filled the room. One of the floodlights crashed to the floor. Then the camera, red light still glowing, tipped to its side.

I heard a thump. The big guy sprawled and struggled to rise.

I took advantage of the chaos and shot up from the chair, but couldn't keep my balance. I ended up on my knees, crawling across the floor in a panic to find an exit.

In front of me, the leader and his men stampeded for the door. "*Terremoto!*" he yelled. "Earthquake!"

CHAPTER 9 – EARTHQUAKE

I got to my feet and staggered forward. The concrete wobbled and swooned like the floor of a kid's bounce house. Pieces of adobe and red clay tile fell around me—choking dust clogged the air. Just beyond, I saw the camera, separated from the tripod—its cycloptic red eye stared back at me. I grabbed it and stumbled forward. As the last of the cartel members rushed out, a loud cracking sound to my left revealed a breach in the wall just wide enough for me to squeeze through.

Outside, I gasped for air and reeled with the moving structure. *Move faster, Max.* Unsteadily, I ran. It was night, and I could only make out the dimmest details as my bare feet tread across the sand and rocks. The rumbling of the collapsing building behind me made me pick up my pace, trying desperately not to trip and fall.

A new sound mixed with the crumbling of the building—gunfire. A firefight with automatic weapons, so like what I'd heard years ago in Iraq. The screams of men who'd been shot echoed in my ears. I couldn't discern reality from memory. Pain. Death.

A wood fence offered shelter. I ducked behind it long enough to look back. The flashes of gunfire lit up the surrounding area. I realized that I still held the camera, and I aimed it at the violent scene sixty meters away.

At first, the LCD was black. I touched each button on the camera. Finally, when I pressed one, the screen sprang to life with a ghostly green glow as the night-vision mode captured the low light levels of the hellacious event.

It was then I realized the ground on which I crouched was not moving. The fence stood firm and solid. Nearby, what appeared to be a small farm, remained calm, quiet, unaffected by the forces that shook the building to pieces.

The only place where the earthquake occurred was at the site of the building from which I had just escaped and its most immediate surroundings. That seemed bizarre. Impossible.

I pressed stop on the video camera, turned and ran up an incline toward a dark-shaped structure at the top of a rise. A barn. Perhaps horse stables. As much as I could tell in the darkness it was rundown and in disrepair but might offer a place to hide.

Once inside, I aimed the camera and used the night vision again to see details of the interior. A line of stalls ran along the right side of the barn. As I rushed passed them, I saw no animals. The last stall was twice the size of the others and served as a storage area for bales of hay.

I climbed the stacked bales and crawled across the top layer to the back corner. I remember helping buck bales at my uncle's farm when I was a teenager. Although they were about sixty pounds each, I knew I could move them and create a void to slip into and hide. With a great deal of grunting and straining, I did just that. Placing the extra bales in front of the void, I settled into my secret place and waited. A narrow separation between two of the bales let me keep an eye on the dark interior of the barn.

The gunfire and rumbling of the toppling building finally faded. I heard the faint flapping of wings and figured bats didn't like my company. Some scurrying sounds gave away the presence of mice. Hopefully, that was the worst I would meet in the barn.

I was afraid to use the camera to keep watch. In the darkness, the green glow would not be missed by someone searching for me. I remained still, breathing shallow and listening for anything beyond bats and mice.

After about ten minutes, I heard someone. First was the soft squeak of the barn door hinge. A long pause. Then footfalls, slow, easy, barely making a sound. It sounded as if he stopped at each stall. I spotted the red dot of his gun's laser sweep the walls and ceiling. Efficient, deadly.

He stopped in front of the stack of bales. The red dot brushed across them and above my head along the rafters and tin roof. He seemed to be considering the possibility of this being a good hiding place but then I heard him say, "She must be dead under the rubble. I'm clear." Unlike the Mexicans, he had no accent.

His exit was not as quiet as his entry, and when he opened the barn door, the pale light of the approaching dawn flowed in. Maybe that's why he wanted to leave—whoever those guys were, they probably didn't want to hang around in the light of day.

I waited for over what I guessed to be an hour before feeling that no one was coming back. While I hid, I watched the videos recorded on the camera. The first was of Colonel Marquez. He sat on the same chair as they had put me on in front of the same banner—he was naked, except for a pair of white briefs. Holding a piece of paper in trembling hands, he read a message almost word for word as the one I'd read. When he finished, the big man grabbed Marquez by the hair, brought the Crocodile Dundee knife to the colonel's neck, and sawed.

"Dear God," I said as I watched blood gush out and flow down his chest. Beheading someone with a knife was not like chopping it off with an ax or using a guillotine. The soft tissues would be easy, but it would take a lot of exertion to go through ligaments and bones to separate the head. There was no mercy in this type of killing. It was barbaric. I looked away for a moment, repulsed by what I saw. When I dared look back, Marquez's head was severed. The big man held his sadistic trophy by the hair and placed it in the victim's lap. Then he walked out of frame.

"*Bueno.*" I recognized the voice of the cartel leader.

Sequoia guy stepped back into the picture. He grabbed the dead body and severed head and dragged the remains in the direction of the door. The video ended.

The next video was mine. My stomach knotted as I watched

the big man hold the blade to my throat. Then came the earthquake, or whatever it was. After the shot of me looking down at the red record light, the next few minutes were filled with blackness and chaotic noise until the night vision shot of the building coming apart and the gunfight.

I turned the camera off and peeked through the crack between the hay bales. The dawn's light seeped in through the holes in the sides of the old stable walls. A rooster crowed, and I knew it was time to get away from this place.

Once I pushed the extra bales out of the way, I climbed down and moved along the stalls. With great care, I cracked open the barn door to a narrow slit. Ahead lay desert, bleak and uninviting. Sticking my head out, I saw mountains to the west and the ocean in the opposite direction—the coast appeared to be a dozen kilometers away. I stepped outside and saw a few lines of fencing and a corral in various stages of decay. To the east, the building from which I'd escaped lay in ruins, not more than a heap of debris as if a wrecking ball had attacked it.

I made my way down the dirt road and around to the opposite side of the wreckage. Vultures already gathered around several dead cartel members. The big Sequoia guy was among the bodies, the knife beside his hand. *Butchering bastard.* Knowing my white bathrobe made an excellent target against a brown desert, I moved among the dead until I found a body about my size. I stripped his clothes and put them on, trying to ignore the two holes and bloodstains on the front of the shirt. The pants were too large. I used the knife that was going to take off my head to slash both sleeves from the shirt. I cut off the cuffs and tied the sleeves together at the ends. Then I twisted them into a cord of fabric, strung it through the belt loops, and tied it in front. That would keep the pants from sliding down.

I slipped on his cowboy boots and hat and tucked his automatic pistol in the waistband at the small of my back. *Rot in hell you piece of shit.*

There was a van and two pickup trucks parked nearby. I

found a set of keys in the ignition of a Nissan pickup and cranked the engine. As I pulled away onto a dirt road leading toward the coast, I had two questions filling my head—what happened to Kenny, and what kind of earthquake can target a single building?

EXCERPT FROM MAGDA SCARLET'S JOURNAL – NEWBORN
Otter Brook, South Carolina—1988

*Y*esterday should have been the most wonderful day of my life. I gave birth to my beautiful baby boy, Christopher Liam Scarlet. I thought the world was perfect when the doctor first laid him across my belly. Craig cut the cord. We were both teary.

Christopher is going to be our new beginning. I have forgiven Craig, but I haven't forgotten. I tried not to think about Ellen Osterling, not on that very special day.

When the three of us, mommy, daddy, and Christopher were alone together, Craig and I talked about what our son might be when he grew up. He was only hours old and already we were envisioning his future. I'd been in labor all night, and both Craig and I were exhausted, but the thrill of meeting our son, becoming parents, kept us high for a while. Finally, when my lunch came, Craig put the baby in the bassinette and went out to grab some iced coffee. He kissed me goodbye, and I thought my true healing had begun.

When the phone rang, I picked it up, ready to hear congratulations from one of our friends. And I was so prepared to brag about our new little one. But there was only heavy breathing at first. I kept saying hello, hello. Finally, the caller spoke. I knew the voice right away. It was Ellen. She said that I didn't deserve the child, that the baby should be hers. And then she hung up.

All those wonderful feelings I'd had flowing through me moments before, disappeared. In three seconds, she'd robbed me of the bliss a new mother is supposed to experience.

When Craig came back I started balling and told him about the call. How did she know I'd had the baby? I accused him of talking to her, and we got into a terrible argument. He said he had no idea how she knew. It took him a long time to convince me that he hadn't spoken to

Ellen. I hope he is telling the truth. I couldn't stand another betrayal.

Why won't this woman leave us alone? She had to be stalking us, watching our every move, to know I'd gone to the hospital and had the baby. I told Craig to go to the police. Do something!

Craig finally calmed me down enough so I could nurse the baby. I can't explain what an experience that is to hold your newborn to your breast, skin to skin. I dozed off, releasing my thoughts of Ellen Osterling. After all, she shouldn't steal these moments from me. I refused to let her.

Craig went home early from the hospital to get some rest. The nurse convinced me to let her take the baby to the nursery so I could do the same. She promised to bring him to me for feedings. I reluctantly agreed. I was so tired. I did fall asleep for a little bit, and when I awoke, I wanted to see my baby. I put on my robe and walked down the corridor to the nursery. There was still a few minutes left during visiting hours, so they had not pulled the curtain covering the window yet. When I turned the corner, I froze. Ellen Osterling had both hands pressed to the nursery window and was staring inside.

I screamed for someone to get her out. Get that woman away from my baby. The nurses were quick to respond, but not as I had hoped. Two of them grabbed my arms and started taking me back to my room. One last glance told me Ellen had disappeared. She had made her point.

I argued with the nurses the whole way back. I told them that woman wanted to take my baby. They said that they had alerted security, but I knew they would never find her. They got me into bed and kept attempting to soothe me like I was some lunatic. And then another nurse came in and stuck a needle in my arm. That's all I remembered until this morning.

I have such horrible thoughts come into my mind that I don't even recognize myself.

CHAPTER 10 – CRIME SCENE

It took a half hour to drive out of the desert and back to San Felipe. I pulled the pickup off the road just south of our villa and crossed the dunes to the beach. If the mystery assault team thought I was dead, they wouldn't be looking for me here. I could see tourists already gathering along the sand on lounge chairs under umbrellas ready for a day of sun and surf. Some already dozed in the tiki hammocks.

I walked along the waterline until I was directly even with our room. Trying not to attract attention in my ill-fitting, bloodstained outfit, I pulled the cowboy hat low over my face and made my way up the beach to the patio outside our suite. Someone had cleaned up the broken beer bottle. I tried the sliding glass door and found it unlocked. Inside, the beds were made and the room tidied up. Housekeeping must have just left because I smelled a strong odor of disinfectant and air freshener.

I went straight to the nightstand and found my iPhone, iPad, and my Walther. Kenny's Glock was also there. As cautious as he was, he would never leave without it. I held it for a moment and thought of our previous night together. As much as I wished he were simply out looking for me, I knew better. There was nothing right about this situation.

I switched the Walther with the Mexican's pistol, and then called Kenny's cell. The call went right to voicemail. Not a good sign.

Then I stripped off the dead man's clothes and headed for the shower. I felt dirty inside and out. I had to wash the night's events from my skin.

This time I took my gun with me. I put it on the toilet seat where I could reach it quickly if needed.

After drying off, I dressed and strapped my Walther just

above my right ankle. I gathered up the Mexican's clothes and my robe and shoved them in a garbage bag. Last, I hung my FBI ID around my neck.

Now it was time to call in the cavalry.

I stood beside Commander Cervantes of the Mexican *Policía Federal* inside the dark tactical assault van parked near the old horse farm. Cervantes was in charge of the *División Antidrogas* which dealt with drug-related crime. He finished watching the video of the beheading of Colonel Marquez and my ordeal.

"Disgusting," he said and handed the camera back to me. "You are very lucky. This group has no regard for human life. They are wild animals."

"What about Agent Gates?" I didn't think it any stranger's business about my relationship with my ex, so I kept my questions and conversation on a professional level. But inside I was scared. We weren't married anymore, but I couldn't imagine my life without Kenny.

"I have ordered a nationwide search by all federal agencies. We will find him."

I was glad he didn't add *dead or alive*.

After contacting the Federales when I was still at the hotel, I had notified my team at the FBI taskforce headquarters in Dallas and OSI Cyber Crime Center in Linthicum, Maryland where Kenny worked. Investigation units from both agencies were on their way. Within an hour, Commander Cervantes had picked me up. By the time we arrived at the crime scene, the collapsed building and horse farm were swarming with combat police, K-9 units, medical examiners, and a CSI team. The search for Marquez's body ended quickly. The corpse had been dumped in a ravine a few hundred meters from the farm. This caused Commander Cervantes to start yelling at anyone within range. I kept my distance to avoid his wrath.

Another truckload of heavily armed police arrived and set up a perimeter around the farm. A helicopter landed with more high-ranking Federales. Then a second chopper swooped in, black with no markings. I watched it land in a nearby field, and a man in a dark suit jumped out. Even from a distance, I recognized my friend, FBI Special Agent Kevin Fender.

A few years back, Kenny and I had worked with Fender to stop a terrorist attack on Las Vegas and recover the ancient artifact, the Blade of Abraham. At the time, Kevin was in charge of the FBI's Las Vegas regional headquarters. He transferred to Dallas to work out of the same task force office as I did. When I asked him why, he said, "I always have more fun working beside you." I warned him to be careful what he wished for. Initially, we had not hit it off well with the Las Vegas case but had now come to have great respect for each other. I trusted Kevin and knew he was as upset about Kenny's disappearance as I was. He waved as he approached.

After a friendly hug, he said, "What do we know about Kenny?"

"They've got everyone with a badge looking for him, but nothing so far. He just vanished." I heard my voice choke up and was sure Kevin also did.

"I'm so sorry, Maxine."

I nodded, knowing there wasn't much he could say to improve the situation. "How did you get here so quick?"

"I was in Ensenada teaching a class at the Mexican police academy. Soon as I got the word, I was on one of their choppers. Only a little over one hundred sixty kilometers." He motioned to the camera I held. "Can I see the video?"

I handed it to him and watched his reaction to each video. Sometimes he grimaced, seemed to recoil and look away. When the video ended he walked off, probably trying to regain his composure. He returned in a moment. "Not an easy thing to watch."

"Every time I watch it, I remember the feel of the knife against my throat."

"Glad you got out of there, Max. There are no rules in drug wars. Not even a shred of morality or civility. These savages have no conscience."

"My gut feeling is that the assault wasn't carried out by a

rival cartel," I said. "If so, they were the best equipped and organized I've ever seen. The guy that searched the barn looked like he was straight out of one of our rapid response teams—body armor, night vision goggles, laser sighted AR-15s, sophisticated coms—he looked more like a Navy SEAL than cartel. Oh, and no Spanish accents."

He played all the clips again, and then scrubbed back to the first night-vision scene of the building being shaken to pieces. "Could this have been the result of demolition equipment brought in during the assault—a bulldozer or front loader on the opposite side of the building?"

I shook my head. "The entire structure started to vibrate and shake and come apart at once—three hundred and sixty degrees of destruction. Plus, when I searched the dead cartel guys out front, there were no heavy equipment tread tracks or evidence of a hauler that could have brought something in. No trace of anything big enough to bring down this building in a matter of minutes. It had all the characteristics of an earthquake." Even as I said it, I knew we were dealing with something much bigger.

Kevin watched the clip again. "I did some calling around to various universities and research facilities while on the chopper from Ensenada. No significant seismic activity recorded in the region within the last forty-eight hours." He handed the camera to me. "That was no earthquake."

"What then?"

Before Kevin could answer, Commander Cervantes approached us. He said he had just ended a call on his cell phone. "Agent Decker, do you know a young Mexican named Ricardo Delgado?"

CHAPTER 11 – LAST STAND

Something dark swept over me with the commander's question about Ricardo Delgado.

"How did you know him?" Cervantes asked.

"He visited Agent Gates and me at our hotel yesterday to discuss my possible assistance in identifying a WWII artifact. He showed us a picture of an object his brother had found, and he believed his brother was murdered because of it. We talked for a while, and I eventually told him I'd help him. He had lunch with us and then left."

Cervantes stared at me for a few seconds, as if considering his next words carefully. "I'm afraid he's dead. We discovered his body near your hotel with your business card in his pocket."

My breath caught, and my hand cupped my mouth. Finally, I said, "He was concerned for his safety. He told us his brother had found the artifact, did some inquiries on the Internet regarding its source and value, and wound up being murdered for it."

"What did the brother find?" Kevin asked.

"Not sure. Looked like a box about the size of a toolbox—perhaps made of brass. Exterior markings showed it was probably from World War II."

"How did you know it was from the war?" Cervantes asked.

Because that's my job. "The markings on the side of the box were the name of a German weapons manufacturer, and there was also a swastika."

The commander's cell phone rang. "Let me know if you think of anything else. For now, I promise that we're making every effort to find Agent Gates." He pulled the phone from his pocket and walked away.

"What do you think, Max?" Kevin said.

"I don't believe in coincidence. First Delgado's brother, then Delgado—both connected by the box. He told two other people about it—Kenny and me. Now Kenny is missing. I'm becoming convinced the assault team last night was there for me and had nothing to do with the cartel. It wasn't a drug war thing. The Mexicans got in the way, and they paid the price."

"So you don't think this was cartel rivals out for revenge?"

"The guy in the barn spoke English. When he finished searching and he reported the place was clear, he said, 'She must be dead under the rubble.' Who do you think *she* is?" I pointed to myself then looked around at the continued police activity.

"If you're right, they won't give up."

"Neither will the cartel. They want me dead, and the other guys want me deader."

It was late afternoon when a couple of the Mexican federal police drove me back to the resort. Kevin had immersed himself with the crime scene investigation and said he would catch up with me later—or call right away with any news. OSI investigators were scheduled to arrive tomorrow.

The police officers accompanied me into the room to make sure it was secure. I thanked them and locked the door as they left. I was dead tired and starving, but before I raided the minibar and then collapse on the bed, I shoved a chair under the doorknob then went to the sliding glass doors for a second check. It's not that I didn't trust the Mexican police—at this point I didn't trust anyone.

Standing in front of the glass, I watched the distant clouds turning shades of evening. The beach was deserted and the ocean flat. What appeared to be a large fishing boat, perhaps a shrimper, sat anchored about 400 meters from shore. I wasn't certain, but I thought someone stood on the deck near the stern.

Kenny carried a small pair of Vivitar binoculars in his bag. He claimed they were for whale watching, but I knew otherwise. Tanned bikini bodies were always on his viewing list.

I pulled them from his bag and focused on the boat. There was a man in a cowboy hat on the deck staring in the direction of the resort through binoculars. At first I thought he was just taking in the scenery. But as I continued to watch, I realized his gaze never drifted from one spot—our room. His image filled the frame, and he knew I'd made him. Slowly, he formed a blade with one of his hands and brought it across his throat. Then he smiled.

Son of a bitch!

They know I'm here and alone. I checked my cell. It was dead. I reached for the room phone on a nearby table. No dial tone.

Shit!

I raised the binoculars for another look at the cowboy. He was still smiling.

But an instant later, the smile disappeared, as did a large portion of his skull. A mist of pink flew backward taking his hat and brains with it. He collapsed out of sight behind the boat's gunwale.

Sniper!

Someone with a noise-suppressed, high-powered rifle had blown the cowboy's head off. The bullet came from the direction of shore—judging from the spray, it could have come from as close as the room next door.

I yanked the drapes shut and ran to turn off all the lights except for the one on the nightstand next to the bed. I pulled open the drawer and removed Kenny's Glock along with the Mexican's automatic. Then I hefted the mattress up and over so it formed a small space in the corner of the bedroom. That's where they would think I was hiding.

I switched off the nightstand light and moved to the corner by the glass doors leading to the patio. With pistols in both hands and my Walther ready in the holster at my ankle, I waited for what might be my last stand.

CHAPTER 12 – O.K. CORRAL

Flashbacks of the last scene in *Butch Cassidy and the Sundance Kid* formed in my head as I crouched with my back to the corner. A tiny glow from the patio light made its way through the thin gaps in the drapes. The only sound was my pulse pounding in my ears. Two minutes went by, then five.

The patio light went out—someone must have unscrewed the bulb.

A faint sound came from the direction of the glass sliding door—someone tried the latch. A few seconds later, a metallic sound—a key or lock pick. The latch clicked.

The door slid open and a hand reached in and pulled the drapes back.

The first dark form, backlit only by moonlight, moved like a cat into the room. I saw the outline of an assault rifle in his hands and the bulky form of night vision goggles on his face. Behind, a second intruder slipped in. Two red laser dots appeared on the bottom of the upturned mattress across the room. Both men opened fire with a series of three-round bursts from the noise-suppressed rifles. The bullets sliced through the mattress and slammed into the wall behind.

The second they stopped firing, I said, "Hi."

They swung to their right to find me, but it was already too late. I rapid fired both automatics at their heads. The night vision devices disintegrated, tearing into their faces as the 9mm slugs did the same to their brains. Both collapsed, not unlike the cowboy on the boat.

I rose and moved to the bodies, making sure others were not about to enter through the patio door.

It was clear.

A pounding came from the other end of the villa. Someone was outside, knocking loudly and calling out my name.

With both guns ready, I moved to within a few meters of the door and pressed up against the wall.

"Who's there?" I called.

"Maxine, it's Kevin. Are you all right?"

"You alone?"

"Yes. Who's shooting?"

I switched on the entrance light then unlocked and opened the door. "Welcome to the O.K. Corral."

It looked as though all the military, police, and forensics teams that scoured the horse farm earlier that day had descended on the resort. Employees and guests were herded into the resort's office and questioned by investigators from the Federales, the FBI, and various other law enforcement agencies. The medical examiner went over the two dead bodies before taking them away. They found no identification on either. Even the serial numbers from the M4 carbine rifles had been removed.

One of the FBI agents told us that the Mexican Coast Guard located the fishing boat adrift 16 kilometers up the coast with no one aboard. It was reported stolen the previous day. Within an hour of finding the boat, the body of the Mexican killed by the sniper was found floating nearby. He was identified as a known member of the Selinas Cartel.

The room next to ours turned up vacant, as I had guessed, and the police confirmed that the patio door was left open, and a firearm discharged close to the glass—gunpowder residue showed up on the frame.

All that meant nothing to me because Kenny's whereabouts was still a mystery.

"Who were those guys?" I asked Kevin as we sat in the resort's café watching the sun rise over the ocean. At this point, I was totally exhausted after a full night of gunfights and police investigations. I'd managed to find food, even though it consisted of candy bars and chips. The strong espresso I now sipped created a tug-of-war with my need to sleep.

"Not the cartel. We got a hit on the fingerprints on one of them—a former Army Special Forces sergeant who served in Iraq. When he left the service, he went to work for one of the private security firms hired by the military to protect our diplomats in war zones."

"Like Blackwater?"

Kevin nodded and took a sip of his coffee. "Stayed in the private security business for a few years then disappeared. Most of the time, guys like him get too old to go running around war zones, so private corporations snatch them up to provide bodyguard protection for executives and such."

"Do we know who hired him?"

"Could be hundreds of companies. Government contractors are big on employing former Special Forces. Makes them feel patriotic. Plus the government has strict requirements covering security qualifications for companies working on top secret projects."

"Well, that's something anyway." I glanced over my shoulder at the Mexican policeman standing near the café doorway. Commander Cervantes assigned me round-the-clock protection, and this guy had become my shadow. Even with a second officer outside my villa, I wasn't filled with confidence, but it was the best choice I had at the moment.

"Max, you look terrible. Why don't you go get some rest? We're going to get you out of here later today. There's nothing you can do. And drinking all that caffeine is only going to make you feel worse."

"Thanks for the compliment, but you're right." I stood. "Call me with any news."

"I promise."

I patted his shoulder as I passed by and headed for the entrance. With a nod and a smile, I waved my Mexican shadow on and we walked across the resort grounds to my new room. The resort had moved me while they worked at cleaning up the blood, patching the wall, and replacing the bullet-riddled mattress. My other guard was waiting at his post outside the door.

"*Buenos días*," I said as we approached.

"*Buenos días, señora*," shadow number two said.

Once inside, I sat on the edge of the bed and removed my shoes. I checked my cell. It was fully charged, so I unplugged it from the charger. I could already feel the softness of the newly replaced mattress—this one minus the bullet holes.

After switching off the light, I dropped back onto the bed and pulled the comforter up over me. *Heaven.*

I took in a deep breath and exhaled slowly. Sleep was coming fast.

Then came the buzzing.

I looked toward the nightstand. An incoming call lit up the cell phone.

CHAPTER 13 – 48 HOURS

I picked up the cell phone and stared at the caller ID.

Kenny Gates.

Suddenly, I was wide-awake, my exhaustion forgotten. I swung my legs over the side of the bed. The blackouts kept it dark, and the darkness caused me to shiver.

I pushed talk. "Kenny?"

"I'm afraid not." The voice was female, mature, and not Mexican. I detected a slight Southern accent, perhaps from the Carolinas.

"Who is this? What are you doing with Agent Gates's phone?"

"First, let me assure you that your former husband is safe and sound. He is our guest for now. Depending on whether you cooperate with us or not will determine how safe and sound he remains."

"How do I know what you're saying is the truth? I need proof of life."

"You'll have to take my word for it."

"You've got to be kidding. Let me talk to him."

"Unfortunately, that's not possible. I'm not with him right now. But my associates are taking good care of Agent Gates."

My anger was about to blow the top of my head off as I tightened my grip on the phone. *Who the hell was this woman? What was going on?* "All right, let's say I believe you for now. What do you want?"

"You have something I desire, and I have something you desire. That means we are in a perfect position to negotiate. Do you want your ex-husband's return?"

"Yes, but I don't have anything of yours."

"Maybe, maybe not. If you don't have it, you know where it

is."

"Where what is?" Was this some Anglo working with the cartel? What the hell would they think I have?

"The object in the photo shown to you by the young Ricardo Delgado."

My mind switched gears. "You're the woman who called Vincente. The one who murdered him. And his brother."

"Agent Decker, I have very little patience when it comes to getting what I want. The Delgado brothers tried my patience. Now they're gone, and all that's left to fulfill my needs is you. Do you want to try my patience, too?"

"I have no idea where that thing is. All I saw was a picture. You want a copy, then give me your email address, and I'll send it to you. I don't even have a clue *what* the thing is. And hell, it's at least 60 or 70 years old. I can't imagine it's worth anything."

"A picture isn't good enough. I want *it*—the object. And aren't you famous for your ability to find things? An atomic bomb hidden in Las Vegas along with the sacred Biblical artifact—the Blade of Abraham? What about the alien artifacts from the Roswell Incident that you located in the Sudan? And so many other priceless objects spanning your career as an archaeologist and OSI agent. It seems to me that there may be no other person with so much expertise and know-how to find what I want."

I hated the way this woman spoke so calmly about killing two innocent young men. And the fact that she knew so much about me, and I nothing about her. "Who are you?"

"Knowing my name wouldn't make any difference in the outcome of our negotiations."

"But knowing your motive and intent might make a difference."

"Just find the object in the photo. Don't involve the authorities. You have forty-eight hours. Don't bother tracing this number. It's a disposable phone with a forced ID to match your ex-husband's. I'll be in touch periodically to check on your progress. Locate the object within the allotted time and you'll get Agent Gates back. Don't deliver it, and you won't. It's that simple."

"How did you get my cell number?"

The woman laughed. "You're not dealing with drug smuggling morons now, Agent Decker. I wouldn't suggest you waste time sleeping. Two days will go by quickly. We wouldn't want time to run out and your former husband winding up joining the Delgado brothers, would we?"

Before I could answer, the line went dead.

EXCERPT FROM MAGDA SCARLET'S JOURNAL—FIRST BIRTHDAY
Otter Brook, South Carolina—1989

*T*he police don't understand. The law is all wrong. It doesn't protect the innocent.

Today was our baby's first birthday. A whole year has passed so quickly. I never knew I could love anyone the way I love Christopher. He's my life. I love my husband. I love my mother and father, even though they're in heaven. I love my friends. But nothing comes near to the way I love my son. I suppose that's the way it is for all mothers. Fathers as well, I'm guessing.

To celebrate Christopher's first year we had a party for him at home. We couldn't have asked for a more beautiful autumn day. About the time the first guests arrived, Christopher woke from his nap. I lifted him from his crib. He nuzzled in my neck, and I swayed back and forth, keeping him close and singing Happy Birthday. I couldn't help but think how blessed I was—how blessed we were as a family.

In the back yard, Craig was grilling and entertaining the guests who had already arrived. When the doorbell rang, I put Christopher on my hip, and we went to greet a guest. I opened the door to see my best friend from high school and her family. We hugged, and my eyes looked over her shoulder out the open door. On the opposite side of the street, Ellen Osterling stood propped up against a white Audi. She waved.

My breathing was so hard and fast I was afraid I was going to hyperventilate. The rest of the day is vague. I operated in a fog the entire time. I didn't tell Craig about Ellen until after the party, afraid there might be a scene. But once everyone was gone, I made him drive us to the police.

I'd never been inside a police station before. Craig had previously gone there to complain about Ellen, but this was a first time for me. The station environment—the smells, the sounds—were all foreign to me. When we finally got to see an officer, I exploded with emotion, telling him they had to do something. That this had gone on long enough. Craig did remind the officer that he had complained before. The man's expression didn't tell me anything about what he was thinking. I told him about Ellen sitting outside our house today on our son's birthday. Then the policeman asked us some questions. Has she threatened us or made any direct threat like kidnapping? Craig said she hadn't, and I disagreed, telling the officer about the call I got at the hospital—that the baby should be hers. I hated the way the officer looked at me with such a patronizing smile as he told me that wasn't a threat, just an opinion. Then he asked more questions, like had she physically harmed anyone? Was she parked in a no parking zone across from our house today? Had she trespassed? The answer to all of his questions was no.

When he said she'd done nothing to break the law, I felt my ears, throat, and face turning hot with anger.

Does this mean we have to wait until she does something terrible before the police can act? Has someone got to get hurt first? I can't believe it.

Craig was as furious as I was, and told the cop that one day something bad, real bad, was going to happen, and when it did, he'd let every newspaper and reporter in the universe know how this department, and especially this officer, had ignored us.

The law is totally screwed up.

We're so frustrated and angry. I look in the mirror and hardly recognize myself. I see the reflection of a miserable human being, and I feel my heart hardening.

CHAPTER 14 – PRIVATE PRISON
San Luis Rio Colorado, Mexico

"Maxine, wake up. We're here." Kevin pulled the car to a stop.

I opened my eyes from a dead sleep and was greeted by the sight of the dusty, depressing, city of San Luis Rio Colorado—Ricardo Delgado's hometown. The drive up the coast from San Filipe had given me the first three-hour stretch of peace in days. After informing Commander Cervantes of the 48-hour deadline, and that Agent Fender and I would be investigating the two brother's deaths, we had headed north.

As I stepped out of the car, I looked around at the neighborhood—although the term didn't apply. It was more like a series of strongholds and compounds. Houses, stores, and other buildings were hidden behind endless rows of walls. Iron gates protected small, block structures—all drab and dreary. There was little traffic. Enough dust and grit covered the cars that it was only a guess to identify their color. Iron bars protected windows and doorways. The odors that permeated the hot, dry air spanned everything from spicy cooking to rotting garbage. My first thought was that I looked upon hundreds of private prisons, each trying to become invisible.

Down at the end of one street, looking north, I saw the Rio Grande and beyond it the United States of America.

Kevin stood beside me. "Can you imagine living here—growing up and trying to have a normal life?"

"Not in my wildest dreams."

He checked his notes. "Looks like this is the mother's

place."

The outer gate was locked. "What do they do if there's a fire?" I asked.

"You think emergency vehicles are gonna respond to this place?"

I saw a small button on the wall and pushed it. From somewhere inside the house, a bell rang—it sounded more like a burglar alarm than a doorbell. After a few moments, a woman came to the door. She was short and plump with long gray hair and a tired expression. "*¿Qué quieres?*" she called out.

"*Señora* Delgado?" I asked.

"*Sí.*"

"We are friends of Ricardo."

"My son had no American friends."

"He came to me for help, *Señora* Delgado."

"And now he is dead."

"I'm so sorry for your loss. For both your sons."

"Your words no bring them back." She turned away.

I knew what she meant. If I could only say some magic words and bring back Francine. This woman's grief was raw and painful, but I had to find a way to get her to cooperate. "*Por favor, Señora* Delgado. We are trying to find out who murdered your sons, but we desperately need your help."

She looked back and bore her gaze into my eyes. "Who are you?"

"I'm Maxine Decker, a consultant with the FBI. This is FBI Special Agent Kevin Fender. Can we have just a few moments of your time?"

She hesitated, but then came forward and stopped a few meters from the wall gate. "Show me identification."

Kevin pulled his cred pack from his jacket pocket, unfolded it, and showed his badge and photo ID. I already had my FBI consultant ID hanging from a lanyard around my neck, so I held it up for her to examine.

Standing this close, I saw the rugged trails of hardship in her face and eyes. This was not an easy life, and violently losing two young boys must have taken what little hope she had for survival to its lowest depths. I needed to go gently with her.

"*Adelante*," she said and opened the wall gate.

Señora Delgado led us into the house where we found sparse, worn furnishings. Religious pictures and objects decorated most of the walls. Photos of her two sons and other family members lined the shelves of a wooden bookcase. A Spanish soap opera played out a dramatic tale on the TV. All in all, a modest family of little means with strong spiritual beliefs and family ties.

She motioned to a couch draped with colorful Mexican blankets.

We sat while she took her place in a recliner with threadbare blue upholstery. "What is it you want?"

"Ricardo told me about what Vincente found in the river," I said. "We believe your sons might have been killed because of it. We think if we can locate the object, we have a better chance of identifying it, and then determine who would want it bad enough to murder your sons."

"I have no idea where the thing is," she said.

"Ricardo mentioned that Vincente kept it hidden in a shed behind your house."

"We would like your permission to search the shed," Kevin said.

"There is nothing there but junk. Only old tires, paint cans, rusted tools. Nothing of value."

"I'm sure you're right, *Señora* Delgado," I said, "but if that's true, then we can eliminate it and look in other directions. Please let us take a look inside the shed. You can come with us if you like. It won't take long, I promise."

She pursed her lips and raised her brows, seriously seeming to consider my request. Then she stood and gestured for us to follow. "Come."

As we passed through the kitchen, she stopped and took a key from a drawer. While we waited on her, pungent spicy aromas overwhelmed me. I saw nothing cooking, so I assumed that after so many meals prepared here, the scents were embedded in the walls, the fabrics, even the wood.

The shed stood at the rear of the yard against the back fence wall. It was about two meters by three, made of wood with a tin roof, and sat on concrete blocks. She unlocked a rusted padlock and pulled open the rickety door. She reached inside and flipped on a switch. A bare bulb lit up the interior. Stepping aside, she motioned us in and then left.

Thirty minutes later, with our clothes soiled and both of us coughing from the dust, we stepped out of the shed. I saw Ricardo's mother nearby, watering plants that seemed withered beyond hope. They needed more than water, perhaps being transplanted to another country would be their only hope for survival.

She twisted the valve, and the water stopped flowing from the hose. Turning toward us she crossed her arms. "I told you."

"Yes, you did. You have a lot of old paint cans, *Señora* Delgado," Kevin said.

I brushed the dust off my shirt. "Thank you for letting us search the shed. We'll leave you to your grief. Again, I'm sorry for your loss."

She walked to the back door with us following.

We halted in the living room, and I turned to thank her once more. Then I stared at Kevin.

"What is it, Max?"

"When we asked Ricardo if he knew where the object was located, he told us he didn't. But he added something interesting. He said that the secret went to the grave with Vincente." I checked my watch, and then faced *Señora* Delgado. "Where is your son buried?"

"Panteon Municipal Cemeterio."

"Is it far from here?" I asked.

"No. Three blocks. Vincente's grave is next to his brother's. Ricardo's just dug. The *autoridades* say his body arrive soon."

"I have one more request."

"If it help find their killer, I do whatever you ask."

"I would like to exhume Vincente's body."

CHAPTER 15 – THE GRAVE

"We're almost there, Commander," I said into my cell phone. "I'll get in touch as soon as we know something." I ended the call. It took most of the afternoon and into the evening, along with numerous calls to the local authorities from Commander Cervantes, to get authorization to dig up Vincente's coffin. Dusk had already darkened the sky as Kevin and I watched the backhoe remove the final load of soil and expose the casket. Two meters away was the freshly dug grave awaiting Ricardo's body—his funeral scheduled for the next day. The cemetery manager and his men, the undertaker, the local medical examiner, and a couple of police officers joined us. *Señora* Delgado had agreed to sign the paperwork, but she decided not to come to the exhumation. I couldn't blame her.

"I hope you're right about this," Kevin said. "None of these guys looks happy. I'll wager they would all rather be someplace sipping a *cerveza* about now."

"So would I." I wiped the sweat from my brow. "But frankly, if this doesn't pan out, I got nothing else." I looked at my cell phone screen. "And we're running out of time."

Panteon Municipal Cemeterio was huge, covering many blocks and, like most everything else, behind high walls. Thousands of tombstones of every size and shape packed the cemetery for as far as I could see in all directions. It reminded me of when I was a kid. My father called them marble orchards. Then he would follow up with his standard joke that people were dying to get in there. Francine and I always laughed.

The cemetery manager waved off the backhoe operator and ordered his workers down into the grave. The casket sat on two planks, and the men worked ropes through the space beneath. Then they secured the rigging to the backhoe scoop. My pulse accelerated, and I chewed on a fingernail cuticle as the coffin emerged out of its resting place and was placed on the ground. The funeral director brushed the remaining dirt from the top of the simple wooden box. He then broke the seal on the side. Everyone took a step closer. Since I was the one responsible for this, they let me stand beside the director as he opened the one-piece lid exposing Vincente's body. I pressed my lips together and steepled my index fingers against my mouth.

Vincente was dressed in a brown suit, white shirt, and blue string tie with the emblem of Mexico on the clasp. Since the funeral had taken place only a few days prior, he looked as if he was sleeping, but his face had that waxy look of an embalmed corpse.

I leaned forward and shined a bright flashlight along the body before turning to Kevin and shaking my head. Then to those gathered I said, "Thank you all for your assistance at such a late hour in the day, but I'm afraid we haven't found what we're searching for."

I heard under-their-breath rumblings as some of the men turned to leave. The funeral director proceeded to close the casket and get it ready to lower into the grave, while the backhoe operator sat on his machine smoking a cigarette. No one seemed interested in remaining around any longer than necessary.

Someone cranked the generator, and the halogen work lights lit up as deep shadows enveloped the graveyard. I walked to the trench where the coffin had rested. Even with the work lights on and my flashlight shining down, it seemed foreboding. I was robbed of the chance to bury my twin sister. My stomach felt queasy as I wondered if I was looking into my future. Then I noticed something interesting.

I moved over to Ricardo's newly dug grave. It was amazing how the backhoe could produce such a smooth, precise rectangular shape in the ground. It was almost perfect. Then I went back to Vincente's grave and compared it to what I'd just seen. "Kevin, would you ask the cemetery manager to come here?"

A moment later, the man approached with Kevin. "*Si, Señora?*"

"I have a question." I motioned for him to follow me. We stood beside Ricardo's grave, and I swept my light across the bottom where the dirt was pressed smooth and flat. "Does the equipment always dig a grave this precise?"

"*Si,*" he said.

I led him back to the other grave. Vincente's coffin was about to be lowered into the hole. "Tell him to wait," I said.

The manager motioned for the operator to stop. He then looked at me.

I aimed the beam of light at the bed of Vincente's grave. The dirt was not smooth and flat but appeared disturbed, as if someone had dug beneath where the coffin would rest. The grade was not as even and level like the one that awaited Ricardo's casket.

"Why is it different?" I asked.

The man stared into the hole for a long time. Then he signaled the backhoe operator to turn off the motor. Finally, he called the two workers and gave them instructions to go into the grave and see, what if anything, was buried at the bottom.

When the first worker shoved the point of his shovel into the dirt, he struck a hard surface. He looked up, and the manager signaled to proceed. Two minutes later, the men uncovered an object and removed it from the grave.

Kevin adjusted one of the halogen lights to shine on the object that now rested near my feet. Moments later, everyone who was still there gathered around to get a look at the toolbox- shaped item with the round tube protruding from one end, and the strange connectors on the other. It was the object in Ricardo's photo, the one found by his brother along the banks of the Colorado River.

My cell phone rang. I checked the caller ID.

Kenny Gates.

CHAPTER 16 – MARBLE ORCHARD

I brought the cell phone to my ear. "Yes?"

"Excellent work, Agent Decker."

I shot a glance at Kevin. Muffling the phone, I said, "It's her."

"And what work is that?" I watched as Kevin pulled out his phone to alert Cervantes.

"You completed your task with time to spare."

I scanned the surrounding cemetery and then got Kevin's attention. "They're here," I whispered. My eyes fell on a black SUV Escalade parked about 90 meters away. I nodded, and Kevin indicated he saw it, too.

"It's all yours," I said to the woman. "Just as soon as I get Agent Gates back safe and sound."

"I see no reason to delay. Your former husband is close. My associates are prepared to deliver him. Take the device and start walking toward the Escalade parked to your south. Come alone. When you're half way, they'll bring Agents Gates to you."

"Are you here, too?" I asked as I picked up the device by the top handle and started off through the marble orchard. When Kevin began to follow, I shook my head. He stopped with great reluctance on his face.

"Oh, heaven's no, Agent Decker. I never cared for Mexico. A little too gritty for me."

"I'd like to meet you. Can we arrange it?"

The woman laughed. "I'm afraid that would be impossible. Besides, just like my dislike for Mexico, I would hate to meet you only to face an army of federal agents bent on my arrest. But thanks for the thought."

"What if I assured you that it would just be the two of us?"

79

"Just keep walking." Her voice grew stern.

She's not here, but she can see me. Video feed from the SUV?

When I was about half the distance to the Escalade, I paused. "How's this?"

"Perfect."

"Let me see Agent Gates."

The door to the SUV opened. A figure emerged dressed similarly to the two I'd shot in my villa. He turned and assisted Kenny out to stand beside the rear fender. Next, he shined a bright flashlight on Kenny's face. My ex's hands were behind his back, most likely secured.

Two more combat-clad men stepped out of the vehicle and came around to bookend Kenny and his handler. Both held assault rifles at the ready.

"Send one of your men, unarmed, to bring Agent Gates to me."

"That's reasonable," she said.

She must have relayed my demand, for I saw the handler remove his sidearm and give it to the left bookend. I assumed he had at least one hidden backup weapon on him, but at this point I didn't want to push my luck. "Send him on," I said.

There were a few streetlights scattered around the cemetery, enough for me to get a decent view of their progress. It was slow but consistent.

Kenny walked with firm steps telling me that hopefully he was not injured. We would know soon.

I heard a muffled pop. Simultaneously, a portion of the tombstone next to me shattered. In the next instance, the old Mexican marble orchard erupted into a war zone.

CHAPTER 17 – AMONG THE DEAD

I dropped to the ground as bullets flew over my head. They seemed to come from multiple directions. There was gunfire from the Escalade aimed at an area a hundred meters to my right. Kevin and the police were shooting at the SUV and the new location. The newcomers were shooting at anything that moved, but mostly at me. Chips of marble flew as thick as the bullets. It was impossible not to hit a tombstone.

I tried to spot Kenny, but the non-stop shooting made me think otherwise. I slipped my PPK from my leg holster. Grasping the handle of the mystery device in my left hand and my 9mm in my right, I maneuvered between the scores of monuments and headstones in the direction I had last seen Kenny. The danger was twofold—getting shot with a bullet or getting hit by razor-edged stone fragments.

"Kenny!" I called over the gunfire. "Where are you?"

I caught a glimpse of the SUV just as one of the black-clad gunmen went down. His partner was firing as he moved around to the protection of the vehicle. The battle seemed to have shifted, with the group to my right turning their attention toward Kevin and the police at the grave site.

"Max!"

Kenny called out from a few meters away. Within seconds, I was at his side. He lay with his hands bound behind him by plastic ties. His escort was motionless on the ground beside him. Even in the dim light, I saw enough blood to tell me the guy was no longer a threat.

I pulled my Adamas fixed blade from its sheath strapped next to my leg holster and sliced through the ties. "Grab his gun." The assault rifle lay beside the fallen gunman.

"Who are those guys?" Kenny motioned toward the direction of the barrage of gunfire coming from across the cemetery.

"My best guess? The cartel. They sure hold a grudge."

We duck-walked between the crypts and markers until we were a short distance from the SUV. The lone surviving gunman was not doing so well. He sat slumped beside the tire of the Escalade holding his right arm. It hung limply at his side.

"Help me out of here," he said, his words wrapped in pain.

As bullets zinged around us, I kicked his assault rifle out of reach. Then I helped him to his feet and maneuvered the man around the vehicle to the SUV's rear passenger door.

"Leave him," Kenny said.

"I would, but he knows the answer to who's behind this." I heaved the guy into the backseat and tossed the mystery device onto the floorboard before jumping in beside him and shoving my Walther into his side. "We're in a cemetery, my friend. It's an ideal place to die. You're half dead now—don't push your luck. Got it?"

He nodded between groans.

Kenny opened the passenger door and crawled over to the driver's seat. The motor was running, and he jammed it into drive. Flooring the accelerator, we shot down one of the narrow access roads between the monuments.

I pulled out my cell and dialed Kevin's number.

"Max?" He was breathless with the sound of gunfire in the background.

"Get to the front gates!"

CHAPTER 18 – THE CROSSING

"Where are the front gates?" Kenny yelled over the roar of the big Detroit V8.

"Keep going north," I said as I jabbed my prisoner in his ribs with my PPK.

A bullet shattered the back window causing the noise from the gunfire and SUV to intensify. Another vehicle was on our tail about 40 meters behind—a large pickup truck with tires that looked as tall as me. Gunfire pelted the back of the SUV. I assumed these were cartel outlaws after my ass at all costs. They wanted to make an example out of me and weren't about to give up on beheading me on video to show the world.

The main gates of *Panteón Municipal Cemeterio* rose out of the dark. Kenny slammed on the brakes, slinging a cloud of dust and gravel. "They'll be on us in ten seconds. Where's Kevin?"

"He'll be here." I saw the headlights of the cartel's truck coming around a corner in the lane—so close I could hear its engine.

The SUV's passenger door flew open and Kevin dove in—he panted as if he had just run the 100-yard dash. "Bum a ride?"

"Which way?" Kenny said.

Kevin sat up in the seat. "Left."

"You okay?" I asked.

He nodded, still breathing hard.

"What about the others?" I never let up on the gouge of my gun in the side of my mystery guy.

"All dead except for one of the Mexican cops. Hard to tell the severity of his wounds in the dark." He glanced out the back at the pickup that had just cleared the gates. "Cartel?"

"Who else loves me this much?"

"What now?" Kenny said.

"Head west on *Alvaro Obregon*," Kevin said. "We're not far from the border crossing checkpoint. There should hardly be any traffic this time of night." He pulled out his cell phone and started dialing. First to the officer in charge of the U.S. Customs and Border Protection command center in Yuma, then the Department of Homeland Security in Phoenix.

The walls and buildings on both sides of the street streaked by in a blur while the barrage of gunfire never let up from the big pickup. I took a few shots back at them, but it didn't slow down the truck. As I watched them gain on us, something caught my eye. Mounted in the upper corner of the right rear window was a small camera aimed outside. That was how the woman on my cell could have seen and known what was going on in the graveyard. The camera was hooked to a compact box behind the backseat. Had to be a video transmitter. In the glass reflection in front of the camera was a tiny red light.

It still glowed. The camera was still recording.

Then another revelation hit me. I slipped my hand into my pocket and fished out my cell phone. I had never ended the call with the woman. With the camera and the phone, she was seeing *and* hearing everything.

"We're cleared through the border crossing," Kevin said as he ended his call. "Head for the inspection lane on your right. And don't slow down."

In the distance, I saw the poorly lit street become awash in red and blue flashing lights. Cars that were lined up to cross into the United States were already being diverted to the side of the road. Mexican border guards waved us ahead. I saw other guards had taken up positions behind barricades with their weapons aimed at our pursuers.

We flew through the inspection lane and a few heartbeats later, passed under the *Welcome to the United States of America* banner that stretched across the multi-lane inspection station.

Kenny brought the SUV to a screeching stop about 90 meters past the border. Instantly, we were surrounded by United States federal agents and sheriff deputies. Kevin was the first out, flashing his FBI cred pack to the border agents.

Next out was Kenny. With his hands up, he let the cops frisk him until Kevin came around the vehicle and verified his identity.

I stepped out of the passenger side door, and the authorities searched me, taking my PPK. The only person left in the vehicle was the wounded assailant who appeared to have passed out somewhere between the cemetery and the border crossing.

"We're going to need a medic," I said to a customs agent. "There's a wounded—"

A flash and muffled bang came from inside the SUV.

I spun around and looked in the vehicle. My prisoner had shot himself in the head. In all the chaos and confusion, I hadn't had time to properly search him. He must have had a small automatic hidden somewhere on him. "Damn. I should have found a minute, just one frigging minute during the chase to pat him down."

The agents yanked open the opposite side door, but the man was already dead. His bullet had done its job.

Kevin ran up, his cell phone to his ear. "I need a medical forensics team here ASAP. We've got a body that must be identified. I want him on a plane to Dallas tonight. Understood?"

Kenny came to me, and we embraced.

"So much for some R and R on a remote beach," I said. We stayed in each other's arms for a few moments. The deputy returned my gun. Then I went to the SUV, reached in and removed the device that had been the cause of this whole mess. I came to stand before the window containing the mounted camera. Confirming the red light was still on, I raised my cell phone to my ear. "Your man is dead."

At first I heard nothing. Then the woman said, "He did what he was trained and ordered to do. I have those who are dedicated, not for the cause, but for the pay. I'm very generous."

"But you didn't accomplish your goal. Agent Kenny Gates is alive and well." Kenny came beside me.

"I see that," the woman said.
"Oh, and I have this." I held up the device.
There was silence. Then the call ended.

EXCERPT FROM MAGDA SCARLET'S JOURNAL – ACCUSATION
Otter Brook, South Carolina—**1991**

*E*llen Osterling has put a knife through our hearts. There had been brief times when I thought she had moved on and wouldn't bother us anymore. But I was wrong. So wrong. She'll never be done with us until we crumple into nothing but a mass of raw flesh. It was hard enough to see the woman outside Christopher's school on several occasions, sitting in her car in the parking lot, waving as we'd leave the school. Now she has done something so foul that if I could take her life, I would. But then who would suffer? Craig and Christopher. I don't care about me. Maybe that's part of her plan, to drive me to attempt something immoral, like murder, so she can even take my freedom from me by having me go to prison.

For the last several days, I've been through hell. Two days ago, I was happy and feeling blessed to have such a wonderful family. On Sunday, we took Christopher to the park. The sky was clear and cornflower blue. Streaks of sunshine pierced the trees' branches and made the purple, green, and yellow maze of the playground equipment seem even more brightly colored. There were no ominous foreboding signs of what was to come.

Christopher loved the slides and the toddler tunnel maze. For the first time, he tried climbing the rope net. We probably shouldn't have let him. If only I could take that decision back. Somehow he became entangled, and the rope twisted around his neck. Craig finally got him loose, but it was a terrible scare. Christopher was fine, but the rope left abrasions and bruises. I think we were more upset than he was. As we left the park, I thought I saw Ellen standing by the fence, but I wasn't sure. I didn't think any more about it.

On Monday, I went to work and received wonderful news. I was promoted, and my boss said I was the new rising star of CoreConcepts. He *gave me the afternoon off. So I went to Christopher's preschool to pick him up. When I got there and asked for my son, the administrator had me come into her office. I couldn't figure out what was going on, and all kinds of red flags went up in my mind. But none of those flags turned out to be the reason the administrator wanted to see me.*

Even as I think about it now, my stomach coils and I feel like throwing up. Someone had made an anonymous call to the school and accused Craig and me of child abuse. The caller alleged that we tied our baby up, tethered him with a rope for punishment. I was dumbfounded. By law, the school had to report the call to the Department of Social Services. They sent someone out immediately and saw the bruises and scrapes on Christopher's neck and took him away. I explained what had happened at the playground, but it didn't matter.

I've called Child Protective Services to find out where they have taken my son, but they won't tell me. Craig and I have called lawyers, but none can see us until next week. I can't wait that long. The system is failing us, and there's nothing I can do about it. I'm mortified and so scared. My baby must wonder why we have abandoned him to strangers. I've cried until there are no tears left. At first I kept thinking it was a mistake. Why would someone make such a terrible accusation? Everyone knows how much we adore our son.

But after the immediate shock and all the hysterics settled down last night, I sat on the couch in the dark with my head on Craig's lap. My mind had cleared, and I realized who was responsible—who the anonymous caller was.

ELLEN OSTERLING

She had been at the park—she'd never stopped stalking us. She is the most evil person in the world. She wants to destroy our lives.

Where is justice?

Where is God?

All I want is my son back. I can't bear this.

CHAPTER 19 – MAGDA
Connors, North Carolina—**Present day**

D r. Magda Scarlet sat at her desk rubbing her temples. Another damn migraine was announcing its impending arrival. She stared at the halo of light that surrounded her office phone, as well as anything else she focused on—all brought on by the headache. Magda shook a pill from its container into her palm, and then tossed the medication into the back of her throat. She swallowed it down with a gulp of cold coffee she'd poured at least 45 minutes earlier.

Donald Penn, her director of research, appeared in the doorway.

She'd sent him a text message to get to her office ASAP.

Penn took a seat across from Magda. His fingers tapped the nailhead trim of the leather chair. "What happened at the cemetery?" he asked. "I thought we had it all worked out, and then I got this emergency-sounding text from you that all had gone to shit."

Magda stood and paced. The lights in the ceiling aggravated her headache. She picked up a remote from her desk and pushed a button, and the overheads went dark.

"It was a fiasco," she said. "We had everything going our way, and then that pack of Mexican animals showed up. Maxine Decker was making the exchange when all hell broke loose. We'll have to find a way to take care of the cartel. They are worse than pesky flies. Swatting won't drive them away."

"That's going to be hard to do," Penn said. "And what about Decker and Gates? Even if they have that old scrap of German metal, it won't do them any good. Maybe you're obsessing over something that doesn't matter."

Magda planted her feet and glared at Penn. "Must I remind you what it's taken for me to get this far, to have GeoDynamiks sought after by the DoE and the DoD? You know full well that it didn't just fall in my lap, Donald. Nothing has ever fallen in my lap except crap." She glanced at an old fading family picture sitting on her desk of her with her husband and their young son. Her gut tightened. No one could understand what she had been through—what had been done to her.

"I think you should focus on the project and leave Agent Decker and Gates wallowing in their imaginations about the device. They'll give it up soon enough."

Magda laughed. "Really, Donald? You believe it's that simple? I don't think so. There have been murders—remember? And now this whole shoot-out at the cemetery."

Penn smacked his lips, a sign she knew he had conceded. "You're right. We do have to deal with them. But I still don't get why you're so hell bent on getting the old Nazi relic. It's such a primitive version of Tesla's invention."

"I've got a meeting with the Under Secretary of Defense next month. By then I'll be ready to propose that GeoDynamiks be contracted to build military weapons based on the design of the device Decker has in her possession. Only ours will be a thousand times better and more powerful. If that Nazi device is shown around and examined, it'll reveal that a weapon like this is possible. I can't have anyone beat me to it. I've spent years developing it. It's mine." She returned to her chair.

Penn's gray eyebrows rose. "Magda, we're already so far ahead of the game. Nobody's going to beat us to it. Forget about that corroded chunk of metal. It's not that important."

It was more than knowing that the Germans built it, she thought. It could lead to uncovering the intended target.

Magda set her eyes on Penn's and stared him down. "I have my reasons."

CHAPTER 20 – MIDGETS
FBI Headquarters, Yuma, AZ

K evin, Kenny, and I sat in the second-floor conference room in the 39th Street FBI offices watching a large screen video monitor. The image of Special Agent Claudia McCue appeared in a forensics lab at Marine Corps Base Quantico in Virginia. In front of her was a stainless steel examination table under intense lighting, and placed on it was the object that we had shipped her by special military courier. Agent McCue, a former University of Georgia mechanical engineering professor turned FBI materials expert had served at the lab for over 12 years. I worked with her twice on previous investigations.

"It cleaned up pretty good, Claudia," I said.

"Not bad for its probable age," Agent McCue said. "My guess is the object spent most of its life buried deep under the highly compacted sandy bottom of the Colorado River. Aside from being dirty and corroded, it was fairly easy to dispose of the caked-on mud and debris. The water discharge from the river delta restoration project must have managed to release it from its grave."

"That makes twice it's risen from the grave," Kevin said with a smile.

"So since you've had a chance to examine it," I said, "give us your best guess. Why kill for that thing?"

"I have no answer to that question, Max. But I've gathered a few bits of info. For starters, the name Friedrich Krupp AG is easy. You identified it right from the start. Friedrich Krupp Germaniawerft was a German shipbuilding company located at Kiel on the southwestern shore of the Baltic Sea, and one of the largest and most important builders of U-boats for the

Kaiserliche Marine in World War I and the Kriegsmarine in World War II. The swastika obviously indicates that the device was built for the Nazi war effort."

"Any idea of its function?" Kenny asked.

Claudia shook her head. "It's packed with interesting components, but the years of corrosion have morphed most into unrecognizable shapes."

"What about the tube on the front end?" I asked. "And the large connectors on the back?"

"The tube may have been a means to point the device in a particular direction, either to receive or send data, such as audio." Agent McCue swung the device around on the table top. "These connectors are probably how it was powered. If mounted in a stationary environment, like a building or military installation, the connections could have supplied electricity. The handle on top suggests it was portable, so my belief is it could have been connected to a bank of batteries."

"Like what you'd find in a Friedrich Krupp U-boat?" Kenny said.

McCue nodded.

"Yeah, but U-boats are large vessels," Kevin said. "It would be hard to miss one sailing up the Colorado River, especially during the war. How could something that big go unnoticed?"

"Funny you should ask," Agent McCue said. "Friedrich Krupp also built midget subs for the Nazis."

CHAPTER 21 – URBAN LEGEND

"They were called *seehund*, German for seal," I said. We'd thanked Agent McCue for her information, then the three of us spent the next few hours on separate workstations digging into the concept of the mysterious Nazi device originating from a midget submarine. Finally, we gathered again around the conference table.

"The *seehund* was a two-man type-127 midget submarine powered by a 60 HP diesel engine," I said. "They came into use in the last year of World War II. The range was around 500 kilometers. The Germans transported them on a mother ship, usually attached to a U-boat until they were within range of their target. Then they were launched and went on to do their dirty work—plant explosive charges beneath enemy ships or smuggle in spies and weapons. They were designed without hydroplanes so they could pass through anti-submarine nets and other obstacles."

"The Allies were well aware of German midget subs," said Kenny, "but I didn't come across anything about a plot to send one up the Colorado River."

"I did," I said. "It's based on a story that in 1944, the ambassador at our embassy in Mexico City notified the State Department of talk of a German U-boat launching a midget sub in the Sea of Cortez near the mouth of the Colorado River. It seems that the mission was to send the midget sub up the river and set off enough explosives to damage the Hoover Dam, thereby cutting the electrical power to the defense contractors in Southern California."

"True?" Kevin asked.

"Urban legend," I said. "Despite it making the basis for a good spy novel, there are a several big problems."

"Which are?"

"Dams, Kevin. Lots of dams—downstream from the Hoover, most completed before WWII. It would have been physically impossible for even a midget sub to navigate the river all the way to the Hoover Dam." I closed my laptop. "Cool idea, though, if you wanted to cripple a chunk of the industrial war effort."

"You're right," Kenny said. "It would make a suspenseful novel. But it doesn't help us in identifying the mystery object."

"Maybe someone just lost it," Kevin said. "What if it was a war souvenir and somehow got dropped into the Colorado."

I looked up from the documents in front of me. "Occam's razor—the simple answer is always the best."

"Whose razor?" Kevin said. "What are you talking about?"

"It's an old problem-solving principle," I said. "William of Occam said that when there are competing hypotheses, the one with the fewest assumptions should be selected. The other, more complicated solutions, may eventually prove correct, but—when not certain—the fewer assumptions that are made, the better. It's basically, *keep it simple, stupid.*"

"Well, excuse me, Professor Max." Kenny gave a symbolic bow of his head.

"So let's suppose it did come from a WWII German midget sub," Kevin said. "I'm only proposing a what if—and the target was the Hoover Dam—what exactly is that thing?"

I raised my brows and shrugged. "And more importantly, after over seventy years who wants it so badly that they're willing to do anything to get it, including murder?"

EXCERPT FROM MAGDA SCARLET'S JOURNAL – BURIAL
Otter Brook, South Carolina—1991

*T*day I buried my son. My world. Christopher was the light that shone inside of me. I hurt so badly, so deeply, that I wonder if I can go on. Craig is also beside himself. Last night I woke and realized he wasn't next to me in our bed. I found him in the garage with a handgun that sat on the workbench. When he saw how scared and undone I became, he finally went back to bed with me. We clung to each other all night.

I didn't sleep, and I don't think he did, either. I feel like there are vermin inside me, eating away at the very fabric of which I am made. It's a torturous destruction of the person I once was. I can't find myself. I'm lost.

Ever since Christopher was taken into custody two weeks ago and placed in foster care, Craig and I have fought with everything we could muster to get our son back. We've jumped through every hoop, followed every protocol, but the authorities have turned a deaf ear. Even our friends have deserted us when we needed them the most.

Four days ago I got a call that Christopher had been airlifted to the burn center at Medical University South Carolina. The news was a shockwave that nearly brought me to my knees. It took Craig and me over an hour to get to the hospital. I folded myself into Craig's arms and body when I heard we were too late. I didn't get to say goodbye to my sweet baby. We were told that Christopher had come down with a cold, and he'd been napping. There was a vaporizer in the bedroom, and somehow a fire started. The foster mother didn't know until she smelled smoke. She was burned while rescuing our son, but not seriously. By the time we got to the hospital, Christopher was dead. I think I went deaf and mute for hours.

I couldn't write about it then, and so my journal is missing those days of catastrophic grief. I take it up again today so that I will never forget. I *still find it difficult to put into words.*

This morning as I stood at Christopher's grave, I wanted to throw myself over his little casket and pray that God would take me with my son. But I didn't cry. I don't understand that. I should have cried and wailed and shaken my fist at the sky. But I didn't. All I felt was unbelievable heartache mixed with rage and hate that gnawed my bones to the marrow.

The wind blew the drizzling rain at us beneath the cemetery tarp. Friends, if I can still call them that, offered stiff, obligatory condolences. Once they left, I took a stone from my pocket. Christopher had picked it up on the preschool playground one day and had proudly presented it to me as a gift. I brought it with me today, and held it in my hand as I stepped closer to his casket. I kissed the stone and then buried it in the center spray of roses draped over the coffin. We had chosen three sprays of white roses, one for every year of his life.

There was one thing I didn't want to enter my mind as I stood graveside because it had no place at my son's burial. But there it was, burning in my brain.

Loud as a train.

Brilliant as lightning.

Sharp as an icepick in my heart.

Ellen Osterling.

It was all her fault.

CHAPTER 22 – U-112

We ordered lunch from Kneaders Bakery & Cafe so we could keep working. Just as it was delivered, I said, "I may have found some answers."

"Whatcha got?" Kenny said as the delivery guy placed paper bags on the conference table.

I leaned back and interlocked my fingers behind my head. "Looks like the Nazi-Hoover Dam plot just might be true."

"How do you figure?" Kevin said. "There was never a confirmed report of a German midget sub. No evidence of any kind. Like you called it—an urban legend."

"We were looking in the wrong place," I said. Kenny slid my turkey sandwich and soda over to me. "We were trying to find hard evidence on the existence of the midget sub. What I found was hard evidence concerning the mother ship." I turned my laptop so they could see the grainy black and white photo. "Gentlemen, I give you U-112."

As my colleagues munched on their lunch, I said, "The U-boat mysteriously sank off the coast of Mexico in the Sea of Cortez in the fall of 1944."

"How do we know that for sure?" Kenny asked me. "And who sank her?"

"Probably the captain scuttled the boat. Commander Hans Wattenberg and a handful of crewmen were captured and taken to the Papago Park POW encampment east of Phoenix. Approximately 1,700 German prisoners were being held there. During their initial interrogation by Army intelligence, Wattenberg admitted transporting a two-man midget submarine to the mouth of the Colorado River and releasing it. The mission dealt with an attempt to damage power-generating facilities, mainly the Hoover Dam."

"Sure didn't make much of a stink," Kevin said.

"The war was almost over. The plot was foiled, or it failed. At that point, it was a non-starter."

"What happened to Commander Wattenberg and the other crewmembers?" Kenny said. He made an annoying sound with his straw through the plastic lid.

"The Papago POW camp was built in a desert location so isolated that the Americans bragged it was impossible to escape. That didn't stop Wattenberg. He and his men got permission to build a volleyball court. With the tools given to them by the guards, they spent their nights digging a tunnel 55 meters long. It became known as *Der Faustball Tunnel*—The Volleyball Tunnel. They had also built a canoe that could be disassembled and carried in three sections."

"Did they get away?" Kenny asked.

"Yes and no. The plan was to use the lightweight canoe to float down the nearby Phoenix Cross Cut Canal to the Salt River. From there to the Gila River and on to the Colorado. Their goal was to make it to Mexico, blend into the background, and somehow work their way back to Germany." I took another bite of my sandwich.

"I guess something went wrong?" Kevin said.

"It's almost funny in a way," I said. "You see, it never occurred to them that in paper-dry Arizona, a blue line designating a river on a map might only be filled with water during certain times of the year. When they got to the Salt River, it was a mud bog."

Kevin said with a snort, "That had to be one helluva surprise for those guys."

"I doubt Wattenberg found it that humorous," I said. "They trudged on with their canoe until they got to the Gila River, which was made up of a few large puddles. As they sat on the dried-up riverbank trying to figure out what to do next, the Army showed up and gave them a ride back to Papago POW camp."

"It does almost sound like a pitiful joke," Kenny said. "What did we do with them when the war was over?"

"They were all eventually sent back to their home

countries," I said. "The commander went home to a seaport village on the Baltic Sea."

"I'd love to pick his brain or any of the crew for that matter," Kevin said. "There's got to be some connection we're missing between the Nazi plot and what's going on today."

"They must all be long gone by now." Kenny collected the trash from our lunch and tossed it into a nearby can.

"They are," I said. "All but one. A young crewman named Dieter Beck. He was twenty-two at the time."

"That would make him ninety-three?" Kenny said.

"And he's still alive?" Kevin said.

"Even better. He's not only alive, he's about a mile from here."

CHAPTER 23 – THE OLD SAILOR
Paradise Springs Assisted Living, Yuma, AZ

"How did Mr. Beck wind up back in Arizona?" I asked the day manager. We followed the tall, middle-aged woman down a series of pale yellow hallways.

"During World War II, he was held at a POW detention center near here," she said. "He has a medical condition that requires him to live in a dry climate. He told me that he never felt better than when he was in Arizona. When the war ended he went back to Germany and worked as a mechanic, but after his wife passed away, and he retired, Mr. Beck decided to relocate in the Yuma area. A few of the other former German POWs did the same. He's been with us for three years following a mild stroke and then a broken hip."

She stopped in front of a door. Like the others we'd passed, it opened to a small, but comfortably furnished bedroom. Beyond the bed, a wheelchair faced the window.

"Mr. Beck, you're visitors are here," the day manager said.

With an effort that demonstrated his frailty, he turned the chair. He was a feeble little man who could not have weighed more than ninety pounds.

Dieter Beck resembled a marionette waiting for the puppeteer to give him motion. His paper-thin skin did little to hide his bones, and his clothes hung off a fragile skeleton. I felt that if I spoke too loud, he would shatter. He looked at us with unblinking eyes.

I stepped into the room followed by the others. "Hello, Mr. Beck. My name is Maxine Decker. I'm a special consultant to the FBI." I motioned to my colleagues. "This is OSI Special Agent Kenny Gates and FBI Special Agent Kevin Fender.

Thank you for allowing us to come see you. We'd like to ask you a few questions about your time in the German navy. Would that be all right?"

He raised one hand from the arm of the wheelchair as he gave me a shallow nod.

"Thank you." I remained standing, even though there were a couple of chairs in the room. "I understand you were part of the crew of the U-112. Is that correct?"

A nod.

"Is it true that in 1944, U-112 helped transport a type-127 midget submarine up the Sea of Cortez to the mouth of the Colorado River?"

The old man's eyes went from mine to Kenny's, to Kevin's, then back to mine. Nod.

"Do you recall how many men were assigned to the *Seehund*?"

His lifted two fingers.

"During the voyage to Mexico, did you have the opportunity to speak to the two crewmen?"

Nod.

"Did they ever talk about their mission? Why they needed the midget sub?"

Nod.

"Was their mission to damage or destroy dams and power-generating facilities along the river?"

"Yes." His voice was more of a squeak as he blinked for the first time.

I turned to Kenny and Kevin. All of us raised our brows. Maybe we would get what we came for.

I focused back on Beck. "Do you know what happened to the two crewmen and the *Seehund*?"

"No."

That was disappointing.

"I have one more question, Mr. Beck. Then we'll leave you to rest. I'm sure this has been more excitement than you usually get in a day."

I thought I saw a tiny smile on his lips.

I retrieved my cell phone from my pocket and pressed the photo icon. Once the photo appeared—a cleaned-up version of the device Agent McCue had texted me—I took a few steps forward until I stood before the old German sailor. I turned the phone so he could see.

"Have you ever seen this object before?"

At first, his stare seemed distant. I could tell he was working hard to call up long-buried memories from a distant past.

Then he nodded and raised his finger, pointing. "*Das erdbeben maschine.*"

"I'm sorry, Mr. Beck, but I don't speak German."

"Zee ersquake machine."

CHAPTER 24 – MAD SCIENTIST

"Yes, I understand," Kevin said into his cell phone from the back seat of our rental. "I don't agree. I think there's more to this than your assessment."

Kenny steered into the parking lot of the FBI building across the street from the Yuma International Airport and switched off the engine.

Kevin ended his call. "Looks like I've been called home to Momma."

We got out and walked to the front entrance. "Seems like an awful lot of dead bodies for them not to be more concerned," I said.

"No one in Dallas feels threatened by a WWII Nazi mystery weapon that's been under water for seventy-one years," Kevin said.

"They should have been with me on that horse farm and seen that building get torn apart," I said.

"Preaching to the choir, Max," Kevin said. "I'll be flying out this afternoon."

"We appreciate your help," Kenny said.

"Hey, you guys kept my ass from getting vaporized in Las Vegas on the Blade case. It's the least I can do."

We had entered the now-familiar conference room for a final recap before Kevin had to depart. I picked up a dry marker and started listing what we knew on the white board. My list covered events, people, and objects. When I had finished, I said, "Here's my big question. If the bad guys who assaulted the horse farm have a working device that can cause a controlled seismic-type event, why do they need to get their hands on the old Nazi version?"

"Either there's something about the Nazi version that

they're missing . . ." Kenny said.

"Or they simply want to destroy the old one, so there's no proof of its existence or the technology," Kevin added.

"I tend to agree with you, Kevin. The components in the old version are beyond recognition—nothing but rusted, corroded blobs. Agent McCue said it would be a shot-in-the-dark to guess their identity."

"Then what we should do is investigate the technology, not the device," Kenny said.

I nodded. "Exactly. If I wanted to create a seismic ground movement event—a controlled earthquake—how would I go about it?"

Kenny typed away on his laptop. After a few entries, he stopped. "Looks like you would have to involve the science of geodynamics. It's the study of how materials move within the planet."

"So the next question is—how do I make them move?" I asked.

Now Kenny and Kevin were both typing away. I sensed a bit of competition between them.

Kevin leaned back first. "Someone already did it."

"Really," I said. Kenny stopped typing.

"A scientist by the name of Nikola Tesla." Kevin paraphrased from what he read on his laptop. "He worked for Thomas Edison but Edison didn't believe in Tesla's invention of alternating currents, and they parted ways. Others took credit for most of his inventions. A lot of his stuff was considered futuristic and farfetched. Some considered him a mad scientist. His research included X-rays, vacuum tubes, trans-Atlantic wireless communications, artificial lightning, death rays, and particle guns—the list goes on and on."

"So what about an earthquake machine?" I asked.

Kevin continued to read from the reference. "Tesla was purported to have once created a small, pneumatic device which would automatically and mechanically seek out the structural resonance frequency of any solid object to which it was attached. Supposedly, he once took this device to a building site and attached it to the girder work of a partially-completed building, causing it to start vibrating so dramatically that the builders abandoned it. Tesla never used the machine again out of fear that it would be used to vibrate the Earth to pieces."

"That certainly qualifies as an earthquake machine," Kenny said.

"And if the Germans were able to get ahold of the device or the plans to build it," I said, "they would have what they needed to damage the Hoover Dam."

The conference room door opened, and a female agent stuck her head in. "Didn't you guys make a trip over to the Paradise Springs Assisted Living facility this morning?"

CHAPTER 25 – CONFIRMED DEAD

"There's been an explosion and fire," the female agent said. "Must have happened soon after you left. They think a gas leak is to blame."

"Anyone hurt?" I asked.

"A couple of residents and one staff member were killed."

Kevin, Kenny, and I exchanged glances.

"Please let us know as soon as you get a list of those who died in the fire," Kevin said to the agent. "And thank you."

Kenny waited until she left and had closed the door. "Coincidence?"

"Everything happens for a reason," I said. "Odds are Dieter Beck is one of the deceased."

Kevin nodded. "I'll bet the staff member is the day manager who stood in the room while we questioned Mr. Beck."

"It's beyond obvious," I said. "Someone wants to destroy all connections to the Nazi earthquake machine. They don't *need* the device—they already have a working model. I was witness to that in Mexico. What they want is to erase any reference to the thing found in the Colorado River."

"And that includes us, Max," Kenny said.

"You know what's weird? The more we research, the more we find that the Nazi plan would never have worked on the Hoover Dam. It's built to withstand earthquakes—ones caused by nature, anyway. No doubt the Germans knew that. Makes you wonder what the Nazis were up to. There's more than one piece of this puzzle missing."

"The device is locked up in a secure lab in Quantico," Kevin said. "Good luck getting their hands on it there."

"I wouldn't be too sure," I said. "These guys have a sophisticated organization—they're armed with the latest in body armor and weapons, well-informed, and powerful. They have highly advanced technology and communications, and can operate across borders. They made mincemeat out of the Selinas Cartel. I'm starting to get the feeling we're up against a private army whose job is to protect the interests of whoever is developing the modern earthquake machine. What we're dealing with is lethal science with teeth."

"If it's a foreign entity that's responsible," Kevin said, "they have what appears to be unrestricted access across our borders."

I shook my head. "There was nothing foreign about the men I heard." I paused. "Except for the woman on the phone. She had a hint of a Southern accent." I thought for a minute about what Kevin had just said. "It could be homegrown terrorists. It wouldn't be the first. There's so much of that these days. Women are as easily recruited as men."

"Okay," Kenny said. "Where do we go for help with this? We need to find someone or some company that specializes in weapon-grade geodynamics or resonant frequency technology."

Kevin and Kenny started typing away, their rivalry still strong. Finally, Kenny said, "The list is long—a lot of branches in this scientific discipline, all highly specialized. There're a couple that come close to having all the qualifications we're looking for, but only one stands out—GeoDynamiks with a K. They're a private contractor for the DoD, and although their current projects are highly classified, their primary field is the study of earthquakes—devices that can predict them, and what can cause them. Who knows what else they dabble in? They might be able to give us some direction."

Kevin searched GeoDynamiks on the Web. "Got it. They're located just north of Charlotte, in Connors, North Carolina."

The door opened, and the female agent popped her head in again. "Confirmed dead include the day manager and an elderly German named Dieter Beck."

EXCERPT FROM MAGDA SCARLET'S JOURNAL – RUE THE DAY
Otter Brook, South Carolina—1992

I *am now positive that I'll never be the same. The old Magda Scarlet no longer exists. She died an agonizing death. Oh, I still carry the name, but the original Magda Scarlet is dead. I have no soul. No sympathy. No love. No kindness. No gentleness. No anything. It's a total fabrication that when one door closes, another opens. There's never a light at the end of any tunnel. The only true thing is a passion that thrives on loathing and fury. The new Magda Scarlet will survive this. Ellen Osterling has taken so much, but she will not have me.*

This morning, three weeks after we interred our only child, I was awakened at 5:30 AM by the doorbell, and then a knocking at the door. I reached for Craig and asked him to answer. Who could be at our door at this time of morning? I wondered. The space beside me was empty. I called for Craig several times, thinking maybe he was in the bathroom or sleeping on the couch as he often did since our son's death. He couldn't get over the guilt. He always traced everything back to his infidelity. I think I forgave him, I hope so, but I'm not sure if I ever truly got over it. Once a trust is broken, it takes a long time to mend.

When Craig didn't answer, I swung my feet over the bed and went to the closet for my robe. Where was my husband? I asked myself. I tread to the front door, still groggy from the sleeping pill I'd taken.

After I switched on the front porch light, I peered through the living room blinds. Two uniformed sheriff's officers stood in the light. Without opening the door, I asked them to show their identification. I moved to the peephole and watched as they held up their badges, and then I let them in.

I didn't believe that there could be any more possible pain than what I already endured. But I was so wrong. The officers suggested that I sit. Their voices were a death knell—the tolling of the bell. And so I sat on the couch, my legs curled under me in a defensive posture.

As soon as they began talking, a buzzing sounded in my ears as if my brain sought a rampart that blocked out what they were saying. I didn't hear full sentences, only a word here and there.

It is evening now, long after the police left, and I have put all the pieces together. Craig went to Ellen Osterling's house in the early morning hours to kill her. But police had the motive all wrong. Ellen had told lies, golden lies that made perfect sense to those who listened. She claimed that Craig had gone to her house because he was still distressed over her ending their affair. That he attempted to rape her. When she resisted, he fired his gun, but Ellen was able to get to her handgun and defend herself.

But this is not what I believe happened. I suppose that in the end, it doesn't matter. My husband is dead. Craig had gone to Ellen's home with the intent to murder her. That was true. He wanted her to pay for what she had done to us—to our family.

She comes from a wealthy and influential background. Her uncle is the governor of our state. I've already heard the news reports on the TV. Support pours out for poor Ellen. I watch, alone and dazed.

Tonight I made a promise to myself—to Craig—to Christopher— that I will not give up. Ellen has power because of her connections, but I'll find a way to climb the ladder to power, also. I'll follow her, watch her from afar, and never let her out of my sight or my mind. One day, she'll have to reckon with me. I don't know when or how, yet, but from this day forward, it is my quest to make her rue the day she hurt my family.

CHAPTER 26 – RED FOLDER
Connors, North Carolina

Magda Scarlet rested both hands atop a red folder on her desk. She kept the folder in the rear of the top drawer of her filing cabinet. Unless she was in the office and needed access, the cabinet stayed locked. Old habits. No one would get into her hardcopies or her digital files. She'd learned that lesson years ago. Early in her career, a co-worker nearly stole one of her projects. That incident taught her how careful she had to be.

The folder's tab had no label. It didn't need one. There was only one red folder.

Magda opened it and lifted the first newspaper clipping. Her eyes skimmed over it. She'd seen it before—many times. The date of the article was 1988, and even though that was a long time ago, the clipping conjured up vivid memories. She peeled away more articles from the stack, now and again glancing at the photo of her family—herself and her deceased husband and child. One of the clippings, dated 1992, included a picture of a woman. Magda glared at it. "I will prevail," she said. "And you'll never see it coming."

"Dr. Scarlet?" It was Donald Penn.

She flinched. He'd taken her by surprise. Quickly she replaced the articles in the folder and closed it. "What is it, Donald?"

"There's been a request for an interview by the two federal agents, Decker and Gates. The receptionist put the call through to me."

Magda felt as if she'd taken a blow to her abdomen. *They couldn't have made a connection to GeoDynamiks.* "Damn it."

"I can take care of it, but thought you'd want to know."

Magda stood, fingers pressed to her forehead. "What did they say? *Exactly* what did they say?"

"I spoke with Gates. He told me they have a problem and believe we can help. Apparently they thought our R and D department was the place to start. But he gave no specifics. He didn't sound like he thought we had anything to do with his kidnapping."

"That's it? They want our help?" She sat back and laughed. "Incredible."

"Seems so. He requested the interview for tomorrow. Would you like me to tell your secretary to check your schedule and set it up?"

"You handle it, Donald. I want to stay out of the picture. I certainly don't want them to hear my voice. Besides, I don't have the time. I've got to get ready for next week's meeting with Under Secretary Rittenberg." She turned away and opened a file on her computer.

Magda sensed that Penn was staring at the red folder. She placed a legal pad over it and then looked up at him. "I'm sure you'll do a good job. Is that all, Donald?"

CHAPTER 27 – DONALD PENN

Kenny and I flew into the Charlotte Douglas International Airport, rented a car, and took I-85 to Connors, a town in the eastern Charlotte metropolitan area. We had parted ways with Kevin Fender since he was called back to Dallas to take part in a new investigation. He promised to be on call if needed. We would have been called back by now, too, if we weren't using up our personal vacation time.

I studied the background info on GeoDynamiks on my iPad while Kenny drove. We were headed to their headquarters and research facility located near Connors. "According to public records, it is a one-hundred-million-dollar, privately owned company that employs 80 people. It has a number of government contracts to develop advanced technology regarding seismic activity. GeoDynamiks also has a pending contract with the DoD, but I can't find specifics." I looked up now and then to enjoy the lush green forests lining the highway.

We passed by northern Connors, took exit 63 and drove along Old Connors Road. Rolling hills and farmland surrounded us, but eight kilometers later, something changed. A tall, chain link fence appeared on our right, topped with large coils of razor wire. Behind it were thick woods. Signs spaced periodically warned of the consequences of trespassing.

"Is this a government contractor or a supermax prison?" Kenny asked.

"Hard to tell."

Half a kilometer further, we came to the GeoDynamiks entrance gate. Kenny turned in and pulled up to a set of chain link gates as high as the surrounding fence. A security officer emerged from a bunker-like building. He was dressed in a dark green, military-style uniform—a Glock holstered at his side. A second security officer followed him but stood back and observed. He was also armed with an automatic pistol in addition to an assault rifle. These guys were serious.

Kenny lowered his window. "Afternoon."

Without returning the greeting, the guard said, "How can I help you?"

"I'm OSI Special Agent Kenny Gates. This is my associate, FBI consultant Maxine Decker. We have an appointment to meet with your head of research, Dr. Donald Penn."

"IDs please."

I pulled my cred pack from my jacket and handed it to Kenny. He passed it along with his to the guard. The man turned and entered the security building. I could see him through the thick glass that made up the upper half of the structure. I assumed it was bulletproof. He scanned our IDs and then made a phone call. He waited for thirty or so seconds before hanging up. The gates slowly opened as he returned to our car and handed back our IDs.

"Proceed. Maintain a constant fifteen miles an hour. Do not stop for any reason. You'll come to a circular drive that leads to the main building. Park in the visitor's space. Leave your keys in the ignition. Enter through the double glass entrance doors. Someone will escort you to your meeting. Don't vary from these instructions. Understood?"

"Got it," Kenny said and started pulling forward. "I had a chance to visit Camp David a few years ago. Not much different."

"The security is impressive."

"Don't forget, they have DoD contracts and probably more with Homeland Security and who knows what else. It's got to be the equivalent of Groom Lake for geeks."

Thick forest lined both sides of the double-lane winding road. Cameras mounted on tall poles covered every curve and bend. Soon the landscape opened up to reveal an enormous, windowless, monolithic structure that seemed to grow out of the bedrock. Across the top of the front entrance was the

GeoDynamiks name and logo—the Earth with a slice taken out, exposing various layers down to the core. Six or so other buildings dotted the campus, all built in a futuristic style.

Kenny pulled into a visitor's spot. There were no other vehicles in sight. He turned the ignition off but left the keys as ordered. We climbed the stone steps and passed through the mirror-polished stainless steel doors. Inside, two security guards stood on each side of a metal detector.

"Please remove all objects from your pockets—cell phones, wallets, coins," one of the men said. "If you're armed, remove your weapons and place them along with everything else in these baskets."

We followed his orders and emptied our pockets. Kenny pulled his Glock from his holster and complied while I slipped my Walther PPK from my calf holster and the Adamas fixed blade beside it. I dropped them both and my cell into the basket. We were waved through the metal detector one at a time. On the other side, the guard scanned us with a hand wand.

"Proceed," he said. "Your possessions will be returned when you depart."

We walked into a spacious lobby with vaulted ceilings. A collection of sleek, modern chairs and couches were scattered around the lobby. All vacant. A woman sat behind the reception desk—the company logo embroidered above her left breast pocket on her green jacket. She smiled as we approached.

"Welcome to GeoDynamiks. I hope you had no problems finding us?"

I expected Kenny to smart off with something about getting into Fort Knox, but he held his sarcasm. "Nope," he said.

"We're here to see Dr. Penn," I said.

"Of course you are."

Interesting reply, I thought.

She handed us visitor's passes on lanyards. "Please wear these at all times while you're on the property. Have a seat. Dr.

Penn will be with you soon."

I nodded, and we wandered over to the first set of chairs. I noted a number of CCV cameras strategically placed to cover every inch of the room, including beyond the doors to the parking area.

"This reminds me of a scene in a James Bond movie," Kenny said. "I expect Ernst Blofeld holding his white Persian to appear any moment."

Right on cue, I heard the sound of a door opening and footsteps on the marble floor. A tall, slender man in a black suit approached. He had a tan face and close-cropped hair as if he had just completed Marine boot camp.

"Agent Decker," he said extending his hand. "Agent Gates. So nice to meet you. I'm Donald Penn, Director of Research."

"Thanks for taking the time to see us, Dr. Penn," I said.

"Anything we can do to cooperate with the FBI is our pleasure." He turned and motioned toward the door from which he came. "Why don't you follow me? We can relax in one of our conference rooms. Have you had lunch?"

As we tagged along behind Penn, I glanced over my shoulder. Our car was gone.

CHAPTER 28 – THE MEETING

P enn led us along a hallway that ended through a set of double doors into a spacious conference room. The table was inlayed with the company name and logo, and surrounded by 24 leather executive chairs. Around the room, additional chairs waited for what I assumed would be second-tier associates. There were no windows, but stylistic crystal chandeliers resembling icicles provided an abundance of lighting. A few paintings hung strategically around the room—among them, I recognized a Monet, Cézanne, and a Mondrian. Somehow I knew these were not replicas. The ceiling extended up three stories, and on one wall near the top was a glass-front balcony probably used as an observation deck. It appeared the government paid well.

"Please make yourselves at ease." Penn motioned to a couple of chairs near the head of the table. "Something to drink?"

"I'm fine," I said. Kenny also declined the offer.

Once we were seated, Penn said, "So how can we assist the FBI and OSI?"

Kenny smiled at our host. "We're involved in the investigation of two murders that took place recently in Mexico and a third suspected homicide that occurred in Arizona."

"And your investigation brought you here? Interesting."

"We're trying to solve a riddle about an old WWII device the Nazi's developed," I said. I showed him the picture on my iPad. "Can you identify this or take a guess what it might be?"

Penn studied it for a moment.

"Our three murder victims are all connected to that," Kenny said.

"What is it?" Penn asked.

"We're hoping you can tell us."

"No idea."

There was a pause before I said, "Just curious. What kind of technology does GeoDynamiks provide the DoD?"

"Now, Agent Decker, you know I can't divulge that. It's the only way we can maintain and protect our government contracts."

"Okay," Kenny said. "We respect that. Are you familiar with the German term *Das erdbeben maschine*?"

Penn shook his head.

"It means *the earthquake machine*," I said. "Near the end of the war, the Nazis used technology from the famous inventor Nikola Tesla to build a portable machine that could detect the vibration frequency of any object and cause that object to vibrate to pieces. Does that sound familiar?"

"Being in the business we're in, I'm certainly familiar with Tesla's turn-of-the-century work. I didn't recognize your German reference."

Kenny went on to tell him about Vincente's discovery of the device in the Colorado River delta and the recent events, and what we knew and didn't know.

"That's it," I said. "As you can see, we need help. Is someone building a modern version of Tesla's invention? And if so, who and why?"

Penn tapped his fingers together. "GeoDynamiks doesn't do much R and D in that particular field. The company was established in 1994 to study earthquakes and earth movement in the hopes of extending prediction times. Over the last twenty years, we've made great advances in the field of seismology—radon emissions, electromagnetic variations, elastic rebound, seismic patterns and such, and have worked closely with various government agencies to extend the warnings. But nothing like what you're describing."

"But you have contracts with the DoD," I said. "That sounds like you're designing weapons using your seismic technology. You've got to be able to tell us something that will help without giving away government secrets."

"Forgive me, Agent Decker, but that's all I can tell you. I'm not at liberty to confirm or deny what or if we are developing anything for the military. I'm sorry, but I have no helpful answers for you."

"But you could give us some advice and guidance, if you gave it some time, right?" Kenny said.

"Maybe. But so much of my time is taken up with the research I do here. I think this interview has covered about all it can." Penn slid his chair back and stood.

"We thank you for your time, Dr. Penn," I said.

Kenny and I prepared to leave. As we moved around the table, I glanced up at the observation balcony and saw a woman, her arms crossed, watching.

CHAPTER 29 – AREA 51

The rental car was back in the visitor's space. I saw it as we exited the entrance doors.

"Your personal belongings should be on the front seat," Penn said.

"Thanks again," I said. I missed the feel of my Walther in its holster.

Moving down the steps, I glanced over my shoulder to see Penn watching us depart.

"Did you see the woman on the observation deck?"

"Yep. Creepy," Kenny said.

"This whole place is creepy if you ask me."

"I wonder why they took our car. They must do a security sweep of it."

"Or a free wash and wax."

"Where to now?"

I checked my Google maps. "The Airport Hyatt looks good. See if I can catch a flight to Dallas tomorrow and you to DC."

My cell slipped from my hand. As I bent to retrieve it, I realized it wound up under the seat. Stretching to reach it, I detected a metal box about the size of a pack of cigarettes duct taped to the floor. On the front end, I felt an antenna about five centimeters long. Without reacting, I grabbed my phone.

"GeoDynamiks was a dry well," I said. "A waste of our time. I'll sure be happy to get home."

"Without me?"

"We still have tonight." I winked at Kenny while I held my cell phone in my lap and sent him a text—*car bugged.* "Got a message from Kevin. I forwarded to you."

Kenny's phone pinged. He glanced at my text and then said,

"Got it."

Thirty minutes later, we pulled into the rental return lot. Taking our carry-ons, we walked into the building and up to the counter.

"I hope everything was okay with your experience." The agent scanned our contract.

"Perfect," Kenny said.

"Keep this on your credit card?" she asked.

Kenny nodded. "Please."

"Then you're all set. Will there be anything else today?"

"Yes," Kenny said. "We'd like to rent another car."

"The bastards bugged our car," I said as we drove back to Connors. "I knew something was up with that place. I mean security is one thing. GeoDynamiks is as secure as the nuclear bunker in Cheyenne Mountain, and he didn't deny they worked on military weaponry. What are they so paranoid about that they'd bug a federal agent's car unless they've got something to hide? Let's go back and take a closer look."

"Got just the plan," Kenny said. "Ask Siri where the nearest hobby store is."

Fifteen minutes later, we parked our replacement rental and walked into SouthPark Mall to find Area 51 Hobbies. Since it was a weekday, the place was nearly empty of customers—I guessed it would be quite different on a Saturday afternoon. A young man in his late teens stood behind the counter working on a remote-controlled racecar.

"Can I help you guys?" he said as we approached.

"We saw your website and read you specialize in drones," Kenny said.

"You've come to the right place." He gestured to a far wall where 12 models hung. "They start at $99.00 and go up from there." He led us to the display.

"We need something that has a high flight ceiling and can be controlled from at least a mile away."

"If you've got a generous budget, the Blade 350 QX3 is

your drone. Flight ceiling is three thousand feet, and you can operate it from up to one and a half miles away. There's a 1080p HD camera mounted underneath and a built-in GPS system. Beginners can fly it out of the box."

"How much?" I asked.

"One thousand plus tax."

"We'll take it."

CHAPTER 30 – GONE FOR NOW

Magda had her secretary call Penn and tell him to meet her in the conference room at 4:30 PM. She watched the clock, and when it read 4:36 she left her office. Her tardiness was purposeful—a subtle demonstration of who held all the power.

"Good afternoon, Donald." She sat in the high-back leather chair at the head of the table. "Beautiful isn't it?" She pointed to the Monet on the wall. "The colors soothe me. I feel I need those beautiful pastels today. I wish I could have Monet's *Woman With a Parasol.* The mother and child resonate with me. I feel like that was me—a long time ago—holding the parasol. And the child was my son. So much has changed."

"You've never mentioned your family before, in all the years we've worked together."

Magda cleared her throat and ignored Penn's comment. "I think I had a touch of claustrophobia being shut up in my office all day. I feel like I can breathe in here. There's more space, more air, more beauty."

She leaned back her head on the chair. "I think I could fall asleep right here, right now." Then she looked at Penn. "But business first. Always, business first. Tell me, how did the interview with the federal agents go? I watched some of it from the balcony, but I couldn't hear as much as I would have liked. Tell me about it."

Penn tapped the eraser of his pencil on the table. "It went fine. They're interested in understanding the Nazi machine and believed we could help. I led them away from that idea. It's ironic that they chose GeoDynamiks to come to for advice."

"Not really," Magda said. "We're the best in the field, and we have our government ties. GeoDynamiks was a no brainer."

"I wanted to make sure they didn't connect us with Agent Gates's kidnapping, and they weren't probing me because they were suspicious that we are producing a version of the earthquake machine."

"And?"

"I had security plant a bug in their car. The only trouble is it's a rental and they've turned it in."

"Did you pick up any of their conversation while they were still in the car? Anything I should know about?"

"The woman, Agent Decker, caught a glimpse of you on the balcony. She thought you watching them was creepy. They also had questions about why we took their car. I did hear them decide to stay tonight at the Airport Hyatt. But right after that, the whole conversation seemed to turn around. In the end, they decided GeoDynamiks was of no use to them. That makes me wonder if they somehow realized the car was bugged."

"It doesn't matter. They know nothing, and now they're gone."

"Dr. Scarlet, Under Secretary Rittenberg is here," Magda's secretary said on the intercom. "Should I send him up?"

Magda hadn't expected him. "No, no. I'll come down and greet him myself. Call Dr. Penn and tell him we'll be meeting with Rittenberg in a few minutes—to join us in the small conference room."

She dropped the folder she'd been reviewing on her desk, smoothed her skirt, and fluffed her hair. She took the stairs instead of the elevator to the first-floor reception area. The stairway was spiral, and her entrance would be grander than stepping out of an elevator.

"Under Secretary," she said, extending her hand. "I'm so happy to see you. What brings you to GeoDynamiks today?"

He shook her hand. "I was on business in Charlotte, and being so close I decided to take a chance that you could fit me in your schedule for a brief meeting. If not, I understand."

"Absolutely, I have time for you." She turned to the receptionist. "Have some drinks and snacks sent to conference room 104 right away, please." The woman behind the desk had an expression of curiosity on her face. Magda guessed it was probably because she knew room 104 was a small conference room, and this was the Under Secretary of Defense for Acquisition, Technology, and Logistics.

"I'll see to it right away." The receptionist stood.

Magda chose the smaller room, believing it would provide a more intimate setting, and make the situation friendlier, less formal. She and Charles Rittenberg had met on several occasions, but usually in Virginia. They had gone to dinner together a numerous times under the pretense of business. During those encounters, they were on a first name basis.

On the elevator ride, Magda smiled at him in the reflection of the polished brass doors. She knew he'd been smitten with her since the first time they met, and she'd played him right up to going to bed with him. It helped keeping contracts coming her way. Some would call it an affair—she called it part of doing business.

"You look wonderful, Magda."

"You're sweet, Charles, and you know I'm always happy to see you."

"I'm staying in Charlotte tonight. Could we get together?"

"Perhaps."

The elevator doors opened, and Magda led the way to the conference room. Seeing Rittenberg tonight would depend on how this meeting went. Donald Penn was already seated—a large portrait of Nikola Tesla hung on the wall behind him. Penn stood when Magda and Rittenberg entered.

Magda sat at the head of the green-glass conference table. The blue glow of a full-wall aquarium backlit her—the placement was no accident. After the greetings and chitchat about the spectacular aquarium and nice weather, they began the formal meeting.

"Dr. Scarlet, I'm happy to report that we're ready to start

receiving the product right away," Rittenberg said. "Every paper has been signed, every 'i' dotted."

Magda laced her fingers and laid her hands on the glass. "But it isn't quite ready yet. We need a short delay."

Rittenberg looked surprised. "But we did have a deadline in the contract. I don't want to put the penalties in affect. We've done a lot of successful business together over the years."

"I understand and I appreciate it. Unfortunately, we hit a small roadblock. It shouldn't take long to fix. I think we can count on two weeks from today as the delivery date."

Penn cocked his head. "Dr. Scarlet—"

"Donald, don't worry." She glared at him and forced a smile. "We'll have everything ready by then."

"Of course," Penn said. "All the glitches will be worked out. Would you excuse me a moment? I apologize. I'm working hard at staying hydrated as part of my newest healthy living plan, and I have to pay the price."

Magda nodded. "While you're out, would you mind checking on the refreshments I asked for?"

Donald Penn left the conference room rubbing his forehead. There was something going on that he didn't understand. Before he rejoined Scarlet and Rittenberg, he needed to get a better handle on what had just occurred between the two. Dr. Scarlet told him she had a meeting with Rittenberg coming up—not here, but in Virginia. Apparently, she didn't have such a meeting scheduled. And when Penn had asked her why she was so obsessed with getting her hands on the old Nazi earthquake machine, she'd told him she was in a rush to get their product to market before anyone else. Now, he'd just heard her say that GeoDynamiks needed more time. They didn't. The machine was ready to go into production. Why was she stalling? Was it a strategy she had in mind that she hadn't told him about?

As Penn's mind tried to untangle the information, he walked down the hall.

As he neared Magda's office, he realized that he'd nearly

forgotten to check on the drinks and food. He'd better do that right away, or she'd have his head.

He stepped into her office and used her desk phone to call downstairs. He was assured that pitchers of ice water, coffee, tea, and a large platter of fruit and cheese were on their way to room 104. As he spoke, his eyes wandered over the various items on Scarlet's desktop. His gaze fell on the folder she must have been examining when she got the call Rittenberg was there.

It was the red folder.

He skimmed through the contents, which were mostly newspaper clippings, some obviously very old. He held up a small obituary. Christopher Liam Scarlet. Penn sat. Magda Scarlet's three-year-old son. He found another article that explained how the child had tragically perished in a fire while in foster care. The boy had been taken from his family by Child Protective Services due to an anonymous accusation of child abuse. The case had never had the opportunity to be fully investigated nor go to court because of Christopher's untimely death.

He glanced at the picture of the family on Magda's desk. How awful for her, he thought. No wonder she didn't speak about her family. It had to be too painful.

Penn thumbed through more of the folder's collection. Many of the newspaper and magazine articles were about an Ellen Osterling. *Osterling? The Supreme Court Justice?* There was an entire chronicle of her career going all the way back to 1987 when she was Special Counsel to the Governor of South Carolina, then on to the Assistant Attorney General for South Carolina. The articles tracked Ellen Osterling through her climb to the top. She clerked for one of the U.S. Courts of Appeals judges. Went on to become a professor of law at Harvard. Appointment to the U.S. Court Of Appeal in DC. And finally, in 2008 she was appointed as Associate Justice of the U.S. Supreme Court.

What was Magda Scarlet's obsession with this woman? And why would she have those articles with the ones about her son?

He was ready to close the folder, afraid Dr. Scarlet might send someone looking for him. But one last clipping shut off his breath.

CHAPTER 31 – ARIAL SURVEILLANCE

We parked the car about half a kilometer west of the GeoDynamiks campus behind an old abandoned BP gas station. Kenny had used a battery charger plugged into the DC port on the dash and got three batteries ready for flight. He performed a couple of test flights in a nearby pasture before declaring he had earned his wings.

"This thing is amazing," he said. "The video quality is better than my flat screen at home."

"You crash and I'm not buying you another one." After using Bluetooth to pair to the drone's control panel with my iPad, I leaned against the hood of the car and watched the streaming video. He was right, it was impressive.

It was growing late, but there was still plenty of light to make at least one pass over GeoDynamiks. If we remained after dark, and needed to make additional passes, we could use the night vision feature on the camera.

"Prepare for takeoff." Kenny started the four motors and slowly let the drone climb. At 60 meters, he dipped the forward edge and sent the aircraft soaring east over the treetops. The drone was not exactly quiet, but the buzzing quickly blended into the ever-growing sound of evening insects.

It only took a minute or so for the GeoDynamiks facility to come into view—what looked to be ten or fifteen acres of open land surrounded by thick forest. It was made up of the main building with its circular drive and six smaller structures that dotted the campus behind it. A parking lot, not visible from the entrance road, held the employee's cars. Walkways connected the structures, and a few figures moved between them—almost like students heading for class. Kenny kept the device at around 850 meters above the company grounds, and judging by the non-reaction of the people outside, no one seemed distracted by the distant buzzing.

Kenny guided the drone through a slow 360 degrees fly-around before spending more time on each building. Like the main building, there were no windows, so the blank gray walls gave no hint as to what was inside.

One car was leaving the visitor parking area. "Zoom in and see if you can get the license plate number."

Kenny dialed the zoom button, and the camera slowly tightened in on the image.

It was a silver Cadillac STS. "Most likely a luxury rental," I said. "Barcodes on the back and side windows, and no dealer ID on the license frame. Virginia tag with the rental give-away white on orange sticker." I typed the tag number into the notes section on my phone. "We'll check on it later."

After another several minutes, employees started emerging from the various buildings and heading for the parking lot. I glanced at my watch—5:00 PM. Rather than leaving by the front entrance road, they started their drive home by way of a road leading out the opposite end of the campus. Kenny followed high overhead as the stream of vehicles wound their way through the forest to a security checkpoint a kilometer away. Each driver handed their ID to the guard. They were then waved through and turned onto a country road that led back to Connors.

After watching a few cars go through the security protocol, Kenny flew the drone back over the GeoDynamiks campus. Most of the cars had emptied out of the lot, only a handful remained. One stood out in particular—a black, 500 Series Mercedes.

"Nice wheels," Kenny said as he zoomed in on it.

"How's your battery?" I asked.

"Fifty percent."

As he pulled back out using the HD zoom feature, I noticed a woman leaving the main building. Dressed in a dark business suit and carrying a briefcase, she headed for the

Mercedes.

"Must be the boss." Kenny zoomed in. "I wonder if she's the one who watched us during our meeting?"

I shrugged and shook my head. "No way to tell from this far away."

"Wanna see where she goes?"

"Doesn't look like anything's happening here. Let's tag along."

Kenny repositioned the drone anticipating the woman would take the back entrance, but she pulled around a drive to the front of the main building and headed for the entrance gate.

"Must be someone important," Kenny said. "She doesn't have to take the back road."

Security flagged the Mercedes through the main gate without having it slow down, much less stop.

"I think you're right. We're following the head honcho."

The woman turned left and drove toward Connors—her progress partially hidden by the treetops and the growing darkness.

"Time to change to night vision." Kenny flipped a switch on his remote control, and the video stream turned ghostly green. We jumped into our rental and pulled onto the country road. As I drove, Kenny kept a close eye on our target about half a kilometer ahead.

"How's your battery?" I asked again.

"Thirty percent." He leaned into the video screen on the controller. "That's interesting."

"What?"

"A van appeared out of a side road and pulled in a few car lengths behind the Mercedes."

"Probably nothing—local farmer, delivery truck, just about anyone."

"I guess." Kenny checked his controls and readouts. "I'm down to eighteen percent. At ten percent, we'll have to recall the drone and swap out the battery."

"And hope we can catch up to her."

"Hang on. She's turning right. Looks like a suburb. High-end houses. Big ones."

"And the van?"

He panned the camera. "It's following."

I sped up until Kenny told me to turn right. It was the entrance to the subdivision. Brick and stone monuments on both sides of the road bore the name *Stone Creek, a private community.*

"She's pulled through the entrance gate and up to a huge house," Kenny said. "Boss or not, she's knocking down some serious money."

"How're you doing on power?"

"Eleven percent. Pull over."

I guided the rental to the curb in front of an elegant, Tudor style mansion. I counted six chimneys, and those were just the ones I could see from the street.

"I'm gonna recall the drone. We can make a battery switch and be airborne in no time." He again studied the controller video screen. "Oh shit!"

CHAPTER 32 – SELF STORAGE

"Kill the lights and scoot down," Kenny said. "They're coming straight in our direction."

"What happened?" I turned the headlights off and slumped in my seat.

"Two guys leaped out of the van, pulled the woman from the car, and threw her in the van."

The van came over a rise in the winding neighborhood street and raced past. As soon as they were out of sight, Kenny jumped from the car and stared at the sky. The drone landed on the street a few meters in front of him. Within seconds, it was airborne with a fresh battery, and Kenny was back in the rental.

"All right, let's go." He concentrated on the video feed. "We can't lose these guys."

I performed a quick U-turn and took off after the van. "Got them yet?"

"They're making a right on Old Connors Rd. Ran the stop sign and almost lost control." He kept the drone just above treetop level—the sound of its buzzing wouldn't be heard from inside a speeding vehicle.

We came to the entrance to Stone Creek and turned onto Old Connors Rd.

"How far ahead are they?"

Kenny never took his eyes off the video feed. "Hard to say, but I'd guess half a kilometer. Don't try to catch up. We don't want them to know we're on their tail. Besides, as long as I can see them with this, they won't know we're here."

"If they get on I-85, can the drone keep up?"

Kenny shook his head. "Hopefully they won't or we'd lose them for sure."

There was more traffic than I expected on what was mostly a county road, but Connors was a bedroom community, and all these folks were probably heading home after a long day in the city.

"They're turning."

"Which way?"

"Left into one of those self-storage places. The van stopped at the gate, and the driver entered a code into a keypad. The gate is opening. There are six long rows of storage units. They're turning down number three. Now they've stopped about midway down the row. I'm going to have to increase my altitude so they can't hear the drone."

I saw a sign ahead that read *U-Stor*, and then the security gate came into view. I kept driving until we were about 150 meters beyond the entrance. Then I turned around and pulled to the shoulder.

"They just opened one of the storage units," Kenny narrated. "Now two guys pulled the woman out of the van dragged her inside the storage unit. There's a bag covering her head."

The vision of the bag over the woman's head made me shudder. I couldn't bear to think this would lead to a possible beheading, but I had to know what was happening. I leaned over to watch the video feed. "The van's driving away."

"Yeah, the driver never got out."

"Wait, one of the men is coming back out. What's that he's carrying?"

"A shotgun. He's looking right at—" Kenny slammed the remote control joystick forward. "The guy's shooting at my thousand-dollar drone."

My cell phone rang. I looked at the caller ID. *Unknown*

I pressed the talk button. "Yes?"

"*Buena noches, Señora* Decker."

CHAPTER 33 – EL DIABLO

"Who is this?" I asked as I watched Kenny maneuver the drone out of the shooter's range.

"A good friend of the late Pablo Garcia." The man had a Spanish accent. "You remember Pablo, don't you?"

"You guys need to get over that and move on. I'm sure you have drugs to smuggle or innocent people to torture. I'm no threat to you or the Selinas Cartel."

"On the contrary, *Señora* Decker. As long as you are alive, you are a symbol of great embarrassment to our organization. It is not honorable for a woman to be responsible for the death of our leader. Until we show our enemies your severed head, you *are* a threat."

"Damn!" Kenny said.

I took a quick glance at the video feed. The green glowing image showed an airborne object moving toward his drone. Kenny had to slam the joystick to the side to avoid a collision.

"I take it you've discovered how we found you?" the Mexican said. "Drones are quite handy these days." He chuckled.

"What do you want?"

"To finish what we started in San Felipe. But your video confession and beheading will have to wait for another time. Right now you need to back off your investigation or the woman will die."

Kenny used body English and the joystick controls to keep from being overtaken by the Mexican's drone. This looked no different from the many times I'd watched him gaming on his Xbox.

"Kidnapping carries enormous consequences," I said.

"It is worth the risk. The device used to destroy the building in San Felipe would be an excellent weapon to deal with our competition, the Federales, and the DEA. We're here to trade the life of the GeoDynamiks CEO for the device. You have nothing to do with this, Agent Decker. Your timing was unfortunate. It is a shame you chose today to visit GeoDynamiks. It may lead to the speeding up of your video premier. But perhaps if you are cooperative, my heart might soften. I am a sentimental and reasonable man. Do you understand?"

"What makes you think GeoDynamiks is the source of the device?"

"We did the same research you did, Agent Decker. I have brilliant tech people working for me. Smart enough to hack into the GeoDynamiks's servers. They built the device, and I'm going to have it."

"How about I call in the local SWAT team?"

"Do that and she'll get a bullet to her brain. Then you will move up to the number one spot on my list."

"Kill her now and you won't get the device."

"Too late, *Señora* Decker. I am a step ahead of you. The machine is already being brought here from GeoDynamiks."

"Got him," Kenny said. "Drove him into a tree." A thud sounded on the roof of the car. Kenny opened the door and grabbed his drone he'd just landed. "Go!"

I floored the accelerator and shot onto the road. "You know my name, but I don't know yours."

"Call me El Diablo."

"Not very original," I said as I steered with one hand.

"But appropriate in this case."

"Okay, El. May I call you El?"

"It is in your best interest to do what I said. Without hesitation. Turn around and leave."

I saw the U-Stor facility coming up on the right, whipped the rental into the entrance drive and blasted through the gates.

CHAPTER 34 – ROW THREE

"Go left," Kenny said. "We'll come in from the back."

I turned and slowed the car as I steered to the end of the first row of storage units. Moving down the row—units on my right, fencing on my left—we soon came to the end. I pulled to a stop and killed the engine. There were security lights throughout the complex, but, fortunately, the one on this back corner was out.

"Who was that on the phone," he asked.

"He calls himself El Diablo. I assume he's the new head of the cartel."

"You look pale, Max. You okay?"

"He claims GeoDynamiks is the manufacturer of the earthquake machine. He wants to trade the company's CEO for the machine. That's the woman they have in the van. If he's right, she's responsible for the quake in the desert, kidnapping you, the death of the Delgado brothers, and she's hell bent on getting me. El Diablo told me to back off." I chuckled. "Fat chance."

"Then let's do what he says. Turn the frigging car around and I'll call every agency there is to send in the troops."

I stared into my ex's eyes. "I can't. You know that. Kidnappings don't end in happily ever after. They'll kill the woman as soon as they get their hands on the device if not before. It'll take too long for back up. We have to go in after her right now."

"Max, it's our *lives* we're talking about."

"No, it's the woman's life at stake. I have to be able to live with myself. No way am I backing down. Are you with me or not because I'm going in with or without you."

Kenny shook his head as if he knew me too well. "All right, all right. I know I'll never win this argument." He got out and placed the drone with its fresh battery on the hood of the car. A moment later, the four motors spun to life, and the little flying machine rose straight up into the Carolina night.

He checked the altimeter readout. At the two thousand-foot mark, he guided the drone toward the third row of storage units. With the night vision on, the video monitor gave the inside of our car an eerie green glow like a science fiction movie.

I lowered my window to see if I could hear the drone motors. Nothing but the sounds of nature.

"Got anything?"

"There's a car coming down row three—moving slow."

I leaned toward Kenny and watched the screen. It was a luxury model, similar to the kidnapped woman's—perhaps a BMW. It pulled to a halt half way down the row.

Kenny zoomed in as much as the camera would allow. "Sure as shit that's where your Mexican buddy is holding the hostage."

The car's lights went out, and the driver's door opened. A man in a suit emerged.

"That looks an awful lot like Donald Penn."

"Agreed." Kenny maneuvered the drone so we could get a better look. "He's taking something out of the trunk. Got it wrapped up in a blanket."

"What do you want to bet it's the device?"

"Think Penn is in on this?"

"I don't know. Maybe just the delivery man."

"The storage unit's door is opening." Kenny made another angle adjustment. "Two guys with guns. They're directing Penn inside."

"I think it's time we get up close and personal."

We stepped out of the rental. Kenny brought the drone home and placed it on the back seat. With guns drawn, we started around the corner.

"Freeze!"

CHAPTER 35 – PORTER AND GANNON

"**D**rop your weapons!
We placed our guns on the ground and then raised our arms.

"Down on the ground. Do it now! Don't turn around."

"On the ground, face down." A different voice. This one female.

We complied.

"Don't move," the female said. "You move and I'll Taser you. Got it?"

I felt her knee on my back.

"Give me your right hand."

Handcuffs clicked around my wrist.

"Now your left."

With a second click, I felt a helplessness I hadn't experienced since my OSI training years ago. I didn't like it.

The woman stood and went to Kenny.

"Don't move, sir. Give me your right hand." Click. "Now your other."

"Officer, I'm with the FBI," I said.

"Face down!" She searched Kenny. "Don't move or you'll be tased." When she finished, she shifted back to me. Running her hand down my right leg, she said, "Knife." She pulled my pants leg up and removed my Adamas and handed it to the other cop.

"I'm FBI," I said. "My ID is in the right pocket of my pants."

The officer's hands ran down my right leg to my pocket. She pulled my ID out.

"Roll over on your side and stand up—slowly."

I made it to my feet. Kenny told her where to find his cred

pack, and we finally stood side by side. The female officer's partner kept his pistol leveled at us. Her nametag read Porter, her arm patch identified her as a Cabarrus County Sheriff's Deputy, and the three stripes told me she was a sergeant—her partner, Officer Gannon, was a two-stripe corporal.

Porter's flashlight beam still shone on Kenny's photo ID and badge, then over to mine. "Interesting combination of federal departments. FBI consultant Maxine Decker and Special Agent Kenneth Gates of the United States Air Force Office of Special Investigations."

"We know who we are, Officer Porter," I said. "And we're a bit short on time. So if you can remove the cuffs..."

Porter gave out a little huff, and then unlocked our handcuffs. She signaled to Officer Gannon and he returned our weapons.

"What's going on here?" she asked.

"We're investigating a kidnapping," Kenny said.

"Who?"

"The CEO of GeoDynamiks," I said.

Porter shot a glance to her partner. "First we've heard of it. The storage company's security system sent an alert that the main gate had been broken into."

"The kidnapping just happened within the hour," Kenny said. "We think we know where they're holding her."

"Who are *they*?" Gannon asked.

"Possibly members of Mexico's Selinas Cartel." I was getting nervous that this delay could cost the hostage her life.

"Selinas Cartel?" Porter said. "Now I know who you are." She moved closer and studied my face. "The agent who nailed Pablo Garcia. You were all over the news."

"You got me. I'd love to reminisce about my Mexican adventure, but we need to move fast before someone gets hurt."

"Call for backup," she said to Gannon. "We stay put until backup arrives."

"No time." I turned and started down row three.

CHAPTER 36 – OFFICER DOWN

The security lamps were spaced far enough apart that they formed light pools between shadows. I moved quickly through the lighted areas into the next dark spot beyond.

"Right behind you," Kenny whispered.

The two deputies positioned themselves on the opposite side of the row and mirrored us from a few paces back. There was nothing up ahead in the glow of the lights, but I couldn't be sure someone waited for us in the dark. My palms were turning slick with sweat. I tightened my grip on the Walther. If there was someone hiding in the darkness, we were easy targets each time we moved under the next light.

Two muffled pops were followed by a grunt. Officer Gannon was hit. I dropped to the pavement and returned fire at the spot where I saw the muzzle flashes.

"Officer down!" Porter called into her shoulder mic. "Shots fired. U-Stor on Old Connors Road. Row three."

I heard the dispatcher repeating Porter's info and request for all units in the area to respond.

Two more pops. One shot hit the side of the building, spraying stucco down on me. No impact from the other.

I fired again. Kenny got off multiple shots. A figure in the shadows ahead fell sideways and hit the ground hard.

"Careful," Kenny said as he slowly hugged the wall and eased toward the body.

"You okay, Porter?" I saw her kneeling over Gannon's body.

"I'm good."

Gannon caught one in the chest. His vest stopped it, but the impact knocked him for a loop. Porter's radio sparked with activity.

I left her and caught up with Kenny. Sixty meters later, we stood over the body of the man we'd taken down. I felt for a pulse. No way to tell which one of us put a 9mm slug through his forehead.

Sirens in the distance.

"All hell's gonna break lose," I said.

A door from a storage unit a couple of stalls ahead flew up. Two men rushed out and started firing wildly down row three. Once again I was on the ground shooting back, Kenny beside me. Porter joined in the firefight, and within seconds the two men fell.

The first police car appeared at the opposite end of row three and roared toward us. A second and third fell in behind. Two more had come around to the back of the storage facility and pulled up next to Officer Gannon.

Kenny, Porter, and I rushed the open door to the storage unit. Other officers did the same from the opposite direction.

I was the first to arrive and took a quick peek inside. "FBI!" I shouted. "Drop your weapon and get down on the ground."

A woman sat in a chair near the back wall. A man stood behind her, a large knife to her throat. Penn was face down, hands tied, the object he removed from his car resting beside him. It was still wrapped in what looked like a blanket. Large cardboard boxes sat stacked along both walls.

"FBI!" I repeated from outside the unit. "Drop your weapon and get down on the ground."

Another quick look told me no one had moved.

"El, is that you?"

"You're very funny, Agent Decker. If you come in, she dies."

"And then what? There's a police convention out here. Your cartel commandos are all dead. You want to end your life in Connors, North Carolina?" I turned to Porter and shook my head to let her know I was just making a point.

He didn't respond.

"Last chance, El."

The light inside the storage unit turned off. The corrugated metal door dropped down and slammed shut.

Silence.

CHAPTER 37 – ROW TWO

The rumble of a large diesel engine broke the silence—the Sheriff's SWAT team pulled in behind the police cars. From the opposite direction, a fire truck appeared along with an ambulance. Row three was awash in red and blue, and throbbing white strobes.

"Get back!" shouted the captain of the SWAT team as they poured out of the truck and rushed toward us. "Everybody get back."

Two paramedics jumped from the ambulance to aid Officer Gannon.

Kenny and I backed away from the closed, roll-down door of the storage unit. I watched as members of SWAT examined the door before trying to pull it up by the handle. Jammed. The captain conferred with the battalion chief who ordered his firefighters to bring tools, including the Jaws of Life.

"Something's not right," I said to Kenny.

Porter had come to stand beside us. "What do you mean?"

"This is a death trap for the Mexican."

"Whether he kills the woman or not, he's boxed in," Kenny said.

I thought for a moment. "Unless he planned for this and has a way out." I turned and retraced our steps with Kenny and Porter following.

We passed police officers, the dead bodies of the Mexican shooters, the fire truck, and EMT vehicle. At the end of row three, I jogged along the back to row two. Cautiously looking around the corner, I saw nothing but the usual light pools and dark shadows. No vehicles.

"What was the unit number on row three?" I asked.

"Twelve," Kenny said.

I took off in a run along row two, checking the unit signs on my right. If the one, where the hostage was held, was 12, then the one that backed up to it would be an odd number on this row. Just before unit 11, I stopped and hugged the wall, my Walther at the ready. I motioned for Kenny to take a position on the other side of the door—Porter was behind me.

I grabbed the door handle and noticed the door was about ten centimeters off the ground. Someone had been in a hurry and not closed it. El Diablo had already escaped. I pulled the handle, and the door slid up its tracks.

Darkness swallowed the interior.

I heard the faint banging and clamoring of the fire department working to open the number 12 door on row three. Moving to the side wall, I found a light switch and flipped it on.

The unit was filled with large piles of materials covered with thick sheets of plastic. A path ran down the middle to the rear of the unit. I moved with caution to the nearest pile and pulled away the covering.

"My God!" Porter said with a gasp.

CHAPTER 38 – ESCAPE

We watched the cops swarm over the two huge piles of neatly stacked bales. Each bundle was the size of a 48-quart ice chest and contained individually wrapped kilos of cocaine. The whole scene took on a surreal atmosphere as the floodlight from the police helicopter created moving shadows.

"First quick count is one hundred and twenty-seven bales—roughly three thousand kilos."

"Around three-hundred million on the street." the captain said.

"That was my take, too, sir."

"Thank you, sergeant." He turned to the three of us. "It's certainly the biggest bust in this region. Excellent work."

I motioned at the dozens of law enforcement personnel. "A team effort."

Kenny smiled. "She doesn't take compliments too well."

"Nevertheless, this will go down in the record books." He pulled out his cell phone and dialed. "I want a search warrant immediately to open every storage unit in this complex. And I want the owner and all employees taken into custody for questioning. Confiscate all video from all cameras. We need to ID the getaway car." As he continued spouting orders, he wandered away.

I looked inside the unit at the trap door at the end of the space between the two piles of bales. It had flung open only seconds after I uncovered the drugs—a fierce-looking SWAT officer aimed his assault rifle at me. Before we could finish identifying ourselves, there were three more officers emerging from the passage between the two storage units. A helicopter aimed its blinding spotlight on us.

"El Diablo must have prepared the tunnel to make a quick exit to the other unit. Only this time he went in the reverse direction. This had to be a major distribution point for the cartel, and a whole lot of folks had to be in on it starting with the guy who runs the place."

"Agreed," Kenny said. "Let's go check on Penn and the kidnap victim."

I nodded and turned to Porter. "Want to join us?"

"I'll catch up. My shift commander wants a written report right away."

We walked along row two, made the turn at the rear of the building and headed down row three. I hoped there would be no emergencies in the county tonight because all the first responders seemed to be here. And the press was starting to arrive. The whopping of the police helicopter and two TV station choppers became unbearable as they took up stationary positions overhead.

We approached the spot where it all started, and I saw Dr. Penn speaking to a couple of men in suits—probably Sheriff's detectives. We waited until they wrapped up their conversation then stepped forward.

"Agents Decker and Gates." Penn reached to shake our hands. "I can't begin to thank you for all you've done. You saved our lives."

Penn's appearance was a far cry from our meeting earlier at GeoDynamiks. Now he was pale, shaken, looking as if he might faint. I wondered if the paramedics had checked him out yet.

"We're just glad you're okay," Kenny said.

"Do you need to sit?" I asked.

He waved me off. "No, I'm fine. Just a bit unnerved."

"Dr. Penn," I said. "The object you brought here tonight, the one the cartel wanted in exchange for your CEO. Where is it?"

"Like I told the detectives, when the lights went out, the Mexican must have grabbed it before he went through the tunnel. By the time the SWAT guys broke in the door, it was gone—so was the man."

"And just what is it?"

"Agent Decker, I'm afraid I can't tell you that. It's highly classified."

"And yet your secret device is now in the hands of Mexican drug dealers," Kenny said. "Men who don't hesitate to kill to get what they want."

"I'm sorry, but I can't reveal the nature of the device."

"Dr. Penn," I said, "we know all about your machine, and we need to have a serious conversation with your CEO. There are accusations floating around about what your organization has been responsible for. We want to know the truth."

"Hello."

I turned at the sound of a woman's voice.

Penn exhaled, probably thankful that my questioning had been interrupted. "Agents, please meet the president and CEO of GeoDynamiks, Dr. Magda Scarlet."

CHAPTER 39 – THE VOICE

I'd heard that voice before. The slight Carolina flavor with a smoky aftertaste. It was the one on the phone in Mexico when I was given 48 hours to find the German WWII device or Kenny would be killed, and again when we were running for our lives through Panteon Municipal Cemeterio. I had no doubt that had been Magda Scarlet. It seemed El Diablo might have told me the truth. I had to be certain, and I needed evidence. My recognition of her voice and the tale from a drug dealer wouldn't fly as far as filing formal charges against her. And what the hell kind of a name was *Magda Scarlet* anyway?

"Why didn't your private commandos come to your aid, Dr. Scarlet?" I asked.

"I assume you're referring to the GeoDynamiks security officers, Agent Decker?" Penn said.

"Yes. I remember killing at least two of them south of the border."

"I'm sure you're mistaken." Penn took Scarlet by the arm. "Perhaps you can make an appointment to continue this discussion some other time. Dr. Scarlet has been through a traumatic series of events tonight. I've convinced the police to let her come in tomorrow to give a statement, but for now I need to get her to safety and away from this awful place. This way, ma'am."

As they walked to Penn's BMW, Scarlet looked over her shoulder and said, "I'm in your debt, Agent Decker."

Yeah, she sure was. We could have let El Diablo have her— simply turned our backs instead of coming in to save her ass.

A moment later she was hidden behind the dark glass of the luxury sedan and whisked away.

"Traumatic events?" Kenny said. "How about getting shot at by GeoDynamiks ninjas while we were diving behind tombstones."

"I've had enough of this place." My ex and I headed back to row one where our rental was parked.

The police captain approached us. "You two mind coming by headquarters tomorrow and giving us a written report?"

"Glad to," I said.

As the officer walked away, Kenny mumbled, "Or we might just sleep in."

"I'm all for that. Scarlet wouldn't dare make a move on us tonight. Not after this. Some peace and quiet are what I need right now."

We passed under the crime scene tape, turned the corner to our car, and walked into a wall of lights. The press found me again.

CHAPTER 40 – CUT TO THE CHASE

"We've gotta find someplace safe to stay," I said as we drove from Connors to Charlotte. "It wouldn't take a Mexican Einstein to figure out we're still around after all those questions from the press."

"They asked everything but your bra size." Kenny steered us onto the interstate. "I could have answered that."

I gave my ex a smile. "Yes, you could, and more."

My iPhone rang. I looked at the caller ID. *Unknown.* "El, is that you?"

"I wanted to thank you for helping deliver the *máquina de terremoto.*"

"Trust me, if there had been any way I could've stopped you, I would have."

"Now you have hurt my feelings, just when we were becoming *buenos amigos.*"

"Are you ready to turn yourself in and hand over the device you stole? You realize every law enforcement agency in this part of the country is looking under every rock for you."

"Actually, the device is why I am calling."

"I'm listening."

"We seem to have a *pequeño problema.*"

"What kind of tiny problem?"

There was a long pause. "We cannot make the device work."

I snickered. "El, I wouldn't call that a *pequeño problema.* Sounds more like a *grande* problem to me."

"I'm glad you find this amusing."

"Look, the device is of no use if you can't make it work. If you don't want to turn yourself in, and I'm guessing you don't, just leave the device where we can find it, hightail it to the border, and hope I don't catch up with you."

"Nice try, Agent Decker. Now here is what is going to happen. As you know, my organization is international. We have connections throughout South, Central, and North America."

"Congratulations."

"We also have a great deal of competition. Dealing with the other cartels along with the DEA would be much easier if we had the advantage of the earthquake machine. Understand?"

"Yes."

"We have distributors in almost every major city including Dallas."

I tried to hide the heat wave that washed over me, and spoke in as calm a voice as possible. "What about Dallas?"

"I believe that is where your friend, FBI Special Agent Kevin Fender, lives? "

I glanced at Kenny whose face revealed that he was reading my body language. "What?" he asked.

I covered the mic on the phone. "Something about Kevin." In the light of the oncoming headlights, I saw Kenny's face harden. "Pull over and stop." Kenny slowed and eased the car onto the shoulder.

"What have you done with Agent Fender?" The words caught in my throat.

"I can tell you no longer find this call humorous, Agent Decker. You've seen some of our videos, so you know how we deal with those who don't fit into our plans."

"Just cut to the chase."

"Do you know where that phrase came from, Agent Decker?"

Before I could say that I didn't give a shit, El continued. "Back in the silent movie days, the most exciting part of the story was the chase scene that always came near the end. The impatient audience would often call out 'cut to the chase' half way through the film. Fascinating, isn't it?"

I said nothing.

"Very well, I *will* cut to the chase—I need the operating

instructions and power supply for the device."

"Why would I help you?"

"Because what happened to Colonel Marquez is about to happen to your friend Agent Fender. Whether he is executed or goes free is entirely up to you. To motivate you to act quickly, I'm sending you a video. *Buenas noches*, Agent Decker."

A message with attachment arrived. I clicked the video file and held the phone so we both could see. Five seconds into the video I dropped the cell, shoved open the car door and threw up onto the side of the road.

CHAPTER 41 – PEACH FLOORS

"I realize what time it is, Dr. Penn," I said, knowing I had awakened him. "It's the middle of the night where I am, too."

I was still shaking from the video of Kevin about to be murdered. It was an image I could never erase. Kenny had fallen into stony silence, but I knew he was boiling inside. We sat on the side of the road while I notified the special agent in charge of the Dallas office, who in turn sent an encrypted message directly to the office of the Director in Washington. A nationwide search involving local, regional, and national law enforcement organizations kicked into gear as word spread that a federal agent had been abducted and was being held by the cartel.

"How'd you get my number?" Penn asked.

"I'm with the FBI, sir."

"So what was it you wanted again?" His speech was still slurred with sleep.

"It's urgent I meet with you and Magda Scarlet."

"At three AM?"

"It's that important."

"What do you need to know?"

"Not on the phone."

"And it can't wait until morning?"

"If it could, I wouldn't have called."

There was a long hesitation. "All right, let me put you on hold and contact Dr. Scarlet."

"Remind her that she owes me."

Penn's BMW was there when Kenny and I pulled into the circular drive of Magda Scarlet's mansion, a pale yellow brick and stone Tuscan-style structure. We had managed to calm down enough along the way to feel we could assume a somewhat normal manner of doing our jobs despite the news of our friend's kidnapping.

Penn greeted us at the entrance—a set of double bronze doors with eight bas-relief panels on each. They must have originated from an Italian cathedral. I'd seen many similar ones during my field work in college archaeology classes.

Inside, we walked on peach-colored marble tiles with oriental rugs placed about to quiet the clicking of shoes. Penn showed us into a great room with a continuation of the tile floors. Overhead, thick oak beams traversed the ceiling. At one end of the room stood a fireplace that appeared to be hand-carved marble. Standing beside it with arms folded as if she were a school principal having two unruly students brought to her office, was Magda Scarlet. A red velvet robe covered her from choker collar to the peach floor. She didn't look pleased.

"Nice place," Kenny said dryly.

Penn started to react to my irreverent ex-husband, but Scarlet moved her hand enough for him to hold his temper. Without taking her glare off me, she said, "I know I said I owed you, Agent Decker. I didn't expect you to cash in your chip this soon." She motioned to the two embroidered, Italian Renaissance couches facing each other in the middle of the room. "You have five minutes. After that, I'm going back upstairs, have some brandy, and hopefully manage to forget this night ever happened."

Kenny and I sat beside each other while Scarlet went to the opposite couch. Penn stood beside her. As I looked at her, I was amazed at her chilling composure. There was no doubt she knew what we suspected of her and GeoDynamiks. She also understood we had no proof.

Scarlet crossed her legs. "Donald said you sounded as if this meeting was a matter of life and death. Explain."

"The Mexican who stole your device—the new leader of the Selinas Cartel, contacted me. Apparently he is unable to make it work."

"I'm not surprised," Penn said with a condescending chuckle.

"Then there's no threat," Scarlet said and held her hands up. "We can all breathe a sigh of relief, and I can go back to sleep."

"Well, not quite," I said. "The cartel has abducted an FBI agent in Dallas and threatens to execute him if we don't supply them with the operating instructions."

"I'm very sorry to hear such disturbing news," Scarlet said. "But what do you expect me to do about it?"

"I expect you to give me the instructions on how to activate your earthquake machine." I paused for effect. "We're certain it's your product."

Scarlet lifted an eyebrow and gave me a dismissive smile.

I ignored her smugness. "The FBI doesn't negotiate with terrorists. That's why I need your cooperation."

CHAPTER 42 – THE CODE

This time we were waved through the GeoDynamiks guard station with no problem. Our rental car was part of a caravan with more flashing lights than a Christmas tree. It was led by numerous North Carolina State Highway Patrol cars, a Sheriff's SWAT team truck, Penn's BMW with Magda Scarlet in the back seat, lots of Cabarrus County Sheriff's cars, one of which was driven by the sheriff himself, a couple of sedans containing FBI agents, and a black SUV transporting the regional FBI rapid response team. A fire and EMT truck brought up the rear.

Rather than pulling up to the front of the GeoDynamiks main building, we paraded around it to one of the secondary buildings labeled Lab E. As everyone exited their vehicles, I should have felt like I was in the most protected spot on Earth. But I had quickly gotten to know El Diablo and had a sour taste in my mouth that made me feel we were anything but safe.

The army of police surrounded the building while Kenny and I followed Scarlet and Penn into the windowless laboratory. Because of the need for the highest of security clearance, no one else was allowed inside. We were the exceptions.

"Lab E is where we research our most experimental devices." Penn led us into a large room filled with racks of electronic gear and work benches covered with video testing scopes and monitors, along with piles of circuit boards and components.

I finally came face-to-face with what looked like a fully assembled *earthquake* machine. There were three or four others on tables scattered around the room in various stages of assembly.

The machine resembled the German relic but only in a general sense. Both were about the same size—around the length of an upright industrial vacuum cleaner but with a great deal more bulk.

"It's quite light," Penn said as he watched me study the device.

"Why was it so important that you retrieve the German relic? You pretty much redesigned this thing, and there was nothing salvageable from the Nazi version?"

He avoided answering my question as if I'd never asked. "It's constructed mostly of magnesium alloys and pure polymers. The whole thing weighs twenty pounds."

"Twenty pounds and it can still cause a building or anything to vibrate until it crumbles?" Kenny asked.

"It's not the weight, Agent Gates, it's what the electronics inside do—automatically and mechanically seek out the structural resonance frequency of any solid object and cause it to vibrate to the point of destruction."

I reached to touch it but Penn shook his head. "Not allowed." He waved for us to follow.

"So this will be the government's newest weapon?"

"Actually, we are about to deliver—"

"Shut up, Donald," Scarlet said. She moved to a spacious desk with a wall of monitors and a computer operator's station. I stood behind her and watched as she typed at an amazingly fast speed. Documents and semantics appeared on the various monitors. Scarlet scrolled each, found a specific line of code and changed a value here and there before moving on.

"And you can cause it to malfunction as I suggested?" I asked.

"Yes. I did this type of modification once before," she said as she typed. "I was forced to leave a company called CoreConcepts that was attempting to steal my ideas. So I modified the code of their flagship product. A snip here, value change there. The product still worked, but not like it was designed. They lost a huge government contract because of that failure."

"So what are you doing now?" I asked.

Penn spoke up. "The brains of the device—the millions of lines of code—are incorporated in the power pack that attaches to the back end. I made sure the device I brought to the storage unit had a dead power pack with no way to recharge it."

"What you'll deliver to the Mexican," Scarlet said, "is a partially charged power pack with slightly modified code. The device will work, but not quite how they anticipate. I'm giving them what they requested—a working model. My part is done."

Kenny and I glanced at each other. I knew we were both thinking this woman has ice water in her veins.

All the monitors suddenly displayed the GeoDynamiks logo. "Done." Scarlet stood.

Penn walked to a nearby table and removed what I assumed was the power pack from its charging and firmware transfer machine. "It's ready and the code is embedded, Agent Decker." He handed it to me—it reminded me of the battery that powered my cordless Ryobi drill. "Now, it's up to you."

I held my cell and dialed the number El Diablo had given me. When he answered, I said, "I have what you want. Now release Agent Kevin Fender."

"First you must listen carefully."

CHAPTER 43 – BUZZING

I breathed in the smell of dank earth and wildflowers as I stood in the middle of a field about a kilometer from the GeoDynamiks's buildings. I was told that the field had once been farmland but was bought years ago by Magda Scarlet for project testing and future expansion. Although I could see few details around me, I knew there were countless sets of eyes watching me through night vision devices. The only light came from the stars and the distant glow of the city. My instructions from El Diablo were to bring whatever was needed to operate the earthquake device and wait in the field, alone.

"Anything?" Kenny whispered in my earpiece.

"Crickets and frogs," I whispered back. "And buzzing insects, mostly mosquitos. You?"

"Same here."

The Kevlar vest made me sweat. I'd worn body armor many times in the past during my years as an OSI agent, but it had been a long time ago. I'd forgotten that it served as a constant reminder someone might want to shoot me. And with night vision technology and advanced sniper weapons, they could probably do it from miles away and pinpoint me between the eyes. I'd never hear the report or feel a thing. And I made a perfect target standing out here.

Knowing Kenny was on the other end of the com system gave me a small sense of security.

"Something's happening," Kenny said.

My body stiffened. I stared hard into the blackness but saw nothing.

"A flying object. Coming from the east. It could be a drone. It's big and coming in hot."

I faced east. Nothing but blackness and the buzzing of—suddenly I realized the buzzing wasn't mosquitoes. If it was, there was a huge swarm coming right at me.

Then it was there, a few meters away. The drone was twice the size of Kenny's and had eight motors rather than four. Below the device hung its payload—what looked like a metal basket the size of a backpack. Dust and dried grass formed a swirling storm around me. I had to protect my eyes with my hands. Kenny said something into my earbud, but the noise drowned him out.

I stepped forward and reached for the basket, which hung at about eye level. The red eye of a camera watched me. I raised the basket's lid and placed the battery and firmware pack inside. The instant I closed the lid, the drone shot straight up as if powered by rockets. The buzzing of its motors faded toward the east, replaced by the chorus of insects and amphibians. The whole thing was over in seconds.

"You okay, Max?" Kenny said.

"Just peachy."

"That thing looked huge on the video."

"I don't think you could afford that one."

CHAPTER 44 – BACKFIRE

Walking back across the field to the GeoDynamiks campus and Lab E, I had plenty of time to think. They manufactured the device that brought down the building in Mexico—I no longer doubted that. Their private ninja army was the one that nabbed Kenny, blew off the head of the cowboy on the fishing boat, and shot up the pillow-top, extra firm mattress in my vacation villa, not to mention getting a few more customers ready for burial in the Mexican cemetery. All this didn't seem to bother Magda Scarlet. But Penn was starting to look a bit paler than the first time we met. Especially after Scarlet ordered him to shut his mouth. According to the company website, all their products were scientific in nature—devices used by geologists, volcanologists, mining companies, map makers and others. They claimed to build machines that help predict earthquakes, but not cause them. *Did we just kick the anthill?*

"Are you all right?" Kenny asked as I approached a group of officers gathered around the back of a police van.

"Just tired."

He put his arm around my shoulders. "I can't imagine why." Then he pointed. "Check this out." The back doors of the van were open exposing racks of surveillance equipment and video screens.

"What's up?"

Donald Penn stood next to Kenny and said, "When the cartel turned on the device, it automatically activated a built-in GPS system. We put it in almost all our products to assist in retrieving lost or stolen equipment."

"They've pulled into a warehouse district in Charlotte near Morehead and Wilkinson," an officer said. "Looks like they stopped."

Another cop turned to me. "That's a high crime area. Lots of drug activity."

Apparently, during the time I walked back from the field, the SWAT and FBI teams had headed toward the city, being directed by the GPS coordinates. What were left were a few sheriff's deputies and state troopers. Scarlet was absent.

"Tactical units are moving in," said the officer who operated the surveillance equipment.

"El Diablo is about to get a big surprise," Kenny said.

"Bigger than you think," Penn said.

We watched the monitor with the blue dot that indicated the cartel vehicle had stopped moving. Five minutes passed. Chatter on the com confirmed that the order to start the assault was seconds away.

"What the!" came a voice over the com. "The place just fell apart."

Suddenly, it sounded like a hundred voices talking at once. I couldn't make out anything other than something big had happened. Dr. Scarlet had done more than we'd asked. Kenny and I stared at each other then at Penn.

He winked. "Backfire."

CHAPTER 45 – DELAYED DELIVERY

"Backfire?" I asked.

"It's a modification to the programming that causes the device to bring down whatever structure is surrounding it rather than a unique target structure," Penn said.

"And that's what Dr. Scarlet did? Program it to backfire?" Kenny asked.

Penn nodded. "The device can also be activated by a built-in timer or by remote control."

"Wouldn't that be an awfully expensive use of a machine that sophisticated?" I asked. "Knowing it will be destroyed?"

"The machine *is* sophisticated, but not all that expensive to manufacture," Penn said. "The Germans did it based on a unique Tesla frequency generation and manipulation technique. We greatly improved on their design and can build it at a fraction of the cost. The tooling up is where the largest investment went."

"But once finished, you would sell it at a sizable profit?"

"Correct, Agent Decker."

"Dr. Penn," Kenny said, "is it considered a weapon?"

He motioned us away from the group of police officers. "It depends on who you sell it to. A demolition company could use it to bring down a building without any risk to surrounding structures. They could charge the same amount for their services but not have to invest the time and man hours to set the hundreds of explosive charges and miles of wiring."

"And if the DoD had your device?"

"We wouldn't ask them what they intended to use it for, Agent Decker. But it would take little imagination to see the value of such a machine for gaining the upper hand in war."

"The authorities said the building destroyed in Charlotte was the result of an explosion. They didn't mention your device. So they have no idea of its capability?"

"No," Penn said. "The explosion they refer to was probably caused by a gas line that ruptured during the focused earthquake event. Convenient for us because we have no awkward explaining to do."

"You've shared a great deal more information with us than you did before, Dr. Penn," I said, "and we do thank you."

"No sense in hiding what you already know."

Kenny scratched his three-day-old beard. "My question is, why haven't you sold this device to the military or commercial customers?"

"We have a contract with the DoD, but for some reason that Dr. Scarlet has not shared with me, we are delaying delivery. The product works as designed, but she's not ready to release it yet. You know, she financed its development out of her pocket. It could be the biggest piece of technology GeoDynamiks has ever produced. But she's holding back for some reason."

I noticed that the deputies and troopers were starting to pack up and leave as the three of us chatted. Soon, there was only a handful of GeoDynamiks security roaming around as if they didn't know quite what to do with us.

"Let us know if you find out anything else, Dr. Penn," I said. "Right now, we need to check on the latest news about our fellow agent."

"I wish you and your friend well," Penn said.

"Thank you." I shook Penn's hand. Kenny did the same, and we headed to our rental car.

Once inside, Kenny started the car and glanced over at me. "Ready to go home?"

My cell rang. The caller ID was the agent in charge of the Dallas task force.

"Yes, sir." I listened for a moment before ending the call. I looked at Kenny with tears streaming. "They found where the cartel held Kevin, but it was too late."

CHAPTER 46 – 99 SCORPIONS

I was a wreck. With the news of Kevin's execution, all the life ran out of me. I was partially responsible for killing my friend, and no amount of consoling from my ex helped. Kenny tried to remain strong, but I knew he was devastated, too. I wanted to curl up in the fetal position and sleep for a month.

Once we got over the initial shock, Kenny and I decided not to drive back to Charlotte. We checked into a Holiday Inn Express in Connors hoping to at least get a couple of hours of shut-eye. As Kenny gave his credit card info to the clerk, my cell rang.

"Decker, here."

The voice on the other end was nearly a whisper. "It's Donald Penn, Agent Decker. Is it possible I can meet with you and Agent Gates? Only the three of us."

I mouthed to Kenny that it was Penn.

"I'm sure we could arrange that. When?"

"Lunch. There's a little out-of-the-way barbecue place called, Soul of the South. They have good food."

"What time?"

"Noon."

Penn gave me directions, and we planned to hook up at the restaurant. When I ended the conversation, Kenny said, "What?"

I explained, and Kenny checked his phone for the time. "Gives us enough time to get a couple of hours of sleep."

At the elevator, he punched the up button.

When we stepped inside, and the doors closed, Kenny hugged me. We said nothing about Kevin. There was nothing to say.

I woke up to the chime of my iPhone alarm. I was certain I was in the same position as I was when I crawled into bed. Every inch of my body told me I'd only had three hours of sleep. I thought of Fender and wanted to pull the covers over my head.

Kenny wasn't his usual playful self. His insides were probably as torn up as mine. But we managed to get our shit together by noon to make our appointment with Dr. Penn. Kenny and I sat side-by-side in a booth with a wood table and benches that must have been painted with at least five coats of polyurethane. We gave a Charlotte brewery craft beer, called 99 Scorpions, a try. The waiter said it was a Mexican imperial lager brewed with agave nectar, serrano peppers, 99 real scorpions, and aged on oak staves from tequila barrels. I hadn't been sold on it for a couple of reasons. Neither the word *Mexican* nor the idea of drinking a beer brewed with scorpions appealed to me.

"Come on Max, live on the edge," Kenny had said.

I fired back at him. "What the hell do you think I'm already doing?" Then I'd given it a second thought and said, "Oh, hell, why not?"

"It's got a little kick to it," I said as the lager traveled to my stomach. "Hope it's not the scorpions."

I checked my phone for messages and then pulled up the license tag number from my notes of the rented Cadillac we'd seen leaving GeoDynamiks. I sent the number in a text to Dallas and asked if they would check with the rental company to find out who had rented the car. I asked for the info ASAP. Ten minutes later our order of fried green tomatoes and onion rings arrived, and I got an answer.

"Kenny, remember that Cadillac license tag you zoomed in on. You'll never guess who rented the car. Under Secretary of Defense, Charles Rittenberg."

"No kidding." Kenny was about to say something else, but his eyes spotted Donald Penn. He elbowed me. "Here he is."

Dr. Penn saw us right away. He slid in on the opposite side of the booth and put a manila envelope he carried on the seat beside him. His face was ashen.

"Looks like you could use one of these." Kenny lifted his beer.

"No, thanks. I haven't slept, and I need to keep my head clear while I talk. I probably shouldn't be here or do this, but I feel like I have to."

I grabbed an onion ring. "What's this all about, Dr. Penn? We might as well get right to the matter." I pushed the basket toward him, but he shook his head.

"I've learned some things about Dr. Scarlet that I think you should know. I'm not sure how all this plays out, but it's troubling me."

Penn described the meeting he'd been in with Scarlet and Rittenberg. "The product is ready, yet Dr. Scarlet wanted to delay delivery. It doesn't make sense."

"You already mentioned that?" Kenny said.

"Why would she lie to the DoD?" I asked.

Penn waved over the waiter. "I've changed my mind. Bring me one of those." He pointed at Kenny's beer, and then rolled his shoulders as if they ached. "I saw a private folder Dr. Scarlet keeps. I didn't go looking for it or anything like that. I had reason to go into her office, and it was on her desk. There are two things I need to talk to you about. Her history and an obsession she has."

I took a slug of the peppery beer, anxious to hear what Penn was about to tell us.

"When Dr. Scarlet was young, she and her husband had a child. Someone anonymously reported her husband physically abused the boy, and the child was taken into foster care. Dr. Scarlet attempted every course possible to have her son returned. From what I read, I believe she'd exhausted the system. There were bruises on the boy's neck that the accuser said was due to the father tethering the child to a rope. Dr. Scarlet insisted it had happened at the playground when her son got tangled in the climbing rope net. Her husband, Craig Scarlet, a teacher, lost his job because of the accusation of child abuse. Unfortunately, before the case could be thoroughly investigated or go to court, the kid died in a fire while in the care of foster parents."

"How horrible," I said, losing my appetite.

"She's never spoken about it to me. Never even mentioned her family, but there's a picture on her desk of her and her husband with their son."

"I don't think I would talk about it either," Kenny said.

"And there were two other things in the folder. One of those things is a collection of twenty or more newspaper and magazine articles that record every event of Ellen Osterling's career."

"Ellen Osterling, the Supreme Court Justice?" I said.

Penn nodded.

My mouth hung open. "Why? What's the connection?"

"There's a big connection. I read a long newspaper clipping in that folder. It reported an attempted murder of Osterling back in 1992, shortly after the Scarlet's three-year-old son died. The perpetrator was said to have been an old lover of hers, Craig Scarlet."

"Magda Scarlet's husband?" I asked.

Penn confirmed. "The article reported that Craig Scarlet and Ellen Osterling had had an affair years before—1986 or somewhere around then—and Osterling had called it off because she found out he was married. Craig Scarlet hadn't taken the news well, and must have let it fester for several years. Then one night he snapped, went to Osterling's home and attempted to shoot and kill her. But he missed, and Osterling was able to get her handgun and defend herself. Her shot was on target, killing Craig Scarlet. Magda Scarlet claimed that it was the other way around—that her husband had been the one who called off the affair even before she was pregnant with their son. In retaliation, Ellen Osterling was the anonymous caller who made a false accusation of child abuse. Dr. Scarlet told the reporter that Osterling had stalked them for years, wanting revenge for Craig Scarlet's rejection. Apparently no one believed Dr. Scarlet, and a lot of sympathy poured out for Ellen Osterling."

"That must have been like salt in a wound," I said.

Penn agreed. "Dr. Scarlet believed Osterling was responsible for her son *and* husband's death. I believe she still does."

Kenny said. "That's a lot of pain Scarlet's been through. How does anybody stay sane after all that?"

"I'm not sure Dr. Scarlet has." The waitress delivered Penn's beer.

"What was the other thing in the folder?"

Penn lifted the envelope from the seat. "Dr. Scarlet had an old journal in the red folder. I skimmed through it." Penn pinched his brows together with his fingers and squinted before he spoke. "I'm not proud that I took the liberty of looking through something so private, but after reading the other articles, I... Anyway, I made copies of some of her entries. We've only seen one side of her—the person she's become over the last thirty years. When you have a chance to read them, I think you'll better understand Dr. Scarlet. You'll know why I'm not so sure she is in her right mind."

He pushed the envelope across the table to me.

"I'd like to ask her some questions," I said.

Penn took a long swig of his 99 Scorpions, then covered his mouth and belched. He took another long pull on his beer.

I knew some bad news was coming.

"I'm afraid you can't."

"What do you mean, we can't?"

Penn knuckle-scrubbed his whiskered jaw. "I went to talk to her about all this. Couldn't find her. I found out she'd left on the GeoDynamik's private jet. I had the flight plan checked. The plane is on its way to Vegas."

The hair on my arms prickled as I readied myself for a bomb I felt Dr. Penn was about to drop. Kenny must have felt the same dread because he squeezed my knee.

Penn stared off into the distance for a moment as if his next words would be painful. Then he faced us, appearing to have aged ten years since he first arrived. "One of the earthquake machines is missing."

CHAPTER 47 – THREAT SOURCE
The Pentagon

After the hour and twenty minutes flight from Charlotte to Washington, Kenny and I took a taxi to the Pentagon. We walked through the southeast visitor screening entrance, showed our federal cred packs and passed through a whole-body AIT imaging scanner. Next, we were given visitor IDs and escorted through a tiny portion of the 28 kilometers of corridors to the office of the Under Secretary of Defense for Acquisition, Technology and Logistics, Charles Rittenberg.

"He'll see you now," the young woman announced.

We entered a large office with wood-paneled walls, dozens of pictures with dignitaries hanging in perfect rows, and a desk the size of a river barge. Rittenberg was tall and appeared fit with a full head of gray hair. His skin told me he was an outdoorsman. A model of a two-masted schooner sat on a credenza behind his chair. There were numerous awards for rowing and sculling. I also noticed three framed diplomas. An undergraduate degree from the U.S. Military Academy at West Point, a Master of Science degree in National Resource Strategy from the Industrial College of the Armed Forces at the National Defense University, Washington, DC, and a Ph.D. in aeronautics from Caltech. I was more than impressed.

"Welcome, agents." Rittenberg came from around his desk and extended his hand. He motioned to two chairs then took his place behind his desk. "It's fortunate you came today. Tomorrow I leave for the U.K. and won't be back for a week. Your expression of urgency and the reputation that precedes you both encouraged me to make time. Although I must advise you, I don't have much more than fifteen minutes. I hope that'll be sufficient."

"Thank you, Under Secretary, for taking the time," I said. "We realize you have a busy schedule. We would never have requested this meeting if we both didn't believe it was of the gravest importance."

"What've you got?"

"We believe that the life of Supreme Court Justice Ellen Osterling is in immediate danger."

Rittenberg sat silent for a moment as if pondering my words. "Well, if true, that's quite serious. How did you come across this supposed threat?"

Kenny replied, "It's based on first-hand intel gathered by Agent Decker and me, and insider information from someone who is close to the source of the threat."

Rittenberg's expression hardened. "Let's start with your informer and the threat's source."

I said, "The insider is Dr. Donald Penn, Director of Research—"

"GeoDynamik's Donald Penn?"

"You know him?" I asked.

"Why, yes. I just met with him…"

I sensed he was becoming nervous. "Then you already know the source of the threat—Dr. Magda Scarlet."

For a moment, Rittenberg appeared to stop breathing.

CHAPTER 48 – BLACK CANYON LODGE

"Dr. Scarlet? Jesus, you must be mistaken." Rittenberg's face paled, and he glanced around as if making sure no one else heard his reaction.

"I wish we were." I let him regain his composure. "How well do you know her?"

"Well, GeoDynamiks has been a government contractor for years. They've designed and built early warning devices to help protect our cities and national landmarks from natural disasters, mainly focused on seismic events. I've had meetings with Dr. Scarlet and Dr. Penn on occasion. But it was always purely business. So I can't say that I know her that well."

Kenny and I looked at each other. "Are you sure?" I asked Rittenberg.

"About what?" he said. "Is GeoDynamiks being a trusted contractor or how well I know Dr. Scarlet?"

"The latter," Kenny said.

Rittenberg shrugged. "We are business acquaintances."

I leaned back in the chair and crossed my legs. "Did you have an affair with Dr. Scarlet?"

The under secretary stiffened. He reached for the phone. "Cancel my next appointment." Hanging up, he said, "What makes you ask that?"

"Penn told us about her trips to Virginia to meet with you," I said. "Only the meetings were in her hotel room after dinner together." I could tell that Rittenberg's thoughts were racing—should he deny everything and ask us to leave or work with us to stop a possible assassination of a Supreme Court Justice?

"We're not here to pass moral judgment on you or anyone," I said. "We're here to save the life of Ellen Osterling. You can help us, or we'll find someone who can."

Rittenberg looked as if he struggled to find the right words. He appeared distressed. I feared rather than getting answers, we might have to dial 911. His words came out as if he strangled on them. "Yes, we have…had a relationship in the past. But it didn't interfere with government business."

"Do you have any idea why Dr. Scarlet would be flying to Nevada?" I said. "Specifically to Las Vegas?"

Rittenberg massaged his chest. He coughed and grimaced, clenching his teeth.

Heart attack? I pulled out my cell, ready to call for medical help. But after a moment, he recovered enough to speak.

"I'm afraid I might know why she's going there."

"Do you need some water or something?" Kenny said.

Rittenberg waved him off. "I'm about to tell you one of the best-kept secrets in our government."

He paused as Kenny and I both leaned forward slightly.

"Have either of you ever heard of The Black Canyon Lodge?"

"No," Kenny said.

I shook my head.

"I'm not surprised. Few have. About four miles east of Boulder City, Nevada is a lodge named after the canyon where the Hoover Dam was constructed. It's built into the side of the mountain near Lone Rock and overlooks the Colorado River, although you can't see it from the river. It was built in 1933 as a comfortable accommodation for visiting dignitaries so they could see the progress of the dam's construction. President Roosevelt stayed there as did many members of Congress and visiting VIPs. Even though the river was diverted during the building process, it still flowed below the dam. Visitors would be shuttled in boats up the river to see the construction site. After the dam was finished and dedicated in 1936, the Black Canyon Lodge was shut down, secured and restricted from the public. During the Cold War, the lodge was reopened and used as a possible safe haven for the President or other high-ranking members of the government. In the event of an attack on the United States while the President was visiting a western state, he would have been rushed to the lodge.

"When the Soviet Union fell, the lodge was converted into a retreat for selective individuals and groups to gather in secret and address issues without the pressure of being in the Beltway."

"If it was so secret, how would Dr. Scarlet know of its existence," Kenny asked.

"You don't have to answer, sir," I said, "I think we can guess who revealed it to her. But what has this got to do with Dr. Scarlet and Justice Osterling?"

"Dr. Scarlet has a private emotional war with the justice. Ellen Osterling did some terrible things to Magda a long time ago. Not just bad things, but horrible and despicable. I think this could have something to do with why she has gone to Vegas. Once a year, at the end of June, when the Court is in recess, the justices meet at Black Canyon Lodge for a few days of private reflection and review. It's not that far from Las Vegas."

"So you think that Osterling is at the lodge?" Kenny asked.

Rittenberg took a deep breath. "All nine Supreme Court justices are there right now."

CHAPTER 49 – THE GREAT ROOM
Somewhere over the Midwest

I stared out the window of the FBI's Gulfstream G550 at the endless farmland below. We had left Andrews AFB and flown back to Charlotte to pick up Dr. Penn, refueled, and then headed for Nevada. Rittenberg had insisted on joining us, repeatedly claiming this was his fault entirely. But in the end, he stayed in Washington coordinating with the Federal Protective Service to lockdown the Black Canyon Lodge and secure the surrounding area. Kenny was sitting in the back of the cabin slowly perusing the swimsuit issue of *Sports Illustrated*. Penn sat facing me.

"How long were you and Agent Gates married?"

"Some days I think it wasn't long enough. Other times, too long. The point is, we do better together not being married."

I turned back to the window. "How did you wind up working for Dr. Scarlet?"

"When she was forced to leave CoreConcepts, she formed a startup that eventually became GeoDynamiks. I was one of her first hires."

"And you never had any indication of her hatred and obsession with Ellen Osterling?"

"Not until I read the news clippings in the red folder. I often thought she had something that fueled a fire that drove her. When I saw the contents of the folder, I knew where that fire came from. This was something that has built over years, decades. It was such a tragic story, in some ways I sympathize with her. But assassinating a Supreme Court justice is madness. How are we going to stop her?"

"The FPS is under orders to use lethal force if she comes

near the lodge."

"Yes, but the problem is she may not need to get near the structure for the device to be effective. Why don't they evacuate the justices and fly them out of the area?"

"Too late. Dr. Scarlet has been on the ground for hours. They feel they can protect the heavily secured lodge, but not the route between it and Nellis Air Force Base. I'm told the terrain is too rugged for a helicopter."

"They don't understand the power of the device, Agent Decker."

I knew Penn was right, but the decisions being made to protect SCOTUS were out of my hands. "You said if you could get your hands on the device, you might be able to disarm it. You still feel that way?"

"I can't promise anything. Dr. Scarlet designed and wrote the code for the earthquake machine. I've worked with the software in its basic form, but she could easily block any attempt to shut it down. She would have had plenty of time to do so on her flight across the country."

Penn didn't sound as convincing as he did on the phone earlier when he asked to come along. "You may be called upon to make some tough decisions before the end of the day," I said. "You need to be ready."

He nodded but didn't look at me directly. *Great. I'm dealing with a super geek who needs to be a superhero.* I closed my eyes and thought of the last time I was in Las Vegas when I came within seconds of being vaporized by an atomic bomb. That device had a Nazi connection, too. In my head, I heard the line from the Indiana Jones movie—*I hate those guys*.

We touched down at McCarran International at dusk. Sin City sparkled in the distance like a giant magical mirage in the desert. Stepping off the plane, we were directed onto a Black Hawk for a ride to the Boulder City Municipal Airport. From there, the last leg of the trip was in a military Humvee along the rugged mountain road to the gated entrance to Black Canyon Lodge. A three-meter-high chain link fence topped with coils of concertina wire stretched out in both directions. A dozen heavily armed Federal Protective Service personnel guarded the gate. After checking our IDs, we were flagged through. Three minutes later, the Humvee pulled up to the single door of the concrete bunker. Two FPS guards protected it. We exited the vehicle and were shown through the door to a set of stairs in a tunnel that led down two stories. We entered a reception area where our IDs were checked again.

"She'll never get within a mile of this place," Kenny said.

"Let's hope not."

"I'm Agent Fowler. This way, please."

The man was dressed in a dark suit, white shirt, and black tie. His shaved head made me wonder if he was Dwayne Johnson's brother, only fitter. We followed Fowler from the reception area to what I would call a great room—moving from bunker-style to mountain-lodge decor. River rock floor, timber beams, animal trophy heads, American Indian wall hangings, Southwestern-designed rugs, a huge rock fireplace with blazing fire, and massive chairs scattered around the room. After taking in the amazing transformation from military fortification to turn-of-the-century, rustic mountain lodge, I realized there were people occupying nine of the chairs—the nine justices of the Supreme Court of the United States of America. I searched each of their faces until I found the one I wanted.

Coming to stand in front of her, I said, "Justice Osterling, I'm Maxine Decker."

She stood and shook my hand. "Agent Decker. Thank you for coming." She motioned to the others in the room. "May I present my colleagues?"

I gave a courteous nod to the other justices.

"Is it true that Dr. Scarlet is coming here to kill me?"

I looked into the eyes of the woman who had shredded Magda Scarlet's life. The woman who was the motivation for what might turn out to be the crime of the century. "I'm afraid it's much worse than that."

CHAPTER 50 – TARGET ACQUIRED

The justices, along with Kenny, Penn, me, and FPS agents, gathered in a rustic dining hall that would have made a medieval king proud. Seated around an impressive, pine-plank dinner table, we listened as Dr. Penn gave a short and sobering tutorial on the GeoDynamiks earthquake machine. When he finished, a few questions were asked, mostly from the FPS agents. I noticed that Osterling sat silent and seemed to gaze off into oblivion. Finally, everyone got up and wandered back into the great room.

"I think they got the point," Kenny said as the room cleared.

Agent Fowler approached. "Based on what Dr. Penn has presented, we're increasing ground patrols inside and outside the perimeter. There are two helicopters with IR and body heat sensors circling the compound. We also have Coast Guard patrol boats on the Colorado River below the lodge in case the subject tries to approach from below."

"Sounds like you've got the place locked down tight, Agent Fowler," I said. "Keep us informed."

"Will do." He turned and left the three of us behind.

"I feel helpless," Penn said. "I know better than anyone what will happen, yet I can't do anything to stop it."

"We're all helpless, Dr. Penn," I said. "Our best bet is for those guys outside to stop her before she can carry out her plan." I turned to Kenny. "Something you said when we were coming in—that she can't get within a mile of this place. If that's true, I don't understand how her mission can be carried out. Dr. Penn, what if she was able to place herself on the opposite side of the canyon—across the river? That's only about two kilometers away."

Penn shrugged. "Maybe, but that's really beyond the range of the device."

"Plus getting over there would be a bitch," Kenny said. "That's rugged terrain. It would take someone young and athletically fit, maybe even with climbing expertise."

"Would that eliminate her showing up outside the perimeter and being able to use it?" I asked Penn.

"Most likely. And like Agent Gates said, she's not in the best of shape."

"Then the target isn't the lodge," I said. I stared at a buffalo head mounted on the wall for a few moments. I realized that next to it was a picture of the Hoover Dam taken during mid-construction. "We understand that GeoDynamiks has seismic monitoring devices installed at numerous locations throughout the country, particularly at national landmarks. Are any of them nearby?"

Penn thought for a moment. "The closest sensor is installed—my God, it's inside the Hoover Dam."

I had already turned and headed for the door. *I can't believe I didn't see this long before now.* I ran across the great room to the first FPS agent I saw. "I need to speak to Fowler right now."

The man touched his earpiece to activate the mic. "Agent Fowler, Agent Decker needs you." He listened for a moment. "This way, please."

I followed him with Kenny and Penn right behind. I stole a quick glance toward the justices. They were gathered in various groups around the room and looked as though this was the last place they wanted to be.

Through a side door and down a hall, we came to a bedroom that had been converted into an office. Fowler looked up from his desk. "Yes, Agent Decker?"

"I need you to call security at the dam and find out if anyone, particularly from GeoDynamiks, has been given access to the secured areas today."

"Explain," he asked.

"The lodge isn't the target. She's going to destroy the Hoover Dam."

CHAPTER 51 – SERVICE CALL

"I've got Chief Meadows of the Hoover Dam Police on the phone," Fowler said. He pushed a button. "You're on speaker, Chief."

"Chief Meadows, this is FBI consultant Agent Maxine Decker. I'm here with OSI Special Agent Kenny Gates and Dr. Donald Penn, Director of Research for GeoDynamiks. We are assisting the FPS in investigating a possible threat within the Hoover-Mead Security Zone, particularly the dam itself."

"How can I assist you, Agent Decker?"

"We understand that GeoDynamiks has one or more seismic event sensor devices installed in or around the dam. Can you confirm?"

"Only one. It's located below the seepage gallery a few feet above the bedrock at the lowest point in the dam."

"Seepage gallery?" I asked.

"Correct. We have pumps running in the gallery twenty-four-seven to handle the fifteen thousand gallons of seepage per minute coming in from the canyon walls."

"So the GeoDynamiks device is under water?"

"Normally. But once a month, a technician comes to download the information from the sensor and upgrade the software. When that happens, we pump the location dry so she can gain assess."

"She?" Kenny said.

"Nice lady," Meadows said. "Comes in, does her work and leaves. She was cleared by DoD security over a year ago."

I shook my head in amazement. "Magda Scarlet has been setting this up for at least a year."

"Magda Scarlet, yeah that's her name." Meadows said.

When was the last time you saw her?" I asked.

"An hour or so ago."

"You pumped the gallery dry for her?"

"Yes. What is this all about, Agent Decker?"

"Where is the technician now?" I asked.

"Gone. Signed out about a half hour ago."

"Is the gallery still dry, Chief?"

"Yes, ma'am. But we're scheduled to stop the lower gallery pumps any minute now."

"Hold off on that, Chief Meadows," I said. "Lock down the dam and stay right there. We're on our way."

"You gonna tell me what this is about?"

"You wouldn't believe me if I did." I turned to Fowler. "We need to borrow one of your Humvees."

CHAPTER 52 – BEDROCK
Hoover Dam

At the Boulder City limits, we were met by two police cruisers that escorted us to U.S. 93 and onto the Hoover Dam Access Road. At this time of night, the dam had long been closed to visitors. Security waved us through the inspection checkpoint. We drove onto the roadway atop the dam, coming to a halt in front of the Nevada elevator. Waiting for us was Chief Meadows.

"This way." Meadows directed us through the brass doors. The trip was short as we got off on a floor restricted from visitors. From there, a brightly lit tunnel with tile walls led us to a set of stairs that appeared to stretch down into the middle of the Earth.

"Coming back up is gonna be fun," Kenny said.

"No one forced you to stop going to the gym," I said.

"You get used to it," Meadows said.

Penn gave out a pessimistic moan.

After the long trip down the stairs, we came to the seepage gallery and another set of stairs. The floor and walls were slick and wet. I moved cautiously to keep from slipping as we ventured deeper into the dam. Constant dripping noises surrounded us as the seepage continuously oozed from the canyon walls.

At the bottom of the steps, we entered a short tunnel that marked the absolute bottom of the Hoover Dam, all four million cubic tons of it as Meadows pointed out during our descent. At this level, he told us, we were standing a few feet away from bedrock with over 700 feet of concrete above our heads. And at the end of the tunnel, we found it—the

GeoDynamiks device.

Unlike the earthquake machine we had seen previously, this was a rectangular box about the size of a countertop microwave oven encased in a container that had to be waterproof. Although the material was opaque, a small portion of the top was clear. I could see a digital number display and keypad on top of the device. It read 23:06 and counting down.

I turned to Penn. "Can't you remove the device? We could take it up top and I'll have a helicopter meet us. They could drop it in the middle of the desert. We can do that in twenty minutes, right?"

"We can try." Dr. Penn got on his knees and worked on the ten clasps that held the waterproof container top sealed to the box. "This is one of our high tech dry boxes," he said and grunted with the strain of pulling the screw-down clamps loose. Kenny picked up on it and assisted him. Once the clamps were released, they lifted the top and set it aside.

Penn studied the device, then shook his head. "Looks like she's got it wired so it can't be tampered with. Mess with it and the timer goes to zero. Good idea, Agent Decker, but it won't work." He continued his examination. "It resembles one of our basic seismic sensors, but the casing has been modified to accommodate the earthquake machine. Quite clever of her."

"Earthquake?" Meadows said. "What the hell's going on here?"

"It's a long story, Chief, but you're looking at an act of domestic terrorism—the goal of which is to rupture the dam and send the contents of Lake Mead down the Colorado River."

"Come on," Meadows said with a crack in his voice. "This is a joke, right?"

"I wish." Turning to Penn, I said, "Can you disarm it?"

"Without the code, probably not. I can't promise anything, but it's worth a try."

My phone rang. Meadows must have guessed my question by the expression on my face.

"We've installed cell repeaters throughout the dam

including its deepest points for emergencies," he said.

I answered and recognized the faint Southern drawl.

"This is a yes or no question, Agent Decker," Magda Scarlet said. "Do you want to save the lives of thousands of people tonight?"

"Yes."

"Then listen and don't say anything. Come to the top of the dam and get in your vehicle. I'll call with further instructions. Come alone. I hope you understand. If you don't do exactly as I've instructed, the Colorado will run red with blood."

The call ended, and I pocketed my phone.

"Who was that?" Kenny asked.

"Rittenberg. He was just making sure we'd gotten to the lodge."

I waited a minute so Kenny wouldn't connect the phone call to what I was going to do. If I told him Scarlet's demand, he'd insist on going with me. For all I knew, it was a setup. If Kenny came along, he'd be a target, too.

"Scarlet's not here," I said. "That means she's headed for the lodge. In case they capture her, I want to be there to convince her to give up the override code."

"I'll make sure my men flag you through with no delay," Meadows said

"You're not going alone. I'll go, too," Kenny said.

"No. Penn needs all the help he can get. I'll let you know immediately if I spot her."

Before leaving, Kenny and I hugged. It was a long embrace like it might be our last. "We used to be married," I said to Meadows who gave me a confused expression.

As I turned to leave, Kenny said, "Hey, look on the bright side, Max. If this thing comes apart, we could be back in Mexico in twenty minutes."

CHAPTER 53 – NIGHT RIDE

I jumped in the Humvee and was about to start the engine when I felt what could only be the cold steel of a gun barrel pressed to the back of my head.

"Good job on following directions," Scarlet said.

In the glow of the dashboard lights, I saw a set of eyes staring back at me in the rearview mirror.

I felt my Walther strapped to my ankle but knew I would never get my hand on it before she fired. "How did you know we were at the dam?"

"When I was leaving, I saw you pull up in the Humvee. Simple. Now, head to US 93."

"Why don't you give me the code for the override, and we can end all this."

"I can't do that."

"I'm sure you realize we don't have time to get out of the way of the water surge if the dam breaks."

"Of course I know that. I'm the one who set the timer. First, we're going to visit an old adversary."

"Ellen Osterling at the Black Canyon Lodge." The gun continued to push against the back of my skull.

"Speed up." Her voice was icy and showed no signs of nervousness. "You've done your homework."

"Be careful with that thing. The road can be bumpy, and it might accidently go off." I felt the pressure of the barrel ease up.

"I'm not going to shoot you unless I have to. I still owe you. But even more than that, I need you."

"For what? A ride?"

She laughed. "I've got to hand it to you for keeping a sense of humor."

"Since we have some time alone, why don't you explain why you're going to the lodge if your plan is to destroy the dam and set free the wrath of the Colorado River? Do you want to be there to witness Osterling's death?"

"Well now, that's an idea. I hadn't thought of that. But, no. I have my concerns that Penn might know enough to figure out the code and disarm the device. Just in case, I'm going to have to do the job up close and personal."

"I understand all the horrors you've been through—losing your son, your husband, the respect of your friends, all stemming from the false child abuse report. You blame Justice Osterling. If I'd been in your place, I might have, too. But nothing you do now will bring them back or change the past."

I glanced in the rearview mirror again. Her gaunt face, tangled hair, and sagging shoulders all expressed intense, deep grief. She had to be recalling painful memories. I felt a pang of sympathy and wondered how the woman had survived it all. From what I'd discovered, she'd been a reasonable and forgiving person at one time—even standing by her unfaithful husband to the end. Osterling had stripped all the goodness away, and there seemed to be nothing left but the craving for revenge.

"He went to her house to kill her, you know," Scarlet said. "But not like they said."

"Who?"

"My husband, Craig. Osterling destroyed him, too. He didn't go to her house because she'd called off the affair like all the reports said. He'd ended the relationship even before our son was conceived. She couldn't forgive him and was obsessed with revenge. She stalked us. She'd sit outside my son's preschool in the parking lot and make sure I'd see her. She parked across the street from our house during Christopher's first birthday party—repeatedly called our house in the middle of the night. Even right after our son was born, I saw her standing at the hospital nursery window, her hands on the glass, staring at my baby. She made our lives hell. And then when our son died because of her lies. It shredded my heart into strands of hatred. Christopher's death killed my husband. He was already a dead man when he went to Osterling's house with the intent of murdering her. He wanted to make Ellen Osterling pay for what she'd done to our family. Nobody ever believed that. But it's the truth. I have no reason to lie."

I could hear the deep, agonizing pain in her voice. The real Magda Scarlet must have become a dead soul like her husband had so many years ago. "I'm sorry, Dr. Scarlet. I can't imagine living such a nightmare. But please, know that what you're about to do won't take away the ache in your heart. It will only create nightmares for thousands more who will lose someone tonight. You don't want that."

"Just drive."

I hoped if I kept her talking, she might soften and give up the code. "Answer one question for me. Why have you gone to so such great lengths? If you wanted to kill Justice Osterling, why didn't you just do it? There had to have been plenty of opportunities over the years."

My eyes met Scarlet's in the mirror.

"I didn't want to get caught, but not because of what you think. I didn't want Ellen Osterling to take one more thing from me—not my freedom or my life. I'll have the final say in what becomes of me. I realized that if I took out the Supreme Court Justices all at once, no one would link her death to me. They'd think it was an act of terrorism. It would be like blowing up an airplane, killing everyone aboard, even though the target was only a single person." She sighed. "It doesn't matter anymore. I knew from the minute the old German earthquake machine was discovered, I'd become more vulnerable. And I did. Now, you and everyone else know my plans." She made a pitiful-sounding chuckle. "My secret is revealed, but Osterling, that vile monster with no conscience, is not going to get out of paying. If you help me get what I want, I'll give you the code."

It all came together in my head. "And that's why you need me?"

"Exactly."

CHAPTER 54 – EVERY FLICKER OF LIGHT

"Turn right at the next road," Scarlet said from the rear seat of the Humvee. "It's going to curl around and head back north and west. Toward the river."

"I know the way," I said.

"Then you know that we're now on government property, and we'll be stopped ahead. Don't do anything foolish. I told you, I don't have any reason to kill you—yet. Let's keep it that way. Pull over, please. Keep your hands on the wheel where I can see them."

I did what Scarlet asked. She got out, came around the front of the vehicle to the passenger side—her gun pointed at me the entire time. "Okay, you can go on, now," she said as she slid in beside me.

I had no chance to go for my Walther.

Soon, the headlights shone on the familiar fencing and guardhouse. I stopped the vehicle when two of the FPS guards waved me down.

"ID, please."

One of the guards scanned the barcode on my ID and then compared my face to the one that came up on his scanner screen. "Agent Decker." He nodded and handed back my credentials. It was as if he'd never seen me before. I supposed his orders were *always to* check ID, no exceptions.

"Yours please," he said shining his flashlight on Scarlet.

She lifted her gun and held it to my temple. "Agent Decker *is* my ID. Let us pass, or her brains will be decorating the Department of Homeland Security patch on your uniform."

The guard hesitated.

"Stand down," Scarlet said. "I have nothing to lose. But

Agent Decker does. Call Under Secretary Charles Rittenberg and have him contact the FPS at the lodge. Have him advise them of our arrival and warn him that any attempt to stop us will instantly ensure Agent Decker's demise. If there's even a hint that FPS isn't cooperating, Agent Decker is a dead woman. I promise that. If all goes well, Agent Decker, eight of the nine Supreme Court Justices, and thousands of others will live to see another day. Tell Rittenberg to pull any strings he needs to, but do it quickly or it won't matter."

Scarlet nudged me with her gun. "Go."

I pulled away. In the outside mirror, I saw one guard on his radio and the other on a cell phone. They took Scarlet's threat seriously. That was a good thing. As she said, she had nothing to lose.

"Are you going to give me the code?"

"I keep my word. First I have to take care of the job I started. Once that's done, the rest is up to fate."

I couldn't imagine how much emotional damage this woman had suffered to bring her to this point. I wondered what I'd be like if I'd been through the same horrors and losses she had. It wouldn't be fair to say, *I would never* because I didn't know. Still, I had to do my job.

We pulled up in front of the concrete building. *Here we go. There is no good ending to this tale.*

We waited with the headlights shining on the single door.

"Are we getting out?" I asked.

"Not yet. Give Rittenberg a chance to get things in order."

"How long before the dam goes? Should we wait? I need the code. Why don't you give it to me now?"

"Sorry. Not yet."

I looked at Scarlet's phone every time she did. The display always showed a timer counting down. Looked like eight minutes and thirty seconds were left. We couldn't just sit here. I counted and figured two more minutes had passed.

"For God's sake, do whatever you're going to do. We're about flat out of time if that readout matches the one on the earthquake machine."

189

"Patience, Agent Decker. I'm a master at it. You should be, too."

"Well, I'm not."

The bunker door opened, and Agent Fowler was illuminated in our lights.

"Let's go," Scarlet said. "You first. Come around to my side of the car and stop. Keep your hands where I can see them. Don't do anything stupid."

I climbed out of the Humvee and went to her side. My heart galloped in my chest. *Hurry up, Scarlet!"*

She got out, held my right arm behind my back and pressed the gun barrel to my head. Fowler moved to the side, giving us room to enter. Scarlet pushed me forward and through the door.

The FPS agent led us down the stairs, through the reception area, and finally into the lodge's belly.

All the justices were seated on the couches and chairs. My eyes quickly scanned the room, finding Ellen Osterling in a wingback chair that flanked the fireplace.

"Stand up," Scarlet ordered. Her eyes also had to be fixed on Osterling.

The justice stood. "Do you honestly believe you can get away with this?"

I couldn't believe the balls Osterling had. So smug, even now.

"No, I don't. And I don't care. Do you know why? Because you stole everything from me that I cared about or loved. You left me empty. There's nothing else of me. So now I want you to look in my eyes and see the hollow darkness inside. Every flicker of light in my soul has gone out."

Scarlet edged me forward. I was still her shield, her key to getting what she wanted.

"Can you see in my eyes, Ellen? Now, I want to see the light go out in yours."

The panic I felt became evident as my body trembled, and sweat veiled my skin. It wasn't the confrontation that terrorized me, it was the time passing.

Suddenly, Scarlet moved from behind me and fired one shot, dead center, into Osterling's forehead, splattering blood and tissue on the rock fireplace.

Osterling dropped.

"Hold your fire!" I screamed knowing security was going to take down Scarlet.

A loud blast told me it was too late.

I knelt beside her. She was still alive—barely. I grabbed my phone, pushed the *home* button twice, and said, "Call Kenny Gates." I put the phone on speaker, and then pulled Magda Scarlet's head into my lap. She peered up at me.

"Christopher," she whispered. "Christopher."

She's hallucinating. "Give me the code. We need the code."

Kenny's voice came through my phone. "Meadows just called from up top. The winged statues in front of the dam are starting to vibrate. They're like giant tuning forks. Max, I—"

"I've got Scarlet," I said. "Keep listening." I touched Magda Scarlet's hand. "Please. You promised to give me the code."

"Christopher." Her head lolled to the side, and bloody spittle spindled out of her mouth.

I shook Scarlet, but there was no response.

I heard Kenny on the phone. "I feel it under my feet now. Like a strong tingle. It's happening, Max."

My whole body went cold, and I gulped down a breath to keep from crying. "Stay with me, Kenny. I want to hear your voice until the end."

Christopher. Christopher. Christopher was all Dr. Scarlet had said. She'd done all this for her son. Oh, my God. That's it.

"Kenny, match the letters of her son's name, Christopher, to numerical digits. Hurry!"

CHAPTER 55 – SHAKE, RATTLE, AND ROLL

Big Bear Lake, Colorado. Two weeks later.

"That was delicious," I said after finishing my share of the cutthroat trout Kenny had caught earlier. He'd baked it with the perfect amount of lemon juice and spices. "It's about time you finally caught one big enough to eat."

"Hey, don't mouth off to the provider." Kenny picked up our dishes and took them to the sink.

"Let 'em soak. Let's go down to the dock and relax. Looks like it'll be a beautiful sunset."

Kenny grabbed us each a bottle of 99 Scorpions from the refrigerator and opened them. "Nice of those folks to ship a case."

We were quiet as we strolled down the path from my Colorado mountain cabin to the dock. The chill of the approaching twilight felt crisp and refreshing. It cleansed me. Both of us gazed out over the darkening lake once we sat on the Adirondack glider. "It doesn't get any better than this," I said.

"No it doesn't."

"I take that back. I'm sorry Kevin can't join us. He was such a pain in the ass when I first met him, and then we ended up being good friends. Strange how things work out. I'm glad we were able to stopover in Dallas for his memorial service."

Kenny raised his bottle. "A toast to Kevin Fender."

I raised my bottle and took a moment to watch the first Colorado fireflies in the woods beyond the lake.

"You know what's weird? Magda Scarlet was about to kill thousands, and yet I felt, and still do feel, sorry for her. She had her own form of post-traumatic stress syndrome. A person can only take so much ripped from them. And to watch Ellen Osterling rise to become a Supreme Court Justice had to have shoved Scarlet over the edge."

Kenny solemnly nodded his head. "Well, sweetheart, she's got some peace now. At least I hope so. I propose another toast in hopes she has."

I met his bottle with a soft tap and clink.

"We saved a lot of lives, Max. If you hadn't figured out the code, I can't imagine the number of people who would be dead. The dam already had a history of taking lives. Supposedly there were a lot of men who died building it. So many, in fact, the workers nicknamed it the Tomb. Rumor is there're plenty of bodies buried inside all that concrete."

I took a sip of my beer. "I like the sting of this stuff."

Kenny followed suit. "That's what makes it so unique." He rested one hand on my knee. "How'd you figure out Scarlet's son's name was the code?"

"She kept repeating it. I guess she was finally holding up her end of the deal."

"She had a lot of faith in your intuition. Glad you're so damn smart."

My mind switched gears. "Did I tell you I got a couple of texts today while you were down here fishing? Good news, plain news, and bad news. Which do you want first?"

Kenny patted my knee then stroked my thigh. "Let's start with the good and move on from here."

"Good news is our boy, Rittenberg, has resigned. Don't know what the consequences will be for him, yet. But at least he's no longer the under secretary."

Kenny raised his bottle again.

"Just plain news is that Dr. Penn's attorney believes he'll get a reduced sentence because of his cooperation and attempt to stop Dr. Scarlet."

I pecked him on the cheek.

"You softening me up before hitting me with the bad news?"

"Nope. I just felt like doing it."

"That was a wussy kiss."

Kenny pulled me close, planted his lips on mine, and drove his fingers up through my hair.

God, I loved this man. Why, why, why hadn't we been able to live together? Maybe we could at this point in our lives. I was older now, and he was mellower. But why take a chance on ruining what we had at this stage?

"Now, that's what I'm talking about," he said after the long kiss ended. "More to come." He grinned and leaned back, looking proud.

I guess he could tell I'd gotten into the kiss. Damn him. He knew me so well and could read my body's reactions with no effort.

I tossed back my hair and collected myself. He winked, knowing I was struggling to get back on track.

"Okay, the not-so-good news," he said. "I'm not ready to hear it, but you're going to tell me anyway. Let's get it out of the way so we can enjoy the sunset and then finish up what we just started."

My face turned somber. "Some new guy called El Martillo, The Hammer, has already taken El Diablo's place as head of the Selinas Cartel. So despite nailing—forgive the pun—Pablo Garcia and El Diablo along with confiscating their east coast cocaine stockpile, we didn't seem to slow them down much."

"You're kidding."

"I wish I were."

"They won't come looking for you, Max. Not here."

The sunset had been spectacular. The sky looked on fire in places—blazing reds and dazzling purples, swirls of gold. We'd finished out beers and held hands until the last glow of the day vanished.

"The dishes can wait," I said as we walked back to my cabin.

Kenny put his arm around my shoulders and gave a little tug. I titled my head so it rested on the inside of his shoulder.

As soon as we locked the door, Kenny danced me through the living room to the bedroom. With every step, I stripped myself of some article of clothing. Shoes first, then blouse. Kenny did the same until there was nothing but our naked bodies pressing together. I lay back on the bed taking Kenny with me. I kept pushing out of my mind that we might not see each other again for a long time. He would leave for Maryland tomorrow. I clung to him, reveling in every touch.

My body shook beneath him. Now I knew what it meant to say *when we made love it was like the earth moved*.

I was so enjoying being intimately entwined, both physically and emotionally, when Kenny lifted up and sprang to his feet. At about the same time, I noticed the cabin shaking.

"Get out, Max," he yelled.

I yanked the sheet from the bed and wrapped it around me. Kenny grabbed my hand, and we ran through the cabin and out the front door." My pulse pounded in my ears, and I couldn't seem to catch my breath. "They're here," I cried. The cartel had found me and had somehow managed to get their hands on an earthquake machine.

Outside, Kenny enfolded me in his arms. The earth shook beneath my feet. And then it stopped.

"Max, it's an earthquake. A real one."

"Not a machine?" I lifted my head. "I never thought I'd appreciate an authentic earthquake."

"It wasn't a big one, thank God."

I looked at Kenny standing naked in the moonlight and started laughing.

"What's so funny?" He looked down at his nude body.

"You're out here in the cold, naked as a jaybird. It's just funny."

"You need to appreciate me more. I provided your meal and cooked it. I let you have the sheet. What do you have to say about that? Show me some respect. Stop laughing and say something nice."

I gave him a big grin. "Baby, you sure know how to make a girl shake, rattle, and roll."

ABOUT THE AUTHORS

Lynn Sholes has worked as a writing trainer for Broward County Schools and Citrus County Schools in Florida. Before writing thrillers her interest in archaeology led her to write historical fiction under the name Lynn Armistead McKee. Lynn is a member of the International Thriller Writers, Mystery Writers of America, Florida Writers Association, and The Authors Guild.

Joe Moore is a former marketing & communications executive and two-time EMMY® winner with 25 years' experience in the television postproduction industry. He is the president emeritus of the International Thriller Writers. Joe writes full time from his home on the banks of the Blackwater River in Northwest Florida.

For more information on Lynn Sholes & Joe Moore, and their thrillers, visit www.sholesmoore.com and follow them on Facebook at www.facebook.com/sholesandmoore

AN EXCERPT FROM
THE BLADE
(BOOK 1)
LYNN SHOLES & JOE MOORE

PUBLISHED BY STONE CREEK BOOKS

"And Abraham stretched forth his hand,
and took the blade to slay his son."
~ Genesis, 22:10

CHAPTER 1 - BETRAYAL
Three years earlier, North of Kirkuk City, Iraq

I lay flat on the ground beside the five-thousand-year-old Assyrian settlement wall and watched the smuggler through my night vision goggles. My partner, OSI Special Agent Aaron Knox, was concealed among the ruins fifteen meters to my right.

"Maxine, what's he doing?" Aaron's voice whispered in my earbud.

"I'm not sure," I said. "Looks like he's fumbling with some boxes in that van."

Just moments earlier, the smuggler had emerged from the farmhouse, glanced in my direction as if he sensed my presence, then headed toward an old panel van twenty meters away. With it parked facing away from me, I had a back view of him as he opened the cargo doors. He kept looking toward the road a hundred meters to the east, probably anticipating the arrival of the transfer truck any moment.

A faint odor of cattle manure drifted from a nearby dusty pasture as I turned my head to the left. A ridgeline ran at an angle across the back of the property, making a perfect hiding place for the Iraqi National Police commandos waiting there.

I shifted my focus back to the van. The smuggler, a twenty-year-old Sunni Kurd, remained at the rear by the open doors. At such a young age, he had already made a name for himself on the black market as part of a smuggling ring that pilfered Iraqi artifacts out of the country through the neighboring Sulaymaniyah Province. Recently, he'd gotten his hands on a few of the valuables looted from the Baghdad National

Museum during the chaotic start of the war back in 2003. Our intel said the treasures included several small Sumerian relics and a number of gold and silver pieces dating back to 2000 BC. The smuggler's take would be hundreds of U.S. dollars, but as the goods moved up the food chain to the ultimate private collectors, they could be worth millions. Because the artifacts were believed to have been originally stolen by U.S. Air Force personnel, the Office of Special Investigations had sent in Aaron and me.

"Truck." The voice in my earbud was now the Iraqi police captain.

I heard it before I saw it. Through the night vision goggles, its headlights glowed green—a ghostly image of a lumbering farm truck appeared over the crest of a hill and headed toward us along the old Kirkuk highway. The Iraqi police would perform the actual apprehension. The two of us were there to observe and assist in the recovery and identification of the artifacts. Nothing more.

I glanced back at the van. "Shit!"

"Max, what's wrong?" Aaron asked.

"He's gone." The van doors stood open like a gaping mouth, but the smuggler had vanished.

I swept the space between the van and the house. Empty.

Back to the van. Dark interior. No movement.

"Maxine?" Aaron's voice was louder.

I looked in the opposite direction and spotted our target hauling ass on foot toward the road. "The little prick is bailing!"

I saw the blurry image of the smuggler running across the flat, barren space toward the highway at a full sprint. He gripped the straps to a bulging backpack, and I realized he had duped us with the cargo van full of cartons. Instead he had all the goods on him. Chances were, nothing of value would be in the van.

"Agent Decker?" The captain was waiting for my signal.

"Hang on." I spotted my partner running behind the smuggler. He was within a meter of being able to tackle the target.

But something wasn't right.

I stood and signaled to the Iraqi commandos to begin their assault.

"Aaron," I called, "Take him down! Stop the bastard!"

My earbud filled with orders from the captain shouting to his men. They were already swarming over the ridge.

Shots came from the van. Someone had been hiding inside. The shooter seemed to be ignoring the commandos and instead was firing at me. *What the hell?* I dropped behind the ancient wall and pulled my SIG Sauer.

Pieces of clay burst from the wall as slugs slammed into my hiding place. *How do they know my exact location?* I heard the Iraqis yelling. More shots. Within seconds, the sound of automatic weapons was everywhere. The guy in the van was relentless.

Crouching low, I maneuvered around the wall toward where my partner had been positioned. New shots fired. I popped up my head for a second and determined they were coming from the farm truck. It had stopped beside the highway, and at least four men were firing at the commandos from the truck's canvas-covered bed.

Whoever was still in the van was spraying bullets across the top of the ruins to keep me occupied. Then I saw him jump out and start to make a run for the truck before the commandos got to him. I moved to the end of the wall, rose, and fired three shots at the gunman. He dropped and didn't get up.

Several Iraqis swarmed the house while the rest headed for the farm truck, their tracers lighting up the night. I took off running to back up my partner but immediately caught the attention of someone in the truck—bullets were now coming at me. The commandos had to seek shelter behind the van as the men in the truck laid down cover fire for the smuggler's escape.

"Aaron, get down!" I yelled into the mic. He was running in the open area. I felt my belt to make sure I had a fresh clip ready before racing along the perimeter of the pasture. I had to help him before he got himself shot.

The smuggler veered off the direct course toward the highway to avoid the line of fire, with Aaron right behind him. They left the open space of the pasture and weaved through the ruins. I took advantage of their detour and sprinted straight toward them for an intercept.

Just before they emerged from the last ancient clay structure, they charged right into me.

I aimed my gun and the smuggler froze. Aaron bent over, hands on his knees catching his breath.

"Aaron!" A voice shouted above the gunfire coming from the truck.

It was American. Not Iraqi.

I ripped off my goggles and glared at my partner. "Who's that? How does he know your name?" The smuggler sidestepped. "Freeze!" I ordered. "Aaron, who's that in the truck?" I had to shout for him to hear above all the racket. "What's going on here?" The pieces were coming together and I thought I already knew the answer, but I desperately wanted to be wrong.

"This has nothing to do with you, Max. Just turn around and walk away." Aaron straightened. "This is my ticket out."

"Have you forgotten that you're a federal agent?"

"Just back off. You're not supposed to get hurt. That was part of the deal."

"Deal? What deal? I'm not backing off. This isn't going to go down. Not like this." Bullets pelted the opposite side of the structure protecting us.

The voice from the truck roared out my partner's name again.

Aaron still hadn't caught his breath, and his words came in a staccato rhythm. "Don't make me do it. I don't want to shoot you."

The truck engine revved.

"Maxine, I'm sorry—"

As he brought his gun up I fired twice.

He collapsed.

"You bitch!" The scream came from the direction of the truck, but closer.

The American. Without my goggles, he was nothing but a dark form rushing at me.

The smuggler took off.

Then a flash.

The bullet struck my side just below my vest. Another slammed into my right thigh. The pain was white hot.

I dropped to my knees and fell forward.

The odor of the cattle manure seemed stronger this close to the earth.

Or was it the smell of death?

CHAPTER 2 - THE VISITOR
Present day, Big Bear Lake, Colorado

As I crested a hill, half a kilometer from my cabin, I spotted a Jeep in the distance. For an instant, the last orange from the setting sun glinted off its shiny paint even as it sat partially hidden in the shadows of the Douglas firs below.

Quickening my pace, I slipped along the path, protected from view by the Gambel oaks and mountain mahogany. I wanted to get a better look at the vehicle.

The Jeep might belong to hikers or wilderness lovers fancying a view of the Rockies in springtime. But this area was not a popular spot, which is one reason I had chosen the location—for solitude. And the signs declaring private property were hard to miss where the dirt road to my place turned off the county blacktop. The Jeep either belonged to a lost soul or to someone looking for me. The latter made me nervous.

The trail leveled off as I came down to the southern end of Big Bear Lake. The path hugged the lake's perimeter in a sweeping arc. Tall blades of grass and sedge kept me partially concealed. Combined with the onrush of night and my dark clothing, I was just a shadow.

I came to the edge of the clearing that cascaded from my cabin down to the lake. Crouching behind a thick fir tree, I poked my head around and scanned the rear of the cabin. That's when I saw him.

The guy was dressed in jeans and a heavy jacket with a baseball cap pulled low over his forehead. Dark hair. Maybe six foot one. Trim. Between 160 and 170 pounds. He walked slowly along the back porch. Judging by the way he moved he was agile and I bet fit beneath the bulk of the jacket.

At each window, he paused to peer in. As he reached the back door, I instinctively went for my sidearm, but the SIG Sauer had long been replaced with a five-inch hunting knife and a Maglite. I hadn't touched a gun since I shot Aaron Knox.

Time to improvise.

I waited until he cracked open the door and entered. Keeping low, I moved through the grass and took advantage of an occasional tree to evade the clearing until I made my way to the side of the cabin. With extra care, I eased open the storm door and slipped into the basement.

It was pitch-black and dank smelling—I'd had every intention of cleaning and reorganizing it, but it was still down near the bottom of my to-do list.

I kept my flashlight off. Moving blind, I felt my way around boxes, tools, and general junk. A rattling thud came when I bumped my shin on an old bedframe. "Damn!" *Had he heard both the collision and my curse?* When I found the thick supports of the wooden stairs, I slid underneath and waited.

The soft creaking of the floorboards told me he was in the kitchen. His steps were slow and light, obviously exercising caution as he searched each room. With my old F150 parked out front and the back door unlocked, it was no mystery that I was home or not far away. Since he wasn't ransacking and rummaging, I concluded that he was not there to burgle. That left one alternative, and I didn't like it.

Narrow slits between the floorboards lit up as the intruder swept his light around each room. He approached the door to the basement.

At the sound of the door hinge squeaking above me, I pushed back against the wall.

He took the first step on the stairs, and his light beam came to rest on an old refrigerator sitting next to a workbench. The Frigidaire didn't function, and the tools on the bench were worn and rusted, left behind by the former owner.

The second step creaked and then the third, slow and easy. A dark leather hiking boot settled on the step level with my face. The next step down, I grabbed his boot laces and he flew forward, head first. With a grunt, he hit the dirt floor hard. I ran out from under the stairs and before he could move, I had my knee planted firmly in his back at the base of his neck and the butt end of my Maglite pressed into his skull.

"Move and you're dead." I stabbed the Maglite against his head for emphasis, hoping it felt like the real thing.

"Maxine, sweetheart, is that any way to greet your long-lost love?"

CHAPTER 3 - KENNY GATES
Big Bear Lake, Colorado

"What did you expect me to do, Kenny? You broke into my home and sneaked around like a burglar. We've got electricity up here in the backwoods. Next time, ring the doorbell. Or call first."

I leaned against the porch railing with my arms folded and watched him baby a cut on his forehead with a Ziploc bag of ice. He sat in a high-back rocking chair and glanced up at me with his apologetic hazel eyes.

"Knocked at your door. No answer. Car was here. You live way out in the middle of bum-fuck Colorado. Anything could have happened to you. I was just checking the place out to make sure you were okay. Of course I loved the extra element of surprise. "

"I'm sure you adored your little perk of scaring the hell out of me."

"So you were going to blow me away with a Maglite?"

"If I had to. It was locked and loaded with double-As."

Kenny smiled as he shifted the plastic ice pack to a new position on his head and looked at the lake in the distance. The stars and fireflies were coming out. "Nice place, Max. You've done good."

He was right. This was what I needed after the long recovery and rehab from my gunshot wounds in Iraq, not to mention the additional hell of going through endless grilling by the Inspector General's Office on the shooting of Aaron Knox. The actual gunplay took a few seconds—the inquiry seemed to go on forever. It didn't take much to push me over the edge. I decided to retire after being shot at three times during my eighteen years as a special agent with the OSI.

The first time was an airman who stood in the parking lot of the Eglin Base Exchange and decided to shoot his girlfriend and any other females within line of sight. I was three cars over. He got the girlfriend and my driver's side window.

Second time, I was conducting an interrogation at MacDill on an officer caught smuggling stolen Peruvian artifacts out of Florida. He came to my hotel room and knocked. When I asked who it was, he fired three bullets through the door. One grazed my arm. I went to the hospital and he went to prison.

The first two weren't anything like Kirkuk. There was also the mental and emotional wrecking of having shot my partner and friend. To make things worse, I was then under suspicion of involvement in the smuggling operation. That nailed my decision to leave the OSI. I didn't just retire, I fled. I *needed* to get out. And I needed to go someplace and be alone for a long time. Big Bear Lake was perfect.

Kenny and I had a long history. We'd met when I joined the OSI. I was only 23 and green. Kenny, on the other hand, was an experienced agent and a good one. While others let me flag and flounder, Kenny found time to coach me through the maze of my new job. He was my personal mentor, even though our fields were different. He was an OSI Computer Crimes Investigator specializing in computer forensics, while mine was the antiquities black market. If a crime was committed by military personnel, we were usually called in to investigate. Kenny had to deal with everything from kiddy porn to falsifying documents, while I dealt with stolen art objects and smuggling.

"Must be boring up here." He put down the ice pack and took a long pull from the Coors.

"Not when I've got people sneaking up on my place and breaking in." I took a drink from my beer. "And why did you park your Jeep up the road? You're lucky I don't like guns anymore."

"My intent was to happily surprise you. But when you

weren't around, I got worried. I screwed up, okay? So sue me."

I shook my head. "And people wonder why I got out of the military."

"What do you do up here all day?"

"Well, I do some painting. Lots of reading. And I've started writing—"

"Really? What kind of writing?"

"Fiction. I've got a few ideas for a novel. I write longhand, then type my work into my laptop. It's fun. They say everyone has at least one book in them."

"Am I in your book?"

I resisted a smart reply and zapped him a *give me a break* look.

"Just asking," he said.

"And I fish. There's some decent trout fishing in the lake. A boat came with the house, so I go out on the lake once in a while. I like being around nature. As a matter of fact, I was coming back from checking on a litter of foxes about a kilometer from here when I saw your Jeep. The mother's been missing for a few days, and I was worried about the kits. But mom showed back up today, although she looked the worse for it."

"Probably a slut fox.

"Or a battered wife."

"Touché," Kenny said, hoisting his bottle.

"So, now that we've had the obligatory idle chitchat and the complimentary beverage, why are you here?"

He set down the beer, rubbed the dark stubble on his chin, and let his face go serious. "We want you back."

I stared at him, wondering if this was someone's idea of a joke. "Back? Back to what? Kenny, there is no back. There's only forward. I'm moving forward with my life. This is my life. Look around you. What could be better than this? There's nothing the government could possibly offer that would entice me to return to active duty."

"Max, you're living in downtown boredomville. OSI is in your blood. You've had your R&R. Now it's time to get back to work. Catch some bad guys. Find an ancient relic or two. Do your magic. I know you."

"Well, for once, you're wrong. This *is* me. And I like me." I walked a few paces away and turned toward the lake, now only a dark mass under a brilliant, star-filled sky. I rubbed my upper arms, enjoying the brisk Colorado mountain air before turning to Kenny. "There's nothing that could bring me back."

"Don't be so sure."

I didn't like the way he said that. He understood me well enough to know what blew my skirt up. Maybe he was just playing with me. He had an annoying habit of doing that. "What do you mean?"

"We think we've got a line on the Blade."

I felt a tingle in my belly and my pulse quickened. Suddenly, that old rush of the chase shot through me. Just to clarify, and with a great deal of anticipation I asked, "What blade?"

"The Blade of Abraham."

CHAPTER 4 - THE ROAD
Austria, 18 months earlier

"Debbie, check this out," she heard her boyfriend call out.

"Where are you?"

"Over here." She looked toward the sound. He was waving at her from among the deep shadows of the forest. He stood in knee-high brush about twenty paces from the remote mountain hiking trail.

"What've you got, Scott?" It took her a few moments to make her way through the brush. "And why did you have to come this far just to take a leak?"

"Took advantage of the moment to see what the woods are like off the trail." He stooped and lifted the edge of a large piece of metal off the ground.

"So what's your big discovery?"

"I found this underneath some brush and ground cover." He pulled the plate up so she could see the bottom. The faded lettering was barely visible among the rust and corrosion. "What's it say?"

Debbie stared at the words. She'd learned German from her mother and maternal grandmother. It was her interest in her heritage and Scott's graduate studies in history that had inspired their summer backpacking trip through central Europe.

"It's German," she said. "Basically says to turn back, that if you go on you'll be shot."

"Turn back from what?" He glanced about at the dark forest as it followed the curve of the mountain. "There's nothing here."

"Well, nothing *now*," she said. "But by the looks of its condition, the sign must've been around for years. Chances are the only reason it's still here is because it's made of metal rather than wood." She leaned forward. "Hang on a sec." Bending, she gave the sign a closer inspection. "Hold the edge up higher. There's something else near the bottom." She brushed away the dirt and caked-on debris. "Wow!"

"What?"

"I'll hold it while you take a look." Tilting the heavy metal plate upright, she waited until he came around. "See it?"

"A swastika. I'm not surprised. The Nazis took over Austria in 1938. Near the end of the war, Hitler had a plan to make a last stand in the Alpine areas of Austria, Bavaria, and northern Italy. They built a number of heavily fortified bunkers to house the army. When that didn't work out, some say they used them to hide all their looted treasure."

Debbie dropped the sign. "I wonder if we're close to one of those treasure bunkers?"

"Plenty of the stuff stolen by the Nazis is still missing. But it's not likely we've found anything after nearly seven decades. Let's get back on the trail or we won't make it to the next hut by sundown."

"Now it's my turn to have to pee." She waved with both hands, motioning for him to turn away. "I'll just be a minute."

Debbie headed for an area a few meters further into the woods. Coming to the top of a slight rise, she looked down onto what she thought was an irregularity below. The brush there was less dense, less lush, and it seemed to form a pattern, like a trail through the thick forest. "Scott," she called out. Her voice sounded small among the thick oaks and sycamore maples.

She ambled down the slope. Kicking at the brush and vines, she noticed the ground felt especially hard and rugged beneath the scrub here. Ripping out some of the plant growth revealed a swatch of cracked and pitted pavement.

"A road," Debbie said. "An old road." So that was why the

brush was less dense. It struggled to survive atop pavement.

Looking around, she saw more evidence of crumbling pavement riddling the area. The remnants of the road continued through the forest up a gradual incline to the left until it curved out of sight.

She wondered if Nazi transport trucks loaded with gold bullion or rare art objects had once traveled along it. A scrabbling sound and a grunt caused her to turn.

Scott had lost his balance as he came down the embankment and landed on his butt.

"That was graceful."

"What are you doing?" He brushed off the dirt before re-securing his backpack. "All of a sudden I turned around and you were gone."

"Look what I found." She gestured like Julie Andrews on the mountaintop in *The Sound Of Music*.

"What?" Scott said, eyeing the surroundings.

"This." She pried loose a piece of the pavement and held it up. "A road. It must date back decades. Certainly hasn't been used in a long, long time."

"That's impressive. Now can we get back on the trail? The hut is hours away. We're losing valuable time."

"But don't you think this is so cool? You found the old Nazi sign, and now I've discovered a hidden road. Think where it might lead. A German treasure bunker could be right around the next bend." She turned, adjusted her backpack and started walking. "Come on, let's explore a little."

"Not a good idea."

"Why? It's headed in the same general direction as the trail. If we get bored, we can work our way west and jump back on."

Reluctantly, he fell in beside her. "We're going to wind up sleeping on the ground, mark my words."

"Where's your sense of adventure? Everyone takes the trail. We're the only ones following this."

"It's just an old road."

"Yes," she said, picking up the pace, "but one with a Nazi warning that beyond this point we'll be shot. You won't find that kind of adventure on the trail."

They followed the road through the forest as it wound around the side of the mountain. After a couple of miles the trees thinned enough for them to see the rugged incline of the mountain.

"I still don't think we should have taken this side excursion," Scott was saying when they rounded a bend and came to an abrupt halt.

What was left of the pavement seemed to run right into the side of the mountain—at least right into a large pile of rocks and debris.

"Landslide?" Debbie asked.

He shrugged. "If it was, it happened a long time ago. No wonder the road isn't used anymore—it doesn't go anywhere."

"So it went somewhere but there was this landslide and now it ends here."

"Now that we've solved the mystery of your phantom highway, can we try to work our way back to the trail? If we move fast, we might be able to make the hut before nightfall."

"Do you think it continued on past the rockslide?" she asked.

"It doesn't look like there's anything beyond the rocks." He walked to the far edge of the debris pile. "I don't see any road beyond. My guess is that it ended right here."

"That makes no sense," Debbie said, heading over to the opposite side of the slide. "Why build a road that dead-ends on the side of a mountain?"

"Deb, we really need to get a move on."

Ignoring him, she passed the base of the rockslide and wandered into the trees and underbrush. She didn't have to look back to know Scott was following her. His grumbling was loud and clear.

"Why are you obsessing over this place?"

"I'm curious, that's all." She climbed over an outcrop by pulling herself up using low hanging branches. "Don't you think it odd?"

"What? That someone a long time ago built a road that

dead-ended into the side of a mountain?"

"That's just it." Standing on a rock, she turned to face him. "I think the road runs *into* the mountain."

"You mean like a tunnel?"

"Maybe. Why would the Germans threaten death to anyone who came up here if they didn't have something to hide? We could be right on top of your treasure bunker."

"So what are you looking for?"

"What's the one thing you need if you're in a bunker inside a mountain?"

"I don't know. Flashlights? Schnapps?"

"Air."

Scott stared at her for a moment before nodding. "So you think if there's a bunker, there might be some kind of ventilation?"

"Maybe. It shouldn't take too long to find out." She started climbing over the next grouping of rocks.

He looked at his watch. "You might as well take your time, now. There's no way we're going to make it to the next hut. We'll sleep back down on the road and head over to the trail tomorrow."

"Be looking for some unusual feature."

They spent the next twenty minutes investigating, climbing, parting vines and weeds, searching the landscape for some anomaly. At last, just as she was ready to give it up, Debbie spotted something. "Over there," she said pointing and heading toward her sighting.

Scott climbed to join her.

"Look at this," she said, pushing the undergrowth aside to expose a man-made stone and mortar slab. "I should be a detective rather than an engineering major." Protruding up from its center was a metal tube about thirty inches in diameter with a cone-shaped lid mounted on top. The lid sat at an odd angle, having been the victim of wind, rain, rust, and more than one falling rock.

Looking inside the small space between the cone lid and the tube, Scott saw a layer of straw and twigs from generations of bird nests. "Well, I've got to admit, you were right. Somewhere inside is a tunnel or bunker, and this probably leads to it." He looked at his girlfriend. "But finding it isn't enough, is it? You're still not satisfied, are you?"

She slipped her backpack off and tested the strength of the cone-shaped lid supports. "Of course not. Now we go inside the mountain."

CHAPTER 5 - EBAY
Big Bear Lake, Colorado

"You're kidding!" I stared at Kenny as I recalled the first time I'd seen the Blade of Abraham. When I was a teen my family took a vacation to Egypt. During our visit to the Cairo Museum, one exhibit especially intrigued me. I remember standing transfixed and staring at the age-worn twelve-inch-long knife with its simple wood and leather-bound handle that rested in a wooden box. I was drawn to it because of the dramatic story it told, one I'd read as a child in Sunday school. Unlike the cold stone statues and endless rows of pottery in the museum, this simple knife suddenly became a direct connection for me to an event over four thousand years ago.

It was the tale of ultimate faith—how Abraham obeyed God's command to sacrifice his son, Isaac. Only at the last moment did God send an angel to intervene. It had a profound effect on me as I stood there staring at the relic in the exhibition case. Throughout my life the Blade of Abraham was my personal symbol of faith and sacrifice.

Not long after our family vacation, I read that the relic was stolen. I suppose that's what helped lead me to pursue my profession. I started following news accounts of other ancient artifacts being stolen and sold on the black market. After I graduated from college, one of my professors told me of his time in the military as an agent in the Air Force Office of Special Investigations. When I found out they needed an archaeologist and welcomed civilian agents, I joined up. But no matter how fulfilling it was to solve hundreds of cases over the years, I never lost my hope of someday finding and recovering that simple blade: the Blade of Abraham.

"We've been down this road before," I said. "Always a dead end, or the piece turns out to be a fake. What's different this time?"

He set the empty Coors bottle on my porch deck. "When was the last time it showed up on your radar?"

"There were rumors of it surfacing in Damascus five years ago and then a year later in Istanbul." I handed Kenny another cold one from an ice chest at my feet.

"Thanks." He twisted off the top. "And nothing since?"

"Right."

"Until last week. You'll never guess where it popped up. eBay."

I almost spit out my beer. "Are you shittin' me?" Wiping my mouth on my sleeve, I decided to drop into the companion rocker beside Kenny. "What kind of moron would auction a priceless religious relic online?" I looked at him. "And a stolen one at that."

"It appeared under the Holy Land Antiquities category. The auction lasted one hour before it disappeared."

"Any bidders?"

He shook his head. "By the time we got wind of it, the listing was gone. Turns out someone hacked the seller's account to post it."

"I can't believe someone would use a public internet site to try to sell a relic like the Blade. Had to be a hoax."

"That was my reaction at first."

"And they actually called it the Blade of Abraham?"

"Takes balls."

"I'll say. What makes you think it was the real thing?"

"We had eBay send us the cached images, which we forwarded to the Cairo Museum. The pictures were high res, so it was easy to compare to what they had on file. Interestingly enough, it was actually the container the Blade was displayed in that gave the most proof. One of the guys at the museum confirmed a small identifying mark on a corner of the wooden box that matched their records and photos perfectly."

"I remember that box from when I first saw it years ago. So the big question—why is OSI involved?"

"The hacked account belonged to an Air Force officer."

I stared at the starlight reflecting off the dark lake, wishing it had gone that easy for me after... My cat suddenly appeared, winding around my ankles and purring. I put him in my lap, stroking his head and back. "Another of my simple pleasures."

"I never knew you were a cat lover."

"After all these years? Surprise, surprise." I hesitated a moment. I was being bitchy and decided to let it go. "Even as a kid I wanted a kitty, but Mom and Fran were allergic. Now that I'm retired and live alone, I tend to indulge myself. So I got a cat. Named him Nanki-Poo. Nank for short. From *The Mikado*."

"Speaking of Fran, how is your sister?"

"Still a free spirit with a big heart. She took off a few months ago on a humanitarian mission to Haiti after the earthquake. They say twins act and think alike, but I never got her wanderlust. She's with a UN-sponsored relief organization. After her work in Haiti, she headed to Cuba to help out with the victims of the hurricane."

I rocked for a few minutes, petting Nank, enjoying his attention as much as he seemed to enjoy mine, and deeply missing my sister. "I have to admit I'm interested."

Kenny gave me that "I know you so well" grin, the one that had rankled me so often over the years—mostly because he did know me so well, and he knew it. But just for an instant, I felt an old cold trail turn warm, maybe even hot. Then the distant sound of a fish jumping out on the black water and the memory of what I'd done that day three years ago in Iraq near the Assyrian ruins brought me back to reality.

"Despite your tempting news, I'm going to have to pass, Kenny. I wish you luck, but I gotta tell you, I'm perfectly happy right here." I leaned back in the rocker and inhaled the fresh mountain air, clearing my head.

"Come on, Max. What's put out that spark in you? Get

back on the horse, as they say. You aren't afraid. Of that I'm sure. The only thing I've ever known you to fear is heights. So why not?"

He wasn't going to quit, and I could feel the fire of my temper flaring. My posture stiffened, and I glared at Kenny. "It's not about fear. How could you even ask me such a thing knowing what I went through after Iraq?"

"Look, Max, I've put my neck on the line for you."

"Maybe that's what you should have done three years ago."

"You're right. I should have. But that's Monday morning quarterbacking. I was wrong. I've told you that before. But I can't change that."

"No, you can't."

"Time and distance make us see things more clearly. I'm not trying to make up for anything. I'm just trying to do what's right."

There wasn't much I could say to that. Yes, he should have done more in my defense and not let me get beat up so badly with the investigation. But looking back, I realize that at the time he was angry. Interesting that I wasn't as bitter anymore. Maybe a tinge of sourness still rose up now and again—that accounted for some of my snippiness with him. Tangled, tangled webs we weave.

Kenny paused a moment, then continued. "You know, at OSI there's still a black cloud that hangs over the name Maxine Decker. People get all weird when your name comes up. Just so you know, when I suggested bringing you in to help with this case, not everyone got excited. I had to remind them that there was never a shred of evidence that you were involved in that smuggling plot, and that killing Aaron had nearly killed you—emotionally. No way would you have shot your partner without just cause. Oh, they agreed that you were the best one suited for this job, but there was resistance in getting you involved. I pushed hard to turn them around. They relented, and I volunteered to come out here and recruit you. They don't have anyone with your level of expertise. You're it, Max, and if you don't say yes, I guarantee they won't get to the bottom of the Blade issue."

I looked away, lowered my head and rocked a few times before I spoke. "Sorry, Kenny." I faced him again, looking into his disappointed eyes. "I just can't. After the Aaron incident, I was severely depressed and I about lost my sanity. It's been a long road back. I finally get out of bed in the mornings instead of finding no reason to get up, take a shower, or get dressed. And I don't think about hurting myself anymore."

He stared into the night for a long time. "I'm so sorry you had to go through all that, Max. I can understand why even a chance at finding the Blade isn't enough to bring you back. No sense in discussing it any further." He stood. "I hope you have a nice life in your mountain hideaway. I'll just be running along. There's no reason to tell you the best part."

I stared up at him and saw a hint of a smile playing at his lips. God, he could be exasperating. "What best part?"

AN EXCERPT FROM
THE SHIELD
(BOOK 2)
LYNN SHOLES & JOE MOORE

PUBLISHED BY STONE CREEK BOOKS

"The presence of unidentified spacecraft flying in our
atmosphere is now accepted as de facto by the military."
Relationship with Inhabitants of Celestial Bodies
(June 1947)

~ Dr. J. Robert Oppenheimer
Director of Advanced Studies
Princeton, New Jersey
&
~ Professor Albert Einstein
Princeton, New Jersey

CHAPTER 1 - NIGHT VISITOR
Big Bear Lake, Colorado

I sat up, startled from sleep. My first muddled thought was earthquake. The walls and windows of my cabin shuddered, shaking a picture off the wall. But then I quickly recognized the thunderous roar of a turbojet helicopter. A beam of bright light shone through the window blinds. Instinct kicked in and I rolled to my side and snatched the SIG Sauer from the nightstand drawer.

The chopper's spotlight swept away and I used the opportunity to run to the living room with both hands locked on the 9mm's grip.

From the light seeping through curtains and blinds I could tell my entire front yard and surrounding area were lit up as if the sun had kicked the moon to the curb. The sound of the helicopter landing was unmistakable.

I stood flush against the wall, gun still gripped with both clammy hands.

A rap on the door made me flinch, and I took aim. I'd already been shot twice in my life and had no intention of this being number three.

"Maxine Decker?"

Another strident knock.

"Agent Decker?"

"Who's there? What do you want?"

"I need to speak with you regarding important government business."

I edged my way to stand beside the door and pulled on a slat in the sidelight mini-blinds for a view of the porch. Backlit by the brilliance of the chopper's spotlight was a man of medium height and trim build. Other than that, he was nothing but a silhouette.

"Identify yourself," I yelled over the noise of the rotors.

"Peter Kepner. I'm with the government and I need to speak to you right away."

"You must be out of the loop, Kepner. I'm no longer a federal agent. I retired from OSI."

"I'm not OSI. I'm an emissary from Beowulf."

"Never heard of it. And if you're not OSI, then why do you want to talk to me?"

"In times of national security issues, Beowulf has executive authority to recruit CIA, FBI, NSA, even Air Force Office of Special Investigations agents. Retired or otherwise."

"Tell the pilot to kill the light and shut down the engine. And tell anyone else on board to stay put. Do it now."

The man relayed my demand through hand signals and his radio. The spotlight dimmed and the rotors trimmed down to a slow idle.

I switched on the front porch light and pulled back the blinds on the sidelight. "Turn around slowly."

Kepner did a 360.

"Show me some ID. And remember I have my weapon pointed at you."

"Got it. But for security reasons, I don't carry any special identification. I can show you my driver's license and a couple of credit cards."

"I'm not Walmart, so you're gonna have to come up with something better than that."

He pulled an envelope from his back pocket. "Agent Decker, I have something for you. I'm sliding it under the door."

I let the blinds snap back and saw the end of the envelope poke through. I picked it up and switched on the lamp on the foyer table. My curiosity was aroused by the embossed seal— the image of a fire-breathing dragon. *Beowulf.* I remembered the ancient epic poem I'd had to study in high school.

I checked to see that Kepner was still there. Then with a zip of my finger I slit the envelope.

I withdrew the stationery, shook it open, and held it close to the light. Seeing the letterhead, I whipped around and glared at the door.

CHAPTER 2 - THE LIGHT BRIGADE
Big Bear Lake, Colorado

My eyes swept the length of the paper. At the top of the stationery was the official White House letterhead. At the bottom was the supposed signature of Guy LeClaire, President of the United States.

Slowly I read the contents, then took a moment to digest it. I retrieved my cell phone from the charger on my nightstand and returned to the living room.

"You still out there, Kepner?" I called.

"Still here."

I did a quick Google search and came up with the phone number I needed to dial according to the instructions in the letter—the White House switchboard. When my call was answered, I continued to follow the directions I was given in the letter. "I'd like to speak with Tennyson."

"One moment, please," the operator said.

A few seconds later, a synthesized voicemail told me to leave a message. I glanced at the letter to make sure I would reply exactly right. "I have read *The Charge of the Light Brigade*."

Then I hung up and waited.

In a moment, my cell rang. "Maxine Decker," I answered.

"Ms. Decker, this is Guy LeClaire."

His words were steady and unmistakable with that distinctive, crisp Boston accent.

My voice had a small tremor in it, both because I was speaking with the President of the United States and because I knew that whatever the reason for Kepner's visit, it was of utmost importance. "Yes, Mr. President?"

"I apologize for this late-night visit and call. We have a critical matter that requires swift and efficient measures. You're needed to participate in a special assignment. Please invite Mr. Kepner inside so he can speak to you. He'll give you more details."

Before I could say anything else, he thanked me once more and ended the call. I stood there a minute trying to absorb what just happened. I unlocked the front door, thankful I wasn't the sheer nightie type, instead wearing long flannel pajama bottoms and a loose-fitting tee.

With a wave of my arm, I invited Peter Kepner inside. I decided to claim the overstuffed chair and leave the sofa to him. Even though I felt confident that the visitor was legitimate, I conspicuously rested the SIG on my lap, one hand atop it. With the kind of business I'd been in for so many years, if I'd learned one thing, it was never to let my guard down. Being betrayed by my partner a few years back had clinched that for me.

I gestured for my visitor to take a seat on the couch opposite me.

Kepner sat, eyed the gun, then looked squarely at me.

"Why the personal visit, Mr. Kepner? Why not a phone call? And why couldn't it have waited until morning? For drama's sake?"

Other than a condescending smile, Kepner didn't react to my jab. "What I'm about to disclose is top secret, and I can't emphasize that enough. As with all electronic communication, there is the outside possibility of unwanted surveillance. That explains my personal visit. And, we need to move on this ASAP. Waiting until the morning would delay our response."

Kepner leaned forward, his elbows on his thighs, fingers laced. "You were a hell of a civilian OSI agent. Top in the antiquities black market. That's why you're Beowulf's choice for this project."

"Like I said, I've never heard of Beowulf."

"And that's a good thing—the way it's supposed to be, Agent Decker."

He wasn't going to let go of the *agent* title no matter how many times I said I was retired.

Kepner steepled his fingers then aimed them at me. "Here's the deal. There's been a serious breach of security at the Beowulf headquarters."

"Excuse me, but first would you elaborate a little more on what exactly Beowulf is? What's the function or mission?"

"I can't give you any more explanation until we are in a protected and secure environment. All I can do at this point is echo the request from the President that your assistance is needed to help with a potentially grave threat to our national security. The United States and its allies are at risk. I would like for you to get ready and leave with me as quickly as you can."

I'd promised myself I wouldn't return to my old occupation in any fashion. I'd consulted on one job after retiring and it had nearly gotten me killed. But this . . . this sounded like something critical that truly put the nation in peril. I felt my resolve softening.

"Where are we going?" I asked.

"I'm sorry, but I can't say."

"So you want me to take off with you to an undisclosed location to help with an undisclosed mission involving a government operation I've never heard of? Right now, in the middle of the night?" I plastered a *you've-got-to-be-kidding-me* expression on my face.

"That's about it."

I chuckled. "Who said the government doesn't have a sense of humor."

His expression quickly reverted to somber and so did mine. This was obviously a no-bullshit situation.

"Just one more thing. Don't pack a bag—no clothes or toiletries. But bring your ID, including your passport. Everything else will be provided for you."

I thought the request to take my passport was strange, especially since he carried so little. "Why my passport?"

"This may eventually require international travel."

I stood, holding the 9mm at my side.

He pointed to it. "And no guns."

CHAPTER 3 - BROKEN PIECES

Five days earlier. JFK International, New York City

The TSA officer watched the travelers passing through the international security checkpoint. A passenger had been asked to step aside after her shoulder bag was X-rayed. Apparently, something had attracted the attention of one of his inspectors. He observed the strikingly beautiful blonde in a fashionable business suit follow the inspector to a side table. There she placed her bag down and stood back while he unzipped it.

The officer wandered over to stand beside the woman and witness the bag search. The inspector was new on the job and the TSA officer wanted to make sure the search was being conducted by the book.

The bag, a leather satchel with a shoulder strap, contained an e-book reader, notepads and pens, some basic office supplies, and a loose-leaf binder full of what looked like design layouts for an advertising brochure.

While the inspector carefully checked the contents, the officer said, "May I see your passport, please?"

With a warm smile, the woman reached inside her purse and removed it—a Canadian passport in the name of Patricia Barney.

"What's your destination, Ms. Barney?" the officer asked.

"Amsterdam."

"Beautiful city."

"Yes, it is. Very European."

"Ma'am," the inspector said, "can you tell me what this is?" He held up a plastic baggie containing three small objects rolled in bubble wrap. He opened the bag and peeled back the bubble wrap. The objects looked identical—triangular in shape, slightly convex, and cream colored. Each was about five centimeters across.

"Those are pieces of a broken porcelain vase. I'm taking them to a specialist in the Netherlands while I visit friends, in hopes he can match the color so I can have a replica made. It belonged to my grandmother, and my goal is to have the new one made before she discovers it was broken." As the woman spoke, she calmly glanced from the officer to the inspector.

The officer took the package from his associate, examined the contents, and then rebundled it. After putting it back in the Ziploc, he held up the bag and jiggled it.

Patricia Barney flinched.

Then he gave it back to the inspector. "Sorry for the delay, Ms. Barney. Sometimes the sensors set off alerts randomly or if an object isn't recognized." He gave a slight nod to the other man and watched as the baggie was returned to the satchel.

"Good luck with finding that replacement," the inspector said as he handed the satchel to her.

"Have a nice day," the officer said. They both watched her rejoin the rest of the passengers and head for the KLM gate. When he returned to his station, he felt a slight tingle in his right hand. Shaking it seemed to make the tingle lessen. As he watched the line of travelers snake toward the metal detectors, he shook his hand again. Probably nothing, he thought, and turned his attention to the next passenger in line.

CHAPTER 4 - NIGHT FLIGHT
Big Bear Lake, Colorado

Did I have some kind of death wish? That was the question buzzing around in my head like a nuisance fly. Brushing my teeth before leaving with Kepner, I glanced in the mirror. What was I thinking to agree to this? I'd been enjoying my retirement. Life was good. The nightmares had dwindled, and I wasn't awakening in the middle of the night in a sweat, my heart exploding in my chest.

Even as I attempted to talk some sense into my brain, I found myself in the closet slipping into khaki pants followed by a pullover sweater and jacket. Next came my high-top hiking boots. As far as Kepner was concerned, I'd be leaving my SIG behind. He didn't need to know about my Walther PPK that I slid inside my boot.

Fully dressed, I emerged into the living room. "All set." I shoved my license and other ID in my pants' pocket and slipped my cell into the inside pocket of my jacket.

Kepner opened the front door. "Let's go."

Stepping onto the porch, I felt the chilly Colorado night air. It was August and the mountains had the loveliest cool temps once the sun went down. I took a big fat lungful of air, knowing I was going to miss it.

Kepner signaled the helicopter's pilot and before we reached it, the turbos spun up and the rotors quickly approached full rotation.

I climbed in, followed by Kepner. He handed me a headset, put one on himself, and adjusted the mic.

The rotors roared and we were airborne.

"Where are we headed?" I asked.

"Grand Junction. Walker Field, to be exact. But that's all you need to know right now. Be patient, Agent Decker."

"Sure." I *was* being patient. What did he expect? I'd been dragged out of bed in the middle of the night because the President said I was needed. But that was basically all I'd been told. If they wanted me so badly, why couldn't they divulge more about *why* they needed me? From all the mystery surrounding tonight's event, I had drawn the single most obvious conclusion. Beowulf was black ops.

Something else was obvious. Kepner wasn't going to call me by my first name. During twenty years as an OSI agent, I never got completely comfortable with the military environment. After all, I was a civilian agent—a trained archaeologist—working on the fringe of the Air Force machine. My job was to locate and identify artifacts, relics, art objects, and antiquities suspected of being stolen or smuggled by military personnel. I did my job better than anyone else, and that's why my less-than-straight-and-narrow attitude was tolerated. Despite my frequent nonconformist approaches, they always kept sending me back into the field to track down the bad guys. And that's what I would still be doing on a regular basis had I not decided I was allergic to lead from one too many bullets. I'd finally had enough and retired to my remote Colorado cabin. But now, here I was. Again.

Thinking about the past, I started to get that old queasiness in my gut. And what made it worse was the dark feeling that the Beowulf operation was blacker than anything I'd come across before.

Just over an hour passed before we reached a private aviation area at the northwest corner of Grand Junction Airport at Walker Field. After jumping onto the tarmac, we walked a short distance to a small Lear business jet, its engines spinning at idle, the strobes and navigation lights washing the immediate area with color and flashes. As we approached, someone inside opened the side hatch and let it drop down, forming steps.

"Our ride," Kepner said.

I tried to pry more information about our destination but he wouldn't budge. "I'll fill you in once we're in the air," was all he offered.

Kepner's long paces and fast gait were difficult for me to keep up with. I double-stepped to almost each of his strides.

"Come on. Give me a break. I feel like a puppy at the heels of his master and I don't like it. Tell me what the mission is all about."

He turned and looked at me. "You are a persistent one."

"So brief me."

"I'm not sure you're going to like it."

CHAPTER 5 - FULL DISCLOSURE
Grand Junction, Colorado

I settled into one of the six leather seats in the small Learjet while Kepner sat across the narrow aisle from me. The pilot and copilot looked like recruiting posters for military fighter pilots—tall, with close-cropped hair, square jaws, and serious expressions. They acknowledged us as we boarded, and then briefly updated Kepner on the status of the plane, weather, and flying time, which would be just under an hour.

Within minutes, the jet screamed down the runway and pulled into a steep climb. One of my Air Force buddies had once told me that small business jets like this one were as close to a fighter as a private civilian could own. I believed it as we rapidly left the lights of Grand Junction behind and shot into the black Colorado night.

"I'm afraid there won't be an in-flight movie or cocktails served, Agent Decker," Kepner said as we quickly reached cruising altitude.

"Tight budget?" My question caused him to smile for the first time.

"I think you'll soon find that we spend our money where we can get the most bang for the buck."

"And where would that be?" As we banked left, I glanced out of the window and spotted the Big Dipper and Polaris swinging past. I knew we were on a southwest heading.

Kepner saw me establishing our direction. "The next leg of our journey ends in Flagstaff."

"Is that our destination?"

"No, only one more hop after that."

I peered back out the window at the sprinkling of lights from small farm communities interspersed with a black landscape. "I'm still waiting to hear what this is all about. And why me?"

Kepner seemed to consider my question.

"You can at least tell me something about Beowulf," I added. "Even if your prediction is right and I don't like it."

Kepner blinked and cocked his head to the side, then looked back at me. "All right," he finally said. "Let me start with this. The organization has been around in one form or another since the mid-1980s. It was one of the many offshoots of Star Wars."

"The Strategic Defense Initiative—Reagan's program?"

"Correct. One of many byproducts of SDI. Beowulf is probably the last one standing."

"Probably?"

He nodded. "The handful of other programs I knew about are all gone."

"So, you've been with Beowulf for, what, twenty-eight years?"

"No, I came onboard in 1993 when SDI was 'dissolved'." He formed quotes in the air with his fingers.

"You mean Star Wars went on even though the public thought it was shut down?"

"SDI didn't continue, but some of the darker programs did."

"Beowulf is a 'dark' program." I repeated his quote gesture. "I kind of figured that out on my own."

"We've covered as much as we need to for now."

"What do you do for Beowulf?"

Again, he seemed to ponder the question.

"Come on. Are you the boss or the night watchman? I at least deserve to know that much."

"Head of security."

"See, that wasn't so hard, was it? Would you like to know anything about me?"

"No need, Agent Decker. I know everything about you."

This ruffled my feathers a bit. "That doesn't seem fair."

"We don't recruit anyone without full disclosure of their history. You've been thoroughly vetted."

"Then you know all about my sordid past?"

In a dry, deadpan delivery, he said, "I know you grew up in Albuquerque alongside your twin sister, Francine. Your mother was a real estate agent and your father taught Economics at the University of New Mexico. You were president of your high school senior class and graduated with honors. You went on to study archaeology and got your masters in the same field. Your sister became an RN and later got involved with global disaster relief organizations.

"Nearing graduation, one of your professors suggested you become a civilian agent for the Air Force Office of Special Investigations. While in civil service, you met and married Kenneth Gates, a fellow OSI agent and computer forensics expert. The marriage ended in divorce. All told, you spent twenty years as an OSI agent before suffering serious gunshot wounds in Iraq—an event in which you shot and supposedly killed your partner, Special Agent Aaron Knox."

At this point I turned back to the window. My chest tightened at the thoughts of Francine and shooting Aaron.

"After recovering from your wounds, you retired to a mountain cabin until your ex-husband brought you back to OSI as a consultant to assist in tracking down an ancient relic called the Blade of Abraham. You wound up stopping a terrorist threat on the city of Las Vegas."

Kepner fell silent for a moment. As I turned back to him, he said, "Did I leave anything out?"

"You've covered enough." It was considerate of him not to mention how Francine died.

"The reason we need you is your talent for finding things that have gone missing, just as you did with the Blade of Abraham and so many other rare, stolen objects. You are one of the best at what you do, and we are on an important journey, one that could change the course of history."

CHAPTER 6 - THE ABYSS
Four days earlier. RAI Center, Amsterdam
The Netherlands

Patricia Barney walked across the sprawling entrance hall, had her ID badge barcode scanned at the security checkpoint, and proceeded along what seemed like endless carpeted aisles separating the hundreds of exhibits. Each interconnected building contained different areas of technology—television production, computers, internet, telecommunications, gaming, and others. The names ranged from the giants of technology like Sony, Harris, Panasonic, and Apple all the way down to small software developers and hardware manufacturers vying for attention. The booth Patricia sought was in Hall 4, companies dedicated to communication. She spotted the modest corner exhibit with its brightly colored sign that read Red Star Innovations.

Three Red Star employees, in matching polo shirts and slacks, were putting the final touches on the various product displays as she approached. The man she was to meet—in his late fifties with a dark, close-cropped beard, and dark eyes— saw her and stepped away from the others. He met her with a polite kiss on each cheek. As he did so, he whispered, "Were you followed?"

She shook her head.

"And you have them?"

"Yes."

"One moment." He grabbed a briefcase from behind a display counter and then waved to the two co-workers. "I shall return shortly."

A few moments later, they sat at a small table in the far corner of the food court silently sipping Douwe Egberts dark roast. His eyes roamed the area around them as if taking a mental picture of the hundreds of attendees moving in steady streams throughout the exhibition hall.

Finally, he placed his cup down. "Any complications?"

"The handoff at the motel went just as planned. My bag was inspected at JFK, but it raised no suspicion." Now it was Patricia's turn to scan the crowd of food court patrons.

"Is there any evidence of your meeting with him?"

"This was a small motel in a small Arizona town, so I doubt it."

"You are very good, Patricia." The man gave a sly grin.

"I believe that's why you hired me."

"So," he said, glancing around again, "it's time to finalize our business." He pointed at the satchel still hanging over her shoulder. "Shall we?"

She slipped it off and placed it next to his feet. At the same time, he reached into his briefcase, removed an envelope, and laid it on the table.

"In euros?"

He nodded.

"I don't suppose you'll tell me what the objects are in the parcel and why you have gone to such extreme measures to get them?" She watched him remove the baggie of triangular objects from the satchel and place it in his briefcase.

"You will be better off not knowing."

"Of course. How about this, then? The Beowulf staff has an exceptionally high level of security clearance. How did you get someone to smuggle the pieces out of the facility?"

"Everyone has skeletons in his closet, as the Americans like to say. Threatening to expose them is more than enough motivation."

"Those pesky skeletons." They both laughed as she retrieved the satchel. "I've been thinking about leaving the game."

"I can see why." He patted the envelope just before she took it. "Is this the most you've made on a single job?"

She dropped the envelope in her bag and slid the strap back

onto her shoulder. "If you call me for anything else and I don't return the call, don't be offended. I'm either on a beach somewhere in the South Pacific or . . ."

"Dead? You're much too beautiful and smart to be caught. Plus, you will get bored on that beach."

She winked. "Depends on who I have snuggled up beside me."

Patricia stood and started to leave but paused. "By the way, be careful how you handle the objects. They make your skin tingle."

"Good to know."

She made her way through the crowds on the long walk back to the entrance hall. Outside to the right was the taxi queue with a few people in line. Judging from their conversations, they were mostly booth-setup crews heading back to their hotels during show hours after working all night. A few businessmen and exhibitors also stood in line.

Patricia took the place at the end of the queue and waited her turn for a taxi. A few others came to stand behind her. The line moved along quickly and she soon found herself at the front. The taxi pulled up and she opened the door and slid into the back seat. She felt someone push in right behind her and slam the door shut.

Patricia turned to complain just as the taxi pulled from the curb. "What are you doing?" she asked the man in the suit next to her. "This is my—"

She knew in an instant she had just made the biggest mistake of her life. She was supposed to be a professional and yet she had let her guard down. So enchanted by the amount of money in her satchel and her new life on some tropical isle, she had neglected to scrutinize those waiting in the taxi queue. How convenient that the taxi had pulled into line ahead of the others. Full of her triumph, she didn't even notice the classic setup. Now she stared at the man pressing his hand against her neck. Patricia knew there was no point in fighting. A second after the sting of the needle, she felt herself surrender to the abyss.

CHAPTER 7 - THE EAST RIM
Flagstaff, Arizona

The jet touched down in the darkness of Flagstaff Pulliam Airport just after 4:00 AM and quickly steered to a collection of hangars south of the main passenger terminal.

Our *Top Gun* pilots taxied the Learjet off the single main runway onto the tarmac. As soon as we came to a halt, one copilot emerged from the cockpit, opened the hatch, and lowered it. Kepner motioned for me to get off. He followed.

He placed his hand at my elbow and hurried me to a helicopter parked around sixty meters away, its rotors spinning, its skin painted midnight black. As soon as we climbed in and buckled up, we lifted off. I saw that our Learjet was already racing down the runway. The whole transfer from jet touchdown to helicopter liftoff couldn't have taken more than three minutes.

Kepner slipped on a set of headphones and pointed to a pair hanging nearby. Once I had them on, I said into the mic, "I really wanted to hit the Flagstaff gift shop during our layover."

He gave me his now-famous blank stare

"How far this leg?" I asked.

"About seventy miles."

I estimated that we were heading northwest. Seventy miles would put us . . . "We're going to the Grand Canyon?"

"Very good. We're headed to a remote area on the East Rim."

"I've always wanted to see it by helicopter."

"Unfortunately, Agent Decker, you won't this trip."

Thirty minutes later, we landed. I couldn't see much except what the full moon illuminated. I noticed that before putting us down, the pilot slipped on what looked like a night vision device. This guy set the bird down with as much assurance as if he were pulling his car into his garage for the hundredth time.

Kepner slid open the side door and jumped out with me right behind. We ducked under the spinning rotors and walked briskly away from the helicopter across hard-packed sand and small stones. Once we were at a safe distance, the black machine rose, banked, and roared back in the direction we had come.

After the sand blasting from the rotor wash blew past, the night surrounded us like a cloak—moonlight swept across a brilliant, starry sky. A whisper of wind cleared the air of the dust from the aircraft's takeoff.

As my eyes became adjusted to the dark, I realized we were standing on a flat expanse of land. In the distance before us ran a dark zigzagging scar gouging the landscape. I assumed it was the Grand Canyon. Not far away in shadow sat a one-story structure the size of a neighborhood 7-Eleven.

"This way." Kepner started toward the building.

As we cut the distance in half, a number of high-intensity floods transformed our surroundings into daylight.

"One second," Kepner said, taking my arm.

We halted and stood silently in the bath of light for ten or fifteen seconds. Then the lamps blinked off, leaving us again wrapped in the blanket of night.

After a moment to let our eyes readjust, we continued on until we came to the front of the building. Even in the muted light I could make out a front porch built of rustic logs and rough-hewn lumber. Strange, I thought, there were no windows. As we stood on the porch, a light over our heads turned on. A plaque with the arrowhead-shaped emblem of the National Park Service was fastened to the wall next to the door. And below it, a sign read "Closed. No Admittance."

"Get many tourists up here?" I asked.

"It's restricted."

Kepner placed his face against the wall beside the door. I wondered what the hell he was doing, and then realized he had aligned his left eye with an iris scanner. An electronic buzz sounded and he pushed the door open. We entered a room about the size of a two-car garage. Fluorescent lights flooded the space.

The room was empty except for a small bare office desk and chair in the corner. I looked across the room. "Are those elevator doors?"

Because he didn't answer, I decided Kepner liked screwing with my head. Either that, or he was just an arrogant dick who didn't feel it necessary to answer my questions. It wouldn't be long before he really pissed me off and I'd bail on this whole deal, presidential request or not.

"Come on," Kepner said. As we walked toward the doors, I heard the click of the lock behind us. The front entrance was secured.

Kepner pushed the *down* button and the elevator doors parted. We stepped inside and he pressed the number 3 button on the control panel, the lowest of the levels. The lift motor spun to life and we dropped. I had no way of knowing how far we descended, but I guessed at least sixty meters, maybe more.

The elevator came to a smooth stop and the doors slid open. What lay before me caused me to take in a sharp breath.

Kepner stepped out, turned, and said, "Welcome to Beowulf."

CHAPTER 8 - CHAUCER
Beowulf Headquarters

Exiting the elevator, I noticed a security checkpoint manned by two ominous-looking men holding assault rifles. The Beowulf insignia patch adorned the breast pockets of their black jumpsuits. The floor, walls, and ceiling were a polished gray material illuminated with indirect lighting. A number of small black globes suspended from above told me we were under video surveillance.

Kepner led me past the two sentries and we entered a hallway like those in a modern corporate office, with a slight dissimilarity. The workstations and terminals that sat dark and empty weren't separated by the conventional portable partitions. Instead, they were divided by glass panels. This was very different from my old stomping grounds at DC3, the OSI headquarters at the Department of Defense Cyber Crime Center in Maryland. To carve this facility out of solid rock had to have been an amazing feat. Money had not been spared.

I assumed that whatever staff occupied these stations would be coming in later, since it was still an hour before dawn. I suppressed a yawn, thinking I should still be home, snug in my bed.

We stopped in front of a set of sculptured stainless-steel double doors that bore the now-familiar Beowulf shield. The nameplate read: Director.

"The director will take it from here. I have some other things to attend to. I'll check in with you later when I get back." Kepner tapped once then opened the door and gestured for me to enter. As I did so, I sensed that he stayed behind. I turned to check. Kepner was gone and the door softly clicked closed.

"Good morning, Agent Decker."

The greeting had come from a man sitting behind a glass and stainless-steel desk. I assumed the 50ish, silver-templed man was the director. He wore a jumpsuit similar to the security guards'. Other than the leather chairs, all the furniture and appointments in the office were also stainless and glass. I wondered what was up with the decor. *Fetish or functionality?*

"It hasn't been that good of a morning," I said. My adrenalin hadn't slowed much since Kepner arrived at my cabin. The shock of it all and lack of sleep were taking a toll.

He came from around his desk and shook my hand. Above the Beowulf patch was a nametag: Chaucer. As I tried to decide whether that was his first or last name, he picked up on my dilemma.

"Please, call me Chaucer."

I acknowledged.

"It's nice to meet you, Agent Decker. You have quite a reputation. All good, by the way."

He returned to his high-back chair, and with a wave of his hand invited me to sit in one of the chairs across the desk from him.

I thanked him for the compliment and sat.

"I have to say, Chaucer, your operation works fast. I feel like I zip lined here."

"Once we set upon a course of action, we waste no time in getting underway." He laid his hands palm down on his desk. "I'm sure you have lots of questions, but maybe I can answer most before you ask."

"Thank god," I said. "Your head of security stonewalled me."

"I apologize. He's very cautious not to give out too much info. Let me see if I can help you out. I'll start with my name. Chaucer isn't my given name. It's a code name."

An English poet. "Like Tennyson for the President?"

"Beowulf deals with extremely sensitive matters and is

answerable only to Tennyson. We never reference the President or use his name. Because of the necessity to operate with ultimate covertness, we are different from other black operations. Congress is not even aware that we exist." He paused a moment, letting that settle in.

"Then how are you funded? Doesn't Congress have to appropriate funds even for black ops?"

"Yes. But not Beowulf. Before I continue, I need to impress upon you that what you are going to learn about Beowulf and our project must be regarded with the highest degree of discretion and confidentiality. Any suspicion of a lack thereof will result in the harshest of responses. You've been selected for your skills and for your character. Two other things were factored in. You don't break under even the most intense situations. And when it isn't easy, you do what you have to do."

I knew what he was referring to—the tragic death of my sister at my own hands, and when I'd been forced to shoot my partner.

"Do you clearly understand what I have just said?"

I gave an affirmative nod.

"Good, because if you can't agree with that, we won't go any further. Look me in the eyes."

Chaucer held my gaze and then continued. "Your help is needed in a critical matter, vital to this country's and others' security and safety. There may be times when you are on your own and things get dicey. I want you to be aware of that. So, if you're going to back out, do it now, not later. Once you're in, you're in."

"You mean I can't decide after you explain what the project is?"

"No."

Whatever the critical matter was, everyone had made it abundantly clear that it was a global-changing issue. If my country needed me that badly, how could I turn my back? My brain urged me to check out now, but my gut said *no way*. I had too many years of service with OSI embedded in me so my loyalty must have become part of my DNA.

"All right. I've come this far. It's a long walk home."

"That means you're agreeing?"

"Yes."

"Okay, Agent Decker. Glad to have you. First, I'll tell you we are a crew of only ten. The fewer who have knowledge of Beowulf, the more secure it remains. There will be no non-disclosure contract for you to sign. There'll be no paper trail that will connect us. This is a verbal agreement only. Please be reminded one last time that any violation will provoke serious measures."

Chaucer sat back in his chair, his eyes fixed on mine.

I got the picture. "Crystal clear."

"Then we'll proceed."

I heard my breath come out in a noticeable sigh. I'd been on some hazardous assignments in my time, but already I knew this was way beyond anything I'd ever been involved in.

"You asked about funding. I'll address that briefly, even though it is irrelevant."

I'd just been reprimanded. For now, I'd shut up and listen. This guy was no candy-ass, and this was no candy-ass operation.

"Every year the Department of Defense has single-line items in their budgets represented by a series of numbers and letters along with a code name—it might read Operation Dragonfly with a vague general description. These line items are simply covers for a black budget. It's a type of slush fund set up by the DoD. It keeps Congress's nose out of the DoD's business—in other words, no congressional oversight. Suppose 2.6 million is budgeted for Operation Dragonfly. But really only 1.2 million actually gets to that project. The rest is funneled to a blacker-than-black op like Beowulf. We are considered beyond black. We arrange to skim enough from each of those line items and, voilà, we have our funding."

"Sounds like government money laundering."

"If looking at it that way helps you understand Beowulf's magnitude and the seriousness of what you'll be working on, then it'll benefit us both."

Chaucer rose and strolled over to a side credenza where a pitcher of ice water and glasses sat. "Would you like some?"

I declined.

He poured a glass and took a deep swallow before returning to lean against the side of his desk.

"Agent Decker, tell me what you know about the Roswell UFO Incident in 1947."

THE BLADE and THE SHIELD are available in print and e-book. For more information on Lynn Sholes & Joe Moore, and their thrillers, visit www.sholesmoore.com and follow them on Facebook at www.facebook.com/sholesandmoore

www.ingramcontent.com/pod-product-compliance
Lightning Source LLC
Chambersburg PA
CBHW060132130626
46556CB00006B/2320